Copyright © 2019 by Alex Lidell

Danger Bearing Press

All rights reserved.

No part of this book may be reproduced in any form or by any electronic or mechanical means, including information storage and retrieval systems, without written permission from the author, except for the use of brief quotations in a book review.

Credits:

Edited by Mollie Traver and Linda Ingmanson

Cover Design by Deranged Doctor Design

ALEX LIDELL

TRACING SHADOWS (Audiobook available)

UNRAVELING DARKNESS (Audiobook available)

TILDOR

THE CADET OF TILDOR

CONTENTS

PART I: RULES OF STONE

LERA

"Watch your left side, mortal." Coal calls to me from where he fights three sclices at once, the fae warrior's sword and dagger a blur of precision. His voice is steady and low, as if we are in a practice corral facing nothing more deadly than sacks of sand.

"I'm. Not. Mortal." Unlike Coal's words, mine come between gasping breaths. My lungs burn, my heart pounding against my ribs as I spin, my sword following the arc of my body to bite into a sclice's thick hide.

The hoglike beast swipes at me with its clawed front limbs, which are long enough to let it run on all fours. It's not running now, though. Standing upright on its back-hinged hind legs, the sclice towers over me, its vertical red eyes, snouted nose, and fang-filled protruding lower jaw all roaring their displeasure.

"Keep leaving your weak side open, and we'll see how not mortal you are," Coal calls, felling the beast before him. In black fighting leathers, his blond hair pulled back with a leather thong, the warrior moves with a preternatural grace that comes of centuries of combat—and still takes my breath. A flick of his powerful forearm, and a second hog beast falls just as it tries to sink its teeth into Coal's shoulder.

Jumping away from the sclice's assault, I force myself to draw a lungful of air. My new immortal body might make me stronger and swifter than I was in my human form, but I've a ways to go before I can match skills with my mates.

I'm not mortal. The words still zing through me, settling uncomfortably into my bones. Only eight months ago, I was working in Master Zake's stable in the mortal lands, with nothing but the bite of his belt and the snap of his temper a reliable promise of the future. When the four fae warriors— Coal, River, Shade, and Tye—appeared from the immortal realm, drawn to me by an ancient magic, none believed our connection was anything but an error. And yet, here I am. Not just the fifth warrior of the quint, but fae myself, mated to all four males by a magic as old as the immortal race.

Now that we're a sanctioned quint, we're charged with protecting Lunos from the dark creatures of Mors—which, if it were up to Coal, would mean roving the lands between the three Lunos courts, Flury, Blaze, and Slait, and battling sclices and piranhas to his heart's content. Unfortunately for Coal, because our commander is also now the king of Slait Court, we never travel far from Slait's capital. The males put on a good front, but after centuries on the front lines, responding to routine reports and checking wards make my males feel like leashed dogs.

Twenty paces away, where the thick fern forest gives way to a clearing, said commander, River, stands with his back straight and eyes narrowed in concentration as his magic opens a great gash in the frost-chilled earth. A future grave for the sclice pack that Tye and Shade herd into the crack while Coal and I deal with the strays. Sclices might have the brains and instincts of rodents, but with their man-sized bodies and insatiable hunger, large packs like this can destroy a village in a night's hunt.

I mark Shade, in his wolf form, snapping at the beasts' hind legs while red-haired Tye plays his fire magic to set off sparks beside their hooves. Swift. Efficient… Competitive. *Stars.* The two have made a game of it, and I'd wager my horse they are keeping score.

The sclice before me snarls its fury, thick yellow drool dripping from its pulled-back lips. The stench coming off the creature is strong enough to make me gag, even here in the Gloom—the normal world's eerie underlining, where Mors beasts tend to congregate—which mutes the colors and smells and sounds. Gripping my sword tighter, I cover my mouth and nose with my elbow as I circle for a better angle.

The hog beast crouches on its hind legs. Growls. Lunges at me faster than I thought possible, sharp front claws pushing off the ground for leverage before raking my left side. Streaks of fire light along my ribs, and I choke back a gasp of pain. My immortal body might heal faster than a human's, but it does nothing to mute the sensations. Shade and Tye are wrangling more than a dozen beasts, and Coal is on to killing his fifth. This one bloody sclice is mine.

Letting the beast's momentum carry it by me, I angle my blade to strike the back of its neck. My ribs burn, my pulse racing in fear-tinged fury as I strike.

The sclice twists around, knocking me off my feet. Pouncing on me as I fall, it lands with its clawed front limbs on either side of my head, its oversized lower jaw hanging open, dripping yellow drool onto my neck.

Arching my back, I kick the sclice off, rolling over my shoulder to reclaim my footing. I feel a tiny pulse of satisfaction when none of the males intervenes to rescue me—

they're making progress. Then I feel Coal's attention on me, as hot and firm as his hands on my sword arm—all right, slow progress.

Reaching inside myself, I feel for the males' phantom limbs of magic that I'm still getting accustomed to living there. Not one but four cords of power wake to my call, the fledgling magics still developing but eager for freedom. Weaving the four cords into a rough braid, I lash out with a messy weave. So far as we know, I'm the only weaver in all of Lunos—but it will take me centuries to grow into the full breadth of my power.

The braid of magic explodes like the crack of a giant whip, echoing through the forest. Bits of earth and fern and slice fly into the air as if caught in some giant shard-filled whirlwind.

"What in the star's name is going on?" River demands, his steady gray eyes taking in the scene while I drop to my knees to catch my breath. "Are you all right, Leralynn?"

I tamp the magic down quickly and back away from the mess. "Yes."

"That's enough for today. Connect," River orders, his crisp words forcing me to my feet. A flash of light has Shade returning to his fae form, black hair swinging over high cheekbones, tan skin, and gleaming yellow eyes. Coal finishes his opponent with an efficient swipe before jogging to where the others are gripping hands.

"Come, lass." Tye extends his hand toward me with a roguish smile and a sparkle in his green eyes, drawing me in to finish the quint's connection. "Playtime's over."

The moment the five of us all touch, the quint's ancient magic fills my body, its thundering power edging out all pain and fatigue. River's competent hands on the magic's reins make short work of pushing the remaining two slices into the cracked earth before sweeping Coal's kills and my mess into the same abyss and sealing it cleanly.

It's over in seconds, but that rush of joint magic, my heart beating in perfect harmony with four others, brushes my soul with the ecstasy of belonging. *Mine.* No matter their war games, their risk-taking, their maddening overprotectiveness, these males are mine.

2

LERA

I feel no such ecstasy an hour later. Sitting shirtless on Shade's worktable in the Slait Palace, I fidget under four fury-filled glares.

"These cuts are deep, cub," Shade says, his usually velvet voice stern as his fingertips probe my ribs gently. The wolf shifter's magic has a healing affinity, just as Tye's power favors fire and River's speaks with the earth. Coal's odd magic is unique, turned inward on himself after years of slavery, giving him even greater strength, speed, and ability to heal than other fae. Shade crouches for a closer look, his scent of earth fresh from rain filling my nose. Even off the battlefield, Shade moves with lupine grace, his fitted gray pants and bare torso revealing a field of tan, smoothly carved muscles. The beautiful angles of his face are tight with concern. "Had the claws gone a bit farther, you'd have a punctured lung."

"I told you to watch your left side, mortal." Coal's blue eyes flash with ice, his tight muscles vibrating with leashed violence. "I didn't know you needed a compass to find 'left.'"

"You needn't have done all that just to win my attention,

Lilac Girl." Tye's crossed arms give away the lie behind his voice's lightness. When the male shifts his weight, I see his fists rolled tight enough to bleach the knuckles.

I rub my arms, hoping the feigned chill will conceal the light tremors of fatigued muscles that are now surfacing. "I'm fine."

"And if you weren't, you'd be dead before you admitted it." River steps up beside me, his gray eyes intent on mine. Despite being over five centuries old, the warrior looks to be in his late twenties, his pointed ears and elongated canines as much a marker of his immortality as his aura of power and command. Here in the privacy of Shade's workroom, he's shrugged off his jacket with the king's crest and the small gold crown his subjects expect to see on him, but still, his militantly straight back, close-cropped brown hair, and broad shoulders carry responsibility like a second skin. Even with me sitting on a high table, he towers over me, the largest of the four males, invading my space with a ruthless precision. The weight of his presence—his overwhelming beauty and anger—sends shivers down my skin. "We were out to combine some exercise with utility. There was no cause whatsoever to put yourself in harm's way. If the sclice was giving you trouble, you should have said something. Do you understand me?"

Reaching into myself, I scrape together enough strength to glare right back at River. "You need to give me some space to try out my skills, River. I'm a warrior of the quint now. Would you be fussing if it was Tye sitting here with a few scratches?"

Tye snorts and takes a chair, turning it around to straddle it, eyes on the show.

"We've fought beside Tye over three hundred years. You became fae six months ago." River's voice drops to a low timbre. "More to the point, Tye isn't my mate. For a fae male, the instinct to protect his mate is overwhelming. The moment you became fae and those mating bonds formed, our lives became even more intertwined with yours than they already were. That is something you need to start getting used to, Leralynn. And respecting."

"I've a better idea, River." I straighten my spine, not caring how the movement stings my ribs or pushes my bare chest out farther. "Shade's wolf's instinct is to mark his territory—yet he somehow manages not to piss on the rug. So perhaps your cock could take some instruction from his."

A muscle in River's square jaw tics. Once. Twice. On the third tic, the male turns on his heel and walks out of the room, the door swinging closed behind him. Shade's small, white-walled workroom with its neat, polished surfaces suddenly feels cavernously empty.

When I open my mouth to shout after him, Shade places his large palm on my cheek, the heat of his body warming the air between us. His yellow eyes are as deep as his voice. "There are very few things in the immortal realm that hurt us more than seeing you in pain, cub." His thumb brushes along my cheekbone the firm pressure sending tendrils of sensation through me. "Protecting you isn't an instinct we *want* to curb."

Strength draining from me, I lean my forehead against Shade's hard chest, the beat of his heart echoing through my skin. "I just want to carry my weight," I whisper, the confession tightening my throat. "Just because magic brought us together—"

"Magic has nothing to do with it." Shade grips my face with both hands, tipping it up to meet his eyes, the fierce possession in them piercing my core. He growls softly, and heat pools in my lower half. "We are your mates, cub. And we would have found you, magic or no, because without you, our souls are incomplete."

Shade leans down until our breaths mix, the heat of his

body cocooning my skin. Still holding my face, he presses his mouth against mine, his tongue slipping in gently before claiming me with a predator's possession that reminds me of the wolf he is. The scent of his arousal saturates the air, one hand now sliding down my neck, my shoulder, my collarbone. Cupping my right breast.

My skin tingles beneath the male's touch, the breast in his hold suddenly full and aching. My insides tighten, as much from the thoroughly claiming kiss as at the thought of Shade's mouth elsewhere. Suckling the sensitive breast he now holds. Dipping lower.

Shade's callused thumb brushes against my nipple, a shudder running though his body when the bud peaks in response. Molten heat flows down my core, my sex, the backs of my thighs, making even my toes tingle with need.

I'll never get used to this. No matter how many times we drown in the mating bond, on how many surfaces in how many palace rooms and quiet passages and curtained nooks we give in to lust, casual talking turning to breathless claiming. I only seem to want them more with each passing day.

"If I knew we were bypassing the healing and scolding and moving right to kissing, I'd have moved closer," says Tye. His deep, amused voice only heightens the ache in my sex, as images of what the three of us could do together right now flood my imagination—the four of us, if Coal would just stop sharpening that damn knife.

Shade chuckles against my mouth, pressing into me until I feel the hardness pulsating inside his breeches. I slide my hand to grip his taut backside, pulling him even closer—

"You need to finish up in here." River's voice cuts between us, the air chilling with the open door. For a moment, I think the male has returned to argue some more, and the frustration gripping my sex mixes violently with the retort bubbling inside my chest. But then I hear it. An uncharacteristic tightness in River's tone—a barely reined-in tension that makes my stomach clench. Shade straightens, giving my thigh an apologetic squeeze, and I slide to my feet.

"What's happened?" Coming up behind me, Tye wraps his jacket around me, his heavy hand staying comfortingly on my shoulder as his eyes watch River's every move.

River runs his hand through his short hair, his one tell surfacing. "A message from the Elders Council," he says quietly. "The wards protecting the mortal realm from magic have cracked."

3

LERA

With Shade's healing magic still tingling along my skin, I let myself into what was once a formal sitting room for River's father, Griorgi, but which now resembles a cross of den and library. Tall windows flood the chamber with brilliant sunlight, illuminating the colorful frescos of fae history covering each wall. Griorgi's high-backed carved wooden chairs have been evicted in favor of more comfortable leather furniture, and a smell of sweet wine and bitter chocolate announces that both Tye and Autumn, River's brilliant sister, have already made themselves comfortable.

"The wards protecting the mortal realm from magic have cracked." River's words echo in my mind, twisting and turning in search of some plausible explanation. A millennium ago, after the fae and humans enslaved in the dark realm of Mors broke free, the most powerful of the immortals combined their magics to separate the world into three realms. The dark realm of Mors, where the terrifying gray-skinned qoru rule. The immortal

realm of Lunos for the fae. And the largest, the mortal realm, where all the human kingdoms find a home.

Last year, Griorgi attempted an alliance with the Mors emperor, opening a portal between Lunos and Mors. That escapade nearly destroyed Blaze, one of Lunos's three courts. A penetration into the mortal realm, whose denizens have little to no knowledge of fae and no way to defend themselves, would be infinitely more deadly.

"Lera!" Autumn looks up from a sea of reference books, her many silver-blond braids swaying. Her fashion, as usual, puts my simple black fighting leathers to shame—a flowing dress of green and turquoise silk belted tight around her tiny waist. The sparkling silver at her ears, wrists, and neck make her look like every inch the princess she is, though it is the small leather cap sitting atop her left ear that the female fingers most often—a gift from her lover, Kora. "River said you are hurt."

I throw River a dagger-filled look. "I thought River wanted to talk about broken wards, not keep worrying over three scratches."

River lifts one brow, his gray eyes unreadable. "I can worry and talk simultaneously."

"Forget I asked," Autumn says quickly, tossing me a quick, conspiratorial smile before turning back to her books.

"Did Mystwood burn down?" I ask, setting a course for my favorite armchair. A shiver runs through me at the thought of the deep, mystical forest separating Lunos from the mortal realm. A forest I used to live at the edge of. It was created to prevent fae—and other, much darker immortal creatures—from walking into mortal lands, a fact my males were able to circumvent to come find me only by way of a highly rare and powerful passage key.

"Mystwood still stands," says River, stepping aside as Shade's wolf streaks across the room.

"Don't you dare," I yell after the beast, who is already leaping from the floor.

Too late. With a self-satisfied snort, Shade lands lightly on my chair and circles in place several times before curling into a large gray ball—one paw, tail, and tongue strategically extended to claim the entire seat.

One yellow eye blinks back at me piously.

I glower at him. "Get off, or I'll sit on you."

"That is not much of a disincentive, Lilac Girl," says Tye, pulling me into his own lap as he settles on the couch. The male's powerful thigh muscles shift to brace my backside, his white-silk-covered arms and scent of pine and citrus flowing like water around me. When I squirm to get free, a set of tiny, very dangerously placed sparks of fire magic nip me beneath my tight leather pants.

I gasp, and Tye clicks his tongue right next to my ear. "You really should stay put, lass. For safety's sake and all that."

"Enough," River says from the middle of the room, his hands laced at the small of his back. With a jerk of his chin, the male nods to the low table where a map and stack of papers are already spread. Scout reports, by the look of them. A great many reports. "While we were out playing with sclices, the Elders Council delivered disturbing news. While Mystwood is intact, there is a weakness in the fabric separating the mortal realms of Light and Gloom. Creatures such as sclices have been spotted in the human world, and our fae scouts have even felt traces of their own magic when the mortal realm should have shackled their power completely. If left unaddressed this one point of weakness will spiderweb out like a crack in a glass."

"I don't understand how that's possible if Mystwood stands," I say.

"Mystwood forest is a wall," says Autumn, rising and pushing River lightly to the side to stand before us. She holds one hand perpendicular to the other palm, her gray eyes blazing with the results of her research. "This wall stops magic and forbids traffic between Lunos and the human world, but it doesn't extend infinitely. Go deep enough into the Gloom and you can get under the wall—but since you can't *exit* the Gloom on the mortal side, this has never mattered."

"Until now," I finish for her.

"Yes," Autumn says. "Since Mystwood is intact, yet traces of magic and Mors vermin have appeared in the human world, we believe there is a rip in the fabric. Fortunately, all the anomalies are centered around a single location. For now. As River stated, if left unchecked, the rip will spread and the impact will become catastrophic."

"The territory with the anomalies belongs to Great Falls Academy, in the mortal realm." Taking over for his sister, River steps toward the table and traces an area on the map, his callused finger circling what looks like a small town surrounded by a great stretch of forested wilderness. "Have you heard of it, Leralynn?"

I wince. Even during my isolated life tending horses at Zake's estate, I'd heard of the place—its reputation precedes it. And then some. "Great Falls is the most prestigious school on the continent, catering to royals and nobles of all ten kingdoms in the Continental Alliance. The king of Ckridel set it up two hundred years ago when the alliance was first formed, following the theory that if you sequester the ten kingdoms' future leaders into joint, high-quality misery for a few years, they'll emerge not only well trained but with an aversion to slaughtering each other in the future. And it's worked."

"Not a bad notion." River runs his hand through his hair. "But rather inconvenient at the moment, as that's the only real place from which to launch a reconnaissance mission."

"I presume the Elders Council wants us to go find out the size and cause of this crack and fix it before the sclices eat the Alliance's future rulers for supper?" says Coal, though we all know the rodents would be the least of the humans' problems if a full passage between the Light and Gloom opened up. Not everyone's ancestors were fortunate enough to escape the qoru, and Coal still wakes with nightmares of his time there as a slave. Emperor Jawrar would jump at another chance to find a foothold beyond Mors's borders, a thought that sends cold dread spiraling through me.

"Yes." River sighs. "With Leralynn being from the mortal lands, and considering the strength of our quint, the Elders believe us uniquely suited for the mission. While my being Slait's ruler on my own court's territory prevents the Council from *ordering* us to go, they are asking us to."

Placing the fate of thousands of lives on our—on *River's* —unerringly responsible shoulders.

The room falls silent, tension in every breath.

The Council doesn't make a habit of requesting anything. That they are doing so now—instead of waiting until River stepped off Slait soil and thus into the Council's jurisdiction— means the situation is dire indeed. There are few quints in Lunos who match the males' experience and skill, and none but the Council itself who rival our joint power.

"They are right," I say, watching River's face tighten even as his hand twitches toward the map. He wants to go. They all do. The six months of staying put since River took the throne is driving the males stir-crazy—their frustration matched only by their bullheaded overprotectiveness. "How would we get into the Academy, though?" I ask, strategically turning the discussion away from *whether* we should be going. "Human legends peg fae for murderous monsters. Anyone in charge of an academy filled with the sons and daughters of the kingdoms' most influential families would order the lot of us killed on sight."

"That problem I can solve." Autumn leans forward, the sparkle in her eyes saying she's been mulling the puzzle over for some time. "You'll get in wearing chameleon veils. Warded amulets that alter the beholder's perception of who you are and why you are there."

"Wait." I hold up my hand. "I thought magic doesn't work in the mortal realm."

"True. With the exception of passive magic, such as our immortality, the mortal realm does shackle all outward power —Tye's fire affinity, Shade's healing, River's earth will all be unusable," says Autumn. "Shifting is all but impossible, and don't ask me about Coal's magic, because the stars only know what that does. But *physical* wards—those attached to objects like this amulet—tend to still function if they are powerful enough."

Opening a wooden box that I hadn't noticed in her lap, the female removes a set of five intricately carved wooden amulets. They're nearly identical circular medallions with a delicate lacelike pattern spreading out in points from the center. "And these are some of the most complex and powerful magics in Lunos. They go beyond the basics and truly build a whole history for each of you, depending on where you are in the mortal world."

"So if Tye were to put a veil on and step into a monastery —" River starts to say.

"—the monastery residents would see him as an acolyte or

a fellow monk," Autumn finishes for him. "Possibly as one who's been there for some time. Moreover, the amulet would use facts from Tye's actual history to build the new legend. So with Tye being a high-level flex athlete, his legend would likely include an explanation for athletic prowess."

"Why would the veil make him appear a monk and not a chamber-pot boy?" asks Coal, earning a dirty look from Tye. "That would fit too."

Autumn shrugs one smooth, bare shoulder. "The veil could very well make him a chamber-pot boy, especially if this monastery made a habit of hiring former athletes to clean rooms—the magic follows the path of least resistance. That is the first limitation of the veil amulets: you've no control over the legend they spin for you, and once the legend is created, it doesn't alter. The amulet is designed to convince the world you belong there—it little cares whether you find the role convenient. For this reason, I'd advise never to wear a new veil into a prison, lest it convinces the guards you belong there as an inmate."

"How will we know what legend the veil created for us?" I ask.

"The amulet will give you an awareness of it, a phantom desire to believe that it is true. This brings me to the veil's second limitation—you must remove the amulet for at least an hour each day, lest you fall victim to the veil yourself."

"Any other limitations?" River asks, picking up one of the amulets and twisting it suspiciously in his fingers.

"One more." Autumn bites her lip, her voice apologetic. "The amulets' magic builds a disguise so complete that it mutes all bonds. You will feel neither the quint nor your mating bond while you wear them."

4

LERA

"I don't think we should go," River says, letting himself into my bedchamber a few hours after our briefing. Closing the door with a soft click, he strides to where I'm already packing, my clothes and weapons laid out neatly atop the four-poster bed. "I can't leave the throne only six months after taking it."

My jaw tightens at both the lie and the reason behind it. "I imagine Autumn can manage the day-to-day operation. Given the few centuries of experience she has at it." Three centuries, to be exact—all the time River stayed away from Slait Court, returning only six months ago to finally depose the monster who sat on the throne.

River has the decency to blush.

I cross my arms, glaring up at him—not an easy feat with how close the large male is standing to me. With his straight back and broad shoulders, corded thighs and mirror-shined black boots spread slightly apart for balance, River eclipses the world without trying. But he isn't going to eclipse me. "If you've come to tell me how much your male instincts will hurt if I—"

"But you *died* six months ago," River snaps, the sudden break of his iron control vibrating the room. His shadowed gray eyes study me with such intensity that my chest tightens. He swallows, a slight tremor running through him. "I still feel the terror of that moment every time I close my eyes. So yes, Leralynn, I hate seeing you in danger. In pain. There is nothing in Lunos or the mortal lands that's worth that for me. For any of us four. Someone else can go."

"Stars. River." The anger simmering my blood softens, and I reach up to trace my fingers along the angle of his square jaw. The tension inside him radiates through the skin, the muscles shifting beneath my fingers. The rare glimpse into my quint commander's vulnerability makes my stomach clench. But it doesn't change reality. "Then I think it's fortunate for both realms that at least one of us can think clearly," I say gently.

"Leralynn." River's voice drops, his hands gripping my hips.

I shake my head. "Someone else didn't grow up in the mortal realm. Someone else isn't a weaver. And someone else is certainly not part of the second most powerful quint in all of Lunos. We might be mated, but we are still a warrior quint. We were chosen by the magic to go out and *do* things. And this is the first of many."

River closes his eyes, his chest expanding with his breaths. A heartbeat later, he pulls me fiercely against him. "Two points of clarification," he whispers, his warm breath ruffling the hair on the top of my head. "First, once we discover the full extent of your new weaving magic, we might be *the* most powerful. And second... No matter how powerful you may one day become, I will always want to keep you safe. It is a hazard you'll be forced to weather for centuries, Leralynn."

"You are blaming the mating bond for making you insufferable?" I swallow, sounding hoarse as that very bond rouses to River's woodsy scent and caresses my soul. "Seems rather convenient."

Taking my chin between his thumb and forefinger, River raises my gaze toward him. His gray eyes study me, shifting into commanding intimacy. "Very convenient," he echoes, his strong face filling my vision, his shoulders blocking the world from view. A purposeful motion, and one that makes my heart stutter in spite of itself.

River's singular undiluted attention fills me, holding me in place as heat floods my sex. My hand twitches toward him, and he stills my motion with a look, my thighs clenching together in a mix of need and outrage.

A pleased, knowing glint fills River's gray eyes, his nostrils flaring delicately. "Yes, I smell it," he whispers into my ear, his gaze trailing down my abdomen until there is no question as to what precisely he refers to.

Heat touches my cheeks.

"You are beautiful when you blush," River whispers. This close, I can feel the pounding of his heart, striking his ribs as hard as my own. His free hand slides down the curve of my hip and thigh, lifting the silk hem of my lavender nightgown. Cool air brushes my thighs a moment before River's warm hand trails up the sensitive skin, dipping unapologetically inside my undergarments toward the dampness I know is there.

Stars. Even after six months, the intensity of my new fae body still comes as a shock. It isn't just the longer, shinier hair and smoother, near-glowing skin, it's the avalanche of sensation. What used to merely arouse me now drives me insane with want.

I squirm on instinct, and River's other hand drops from my face to cup my backside firmly, keeping me in place as he slides through my slickness. Extracting his glistening hand, he licks his fingers clean, growling with soft pleasure.

Stars. I open my mouth to—

River's lips capture mine, swallowing whatever protest I was about to utter.

My body tenses, River's claiming flooding me with sensation so intense, I can't stay still. Yet I can't move either. Not with the male's hands and mouth on me, his feet shifting to trap mine between them. Giving me no escape. No chance to do anything but feel him. Feel us.

One heartbeat builds on the next until the slow throbbing vibrating through my core grows so insistent, I am gasping for air. Pulling back slightly, River scrapes the points of elongated canines along my bottom lip, making me writhe beneath his hands despite certain consequences.

River chuckles, his hand slipping right back beneath my skirt, up my damn inner thigh and—I gasp as a finger slides inside me, his thumb flicking over the sensitive apex. A zing spiders along my skin, my sex clenching around the glorious intrusion, the burst of sensation both too much and not nearly enough. When the callused tip of River's finger traces my hood, I whimper outright, rising onto my toes for relief that won't come.

River's lips brush my ear. "I can ignore the mating bond's instinct no more than you can ignore this, luv." Another trace along my hood, coupled with tiny flicks on either side of my apex until I'm squirming despite his hold. "But please, try as hard as you like."

"Bastard." Raising my hands, I rake them over River's

back, the press of his hardness against my mound dizzyingly satisfying.

With a growl, he pushes me away to arm's length, his breaths ragged, his gray eyes gleaming with barely restrained need. A predator targeting prey. With the next breath, River shoves me back and back, until my thighs press against the edge of my bed and my breaths come in ragged, desperate gasps. With a sweep of one thickly muscled arm, my neat piles are strewn across the floor.

"Those are my travel clothes," I warn.

"I'll get you new ones." The sound of ripping silk swallows River's words, the room's cool air brushing my exposed skin for a moment before his muscular body settles atop mine.

River frees himself in one practiced movement, the thick head of his engorged cock coating itself in my wetness. Even after all these months, the size of him sends ripples of warning through my body, my channel already tasting the stretch—the fullness—to come. Gripping my thighs in an undeniable hold, River finds my eyes as he positions himself at my entrance, his eyes shining with desire and conquest. Savoring my anxious anticipation, the bastard.

"I'll murder you in your sleep," I warn through clenched teeth, my empty, empty sex clenching around nothingness while the thoroughly aroused apex sends zinging pulses down to my toes.

River's teeth flash, the power of him suddenly filling every inch of air in the room. Five centuries of battle-honed muscles, of leading the realm's greatest warriors, all flash in reminder of who exactly stands between my open thighs. "Just for that…" The warning in River's voice shoots through me a moment before he lowers his mouth right atop my bud and *sucks*.

My whole body tightens, the pleasure mounting so fast

and hard that it turns to liquid agony and back, a bow stretching further and further and—

River stops.

No. No. No. My body trembles in anticipation, in the all-consuming need to release that tautly pulled bow. I buck desperately, come up against River's unyielding hold, and finally whimper.

With a pleased chuckle, River sheathes himself inside me, his thickness everything I wanted and feared. In and back, in and back, the powerful *thrust thrust thrust* of his cock gathers all the needy nerves inside me. My heart quickens, my breath coming in little pants while my eyes see nothing but the strong line of River's jaw and the flex of corded muscle beneath his well-cut tunic.

Thrust thrust thrust.

River's shaft pulses, my channel clenching around it. Every fiber in my lower body screams, feeling the approaching abyss. This time, my wild, needy, desperate bucking is beyond my control. But not beyond River's, who holds my thighs with unyielding command.

Thrust, thrust…

The explosion of pleasure rakes through my body, lighting every nerve. Anguish so fierce, it is pure bliss. My muscles tighten, my sex clenches, my vision blurs. Tumbling into the great abyss inside me, I feel River's own release filling my channel and realize the warrior is trembling as badly as I am.

THERE ARE FOUR WRAPPED BUNDLES, in addition to Autumn, Kora, and the males, waiting for me in the stables the following morning. Settling my saddlebags beside Sprite, the dapple-gray mare River gifted me with when I first came to

Lunos, I study the gathering suspiciously. "What's happening?"

"We—" Autumn starts, then rolls her eyes at the males and picks up one of the larger bundles, thrusting it into my arms. "*I* thought that your first official mission as a quint warrior was worth celebrating. So, here. This is from me."

"Wasn't dethroning King Griorgi the first?" I ask.

"No. That was housekeeping." Autumn nods at the package that I unwrap to reveal a gown of soft red silk, a matching shawl completing the look. "Dress in this before you put on the veil and enter the Academy, all right?" She pulls her own shimmering silver wrap more tightly around her slender shoulders and looks down, suddenly finding its woven edge endlessly fascinating. Her eyes glisten slightly in the morning sun. "The veil can't make you a chamber-pot girl in that. At least I don't think it can. I—"

I throw my arms around my friend, who hugs me back fiercely, letting go only when Kora puts a comforting arm on Autumn's shoulder, drawing her lover away.

"Thank you." I kiss Autumn's cheek before looking up at her brother, who holds his package with uncharacteristic hesitation. Taking River's gift, I unwrap the paper gingerly and feel my chest tighten at the intricate handiwork. Four cords in different sparkling shades of gold woven together into a braid, the pendent hanging from them a complex knot of the same strands. I look closer and gasp in recognition. One strand is studded with amethysts—Coal's strange purple magic; one with deep brown-red garnets—River's earth magic; one with yellow-orange diamonds—Tye's fire; and one with gleaming silver—Shade's healing. "The cords of your four magics plaited together with my weaver's gift," I whisper, running my fingers over the priceless piece. "This must have taken the jeweler months."

River shrugs one massive shoulder, but there is a bit of color in his cheeks when I turn to let him fasten the treasure around my neck.

Shade steps up next, his package holding a pair of gray mittens. Inhaling the wool's familiar earthy scent, I narrow my eyes at the shifter. "Where exactly did you get these?"

A flash of light has a wolf replacing the male, the animal's long tongue licking the tip of his nose virtuously. Now that I'm paying closer attention, I see the wolf's shortened coat and wince. "How many weavers did you bite in the making of these mittens?" I ask.

"Four," Autumn informs me dryly. "Two of them submitted resignations."

The wolf, suddenly finding a tree in need of careful sniffing, trots off while Tye hands me the heaviest package yet. Instead of paper, this one is wrapped in sturdy cloth, rolled up tightly and buckled closed. He winks as I take it, making my heart beat faster. He's ridiculously handsome in his fitted leather riding pants and billowing white shirt, opened at the collar to reveal the muscled flare of his pectorals. And he knows it. I roll my eyes, making him grin wider.

Laying the bundle on a nearby tree stump, I unroll it carefully and stare at the thin polished instruments. No. No, it can't be. "Are these…"

"Lockpicks," Tye supplies helpfully. "Aye."

River curses.

"These are…" I struggle to find the right word. "Gorgeous" doesn't seem to fit the objects and "a sure way to get arrested" doesn't fit the mood. "High-quality tools of a trade I don't quite know."

Tye sighs gravely. "I was afraid of that. I will have to teach you, then, lass." His emerald eyes sparkle. "Though I must warn you, I'm a very hands-on type of instructor."

I snap the kit closed very quickly, then stuff it into my saddlebag. When I step away, I find Coal's blue eyes watching me from the side. Five fae and four packages. Coal isn't the type for sentimentality. I nod my understanding at him.

Coal turns away.

A heartbeat later, a glistening boot dagger whizzes so close to my ear that I hear the whistle of air as it flies by. With a dull thump, the blade impales itself into a tree, the hilt still vibrating from the impact. Saying nothing, Coal mounts his horse, leaving me to collect my final gift in silence.

With everyone mounted up, River lays a large hand on his sister's shoulders, Autumn reaching up to grasp his muscled forearm. The siblings trade no words, and I wonder how many such goodbyes they've exchanged over the centuries—each time knowing they might not be quite the same beings when they meet next. Before I can dwell on the thought, River clicks to his stallion and leads us to Great Falls Academy.

5

LERA

he ride to Mystwood's edge is quiet and efficient. Letting the horses rest and water before we enter the warded forest, River pulls out a saucer-sized disk carved with runes—one of the few keys permitting the bearers passage through the forest. The magic radiating from the relic tickles my skin, drawing me toward it.

"Stay together. We've a small radius," River says, his calm voice a beacon as I ready to step into the Gloom—one of the new and rare skills my fae body came equipped with. Which makes entering it no more pleasant than it was when the males had to tow me along.

The air around me thickens, a moment of viscous blackness pushing against me on all sides, and then I'm in the dull echo of the world. The colors and noises and smells are all short of what they should be—shades of gray and strange echoes. Wrong. But travel is faster here—and when it comes to Mystwood, traveling through the Gloom is the only way possible to traverse the place. Even with the key.

River once explained the Gloom as an underlining to the

33

normal world—what we call the Light—a slippery undercloth that shifts and moves with the main cloth but is separate from it as well. Some of the stitching, like many of Mystwood's ash and maple trees, penetrate all the way through. Other pieces, like much of the shrubbery, exist only in the Light. Poetic, but I've worked out my own, more practical, definition.

The Gloom is where creatures of darkness and evil thrive and roam, unseen in the Light until they are ready to rise and strike. Something that can never be permitted to happen in the mortal realm.

This is my second time crossing Mystwood, the first being when the males whisked me away from servitude in Zake's stable. Now, returning as a fae warrior myself, I expect the forest to seem less oppressive. In reality, the opposite is true.

"One nice thing about being human is that you don't know what goes bump in the shadows, Lilac Girl," Tye says, stretching lazily beside me—seeming to read my mind as usual. "Which is why I make it a personal goal to know as little as possible about everything."

We move along with little conversation, Shade's wolf keeping as close to us as the horses will tolerate. When the five of us clear Mystwood less than six hours later, stepping into the Light just before the edge of the mortal realm, the muted oppression of the Gloom finally melts away—only to reveal a new set of shackles one step later. My magic. Lashed down as tightly as a ship's furled sails.

Having lived most of my life without the magic, I thought this part would little bother me, but the emptiness grips my throat. Looking around with my immortal's heightened senses, I mourn the loss of Lunos's lush intensity even as I pick up each sound and smell the way my human body never could.

With so few humans willing to live anywhere near the edge of Mystwood, it's relatively easy to keep out of the humans' sight during the four-day ride to the town of Great Falls, which takes its name from a tall, narrow waterfall rushing over a cliff high in the mountains on the right. Its roar echoes distantly around the small, steep valley, over the patchwork sheep meadows and neat timber-frame houses. The lonely screech of circling ravens and a stiff breeze mark our passage across a bare, grassy ridge above the valley.

Stopping at an overlook a mile off, I raise my hand to block out the sun as I examine the Academy's estate sprawling at the top of a foothill overlooking the town. An immense walled-off fortress of gray stone, blending into the mountains behind it, its gilded red standard flapping on the cold wind. The hiss and crack of the fabric cuts into my hearing. I frown. Even with my fae senses, the flapping cloth is too far away to be heard. No, the hiss and crack is coming from something else, though it certainly sounds like a flapping flag.

I glance around, Sprite dancing beneath me enough to earn a disapproving glance from Coal. Nothing about him or the other males suggests they hear anything amiss. In fact—I realize with a start—River is speaking.

"…A generation of influential youth all in one place." The quint commander pats his stallion's neck, his voice filled with a responsibility he can't help. Perhaps that need to take charge is what makes River who he is. "I hope the staff have a firm bit in the youngsters' mouths before the would-be kings decide to compare the size of their cocks and do something unusually stupid."

Hiss crack crack.

My pulse jumps.

"Lass?" Tye frowns. "Are you—"

"They aren't children," I say quickly, forcing my voice into mild outrage to knock Tye's inconvenient perceptiveness off scent. After all my insistence over us coming here, at the first sight of our battleground, I'm already hearing phantom noises. "Twenty years might be nothing for fae, but for a human, it's rather significant. It also happens to be my age."

"My point exactly," says River. "Let's get this done. Remember what Autumn said about muted bonds and brace yourselves for the change." Taking out the veil amulet, the male snaps it around his neck with no ceremony, the others wordlessly following his example. The intricately carved wood medallions fall against their sternums until they each tuck them away under their shirts.

Hiss crack crack.

I fumble for my own amulet, a chill running over my skin as I settle it around my neck. The soft click of the clasp is one of the loudest sounds I've ever heard—a slamming door cutting me off from the males. My lungs tighten painfully, and it takes all my willpower to keep my hands light on Sprite's reins. To raise my chin. To smile with a cockiness I wish I felt.

"So, then," I say, realizing too late that I've forgotten to don the dress Autumn gave me. Damn it. I'll do it as soon as we find a less exposed spot on our way to the Academy. In my black pants and favorite fitted blue tunic, belted around the waist, the magic could give me a disguise for just about anyone. "What am I now?"

"A pain in the ass," says Coal, the carved angles of his face still as he cocks a brow at me.

"We know you, cub. The amulet won't spin a veil for those who know the truth," Shade, now in his fae form, says gently. "We look like ourselves to you too, do we not?"

"Right. Of course." I rub my eyes with the heel of my hand.

"What's wrong, Lilac Girl?" Tye asks.

"Nothing. I mean I can't feel you with the amulet. And—"

Tye winces. "It does hurt me to see you lie so poorly, lass. We need to work on that. What is it?"

I sigh, shaking my head. "Just an odd noise I heard. A hissing sound, like…static, but louder. Do you hear it?"

They pause, cocking their heads in concentration.

"No," says Tye after a moment, Shade, Coal, and River echo their agreement, their eyes kind—and somewhat worried.

Heat fills my cheeks, but River raises his hand, stopping my attempt to apologize. "Us not hearing it doesn't mean nothing is there. Your magic is unique, Leralynn. A human made fae, a weaver to boot. It is entirely possible you are hearing escaping magic. Perhaps the very rift we are here to find."

"Or my own imagination."

River shrugs one shoulder. "Indeed. But, being immortal we've the time to check. Where is the sound coming from?"

"It's…" The words die in my mouth. Nothing. I hear nothing now but my own racing heart. The heat already touching my cheeks spreads to make the tips of my ears tingle. Swallowing, I close my eyes, willing myself to find the sound again. Nothing. "May I take the amulet off? Perhaps it's interfering with the sound."

River's gaze weighs the distance to the Academy before he nods. "For a bit."

I open the clasp and shove the amulet into my breast pocket, relief flooding me as the mating bonds call to me once more—and the static. At least I wasn't imagining the noise. "This way." Nudging Sprite into a trot, I lead the males toward the sound, which grows louder with each step. Overwhelming. We cross into a whispering green aspen wood, light flickering through the leaves in dizzying patterns. My muscles tense, my breath and heart speeding as Sprite picks up a gallop along a narrow uphill trail. The hooves of the males' stallions keep pace, staying far enough back to avoid sending the horses into a competitive race, which would likely end with me on the ground.

Hiss crack crack. Hiss crack crack.

The trail swings sharply to the right, but with sound coming so clearly from behind a cluster of huge boulders on the opposite side, I nudge my mount that way. Sprite takes the left at alarming speed, her body angling sharply. I have no time to twist around and make sure the males saw me turn off the trail, no ability to do anything but cling on with every muscle fiber. Sprite's hooves pound the uneven ground, the horse out of control as she races for the boulders, which prove farther away than I'd guessed. Branches whip, clumps of earth flying into the air. I grab the pommel of my saddle to keep my seat, the reins loosening in my hands. My legs squeeze the horse's sides, my instinctual clinging unfortunately signaling Sprite to run faster still.

HISS. CRACK—

I see the crumbling rune-carved stone embedded in the ground a heartbeat before Sprite trips over it. The tenuous hold I have on my saddle breaks, sending me to the ground. My head cracks against a rock, the sound coming before the pain. Then the world flashes in a blaze of blinding light before darkness comes.

6

LERA

I wake with a horse's nose poking my back, the clicking aspen forest sprawling its spring glory before me. My head hurts, but I find no blood when I touch my skull. Small miracle. I also find no one else beside me.

"River?" I call, my pulse hammering. "Coal? Tye? Shade?"

Silence. A few paces away, the rune-carved stone Sprite tripped over is broken into hand-sized bits. By the looks of it, the thing was a square slate about the length of a man's forearm on each side and pushed into the cold earth like a misaligned paving stone. The noise from it—if there ever was a noise—is gone. Picking up one of the shards, I realize the thing wasn't stone all the way through, but rather just a hard shell protecting a softer claylike core that leaves dust on my fingers.

"River?" I call again. "Anyone?"

Only chattering birds answer, and the ghostly whispering of bright-green leaves.

Sprite whinnies, stomping one foot with a loose shoe.

Damn it. Bending down, I pull the shoe the rest of the way off and toss it away. I'll be walking the horse from here on out. But walking her to where?

Holding Sprite by her reins, I slowly retrace the path we galloped, through slants of golden evening light. The tracks curve downhill, turning sharply toward the narrow trail Sprite and I had run. Here, several sets of diverging hoofprints lead in all directions. As if some riders had followed the trail to the right—where I'd gone left—and others turned their horses around completely, heading back to a wider road. Or perhaps the mounts had spooked and run.

I shake my head, instantly regretting the motion as pain slices down the back of my skull. *Think, Lera. What exactly happened?* Forcing my breathing to steady, I think back. I recall cantering. No, galloping. The males giving me space, but not staying far back. Then the trail went right. But I didn't. I turned off the trail and headed sharply left. Sprite broke into a gallop over bad terrain. She tripped. I fell, hitting my head. Losing consciousness. With the thick green foliage and sharp turn, the males might not have seen me take the turn and fall, but surely they should have found me by now.

Except they didn't.

By the looks of the horse tracks, they went the other way entirely. I sigh, pulling myself together. I've no notion how long I was unconscious, but from the sun's movement, it was some time. Whatever the reason the males left, they are now either too far to hear me yell or not in a position to answer. Perhaps, with the mating bond muted by their amulets, they don't feel me—or their fear for me—as fiercely as they normally would. I don't feel them at all, though my fear is perfectly intact. The reality of existence without the bond's pull sends a chill down my spine, despite knowing it would happen. Bracing a hand against a tree, I take a deep breath and force my mind to function. Plan. I've two choices now by my reckoning: either stay here in the middle of the woods, hoping to be rescued before the predators decide I'm dinner, or continue to the Academy as planned and work things through there.

My hands tremble as I take up Sprite's reins, leading the mare down the path. I slip on my veil amulet lest I cross paths with anyone, shivering at the feelings that pass over me—the deadening of deafened mating bonds, the faint vertigo that comes from pulling an alternate identity over me like a cloak.

To my relief, the amulet remained intact during the fall, along with my saddlebags. I try to focus on that. On anything except why no one is here. There is an explanation for this. There has to be. This is but a hiccup, I promise myself, refusing to let the thickening woods and lengthening shadows, the rising hoot of an owl, the crunching step of an unseen animal, close around me.

With the Academy clearly visible atop high ground, I keep my course set on its flapping standard. Winding trails come and go along steep hills, but I keep straight and move quickly, talking to Sprite softly as we walk unwaveringly between trees. "We are Sprite and Lera," I tell Sprite, who nickers in agreement. "I am a fae female of a warrior quint. And we are here to discover what's letting magic leak into the human world. We are here to save people. We aren't afraid."

It's well past sunset by the time Sprite and I finally make it to the Academy wall, dark-gray stone rising into the blackness above me, topped with flickering torches. A heavy wooden gate with iron spikes the width of my thigh rises on creaking pulleys to let me into a vestibule, the secondary gate remaining closed.

The uniformed guard who let me in frowns, lowering the spiked gate back down behind Sprite and me. Trapping us between the two exits. "It is past curfew," he says, his black brows narrowing. He's the first human I've seen up close in months, and I instantly notice the differences—the blunter features, as if seen through a foggy lens, the shorter stature and softer frame.

I lick my dry lips. "I'm…" The amulet warms against my sternum, phantom memories shimmering in my mind, changing my history.

The estate that I grew up in as Zake's indentured servant becomes a mansion with high vaulted ceilings and plush rugs. My old clothes shift from a stable hand's ill-fitting rags to a too-tight tailored dress embroidered with a coat of arms. The belt that beat me raw still remains in my memories, though the lord wielding it now presses me against an upholstered wall instead of a stable's rough wood for the lashings.

I'm a noble-born orphan, my new memories tell me. Taken in by Lord Zake of Osprey and raised as his ward. I have no friends.

I clear my throat and try again. "I'm—"

"Leralynn of Osprey," the guard finishes for me. "I'm aware of who you are. But not why you are late. Great Falls Academy, you will discover, does not tolerate tardiness. Nor do we tolerate students roaming the wilderness. In fact, Commander River—that's the Academy's deputy headmaster who took up the late Commander Jun's vacant post five months ago—has ordered that anyone found in violation of curfew be sent directly to him."

"River?" My breath catches, relief and anxiety filling my chest. The amulets are working, and my males—at least one of them—is here. It's all right. Whatever the reason River never circled back to get me, I'll discover it shortly. I am not alone. "River is here?" I repeat, not realizing I've grabbed the guard's wrist until he cocks a thick brow at me.

"Take a breath, girl." The man softens his voice, apparently taking my behavior as a sign that the appropriate level of terror has been instilled. "I won't report you, just this once. Though if I were you, I'd endeavor to know as little of the captain as you do now." He motions for the inner doors to be opened and leads me into the Academy's sleeping campus, while one of the other guards takes charge of Sprite.

A quick mental analysis confirms I have no choice but to follow him, to play along with my disguise until I can gather more information. No matter how much I long to run through the Academy shouting River's name, I'm here for a mission—one that I can't risk because I'm too frightened to spend a night alone. Plus, the danger of being discovered as fae in these parts is not lost on me either—I little need a farmer or hunter trying to plant an axe between my shoulder blades. Avoiding the desire to finger my amulet, I follow the guard meekly.

Even in the night's darkness, my immortal eyes mark the Academy's grand sprawl. Stone buildings rising several stories into the air on all sides of us, the distant neigh of stabled horses, cobblestone passages, and quietly burbling fountains.

"The physical training and maneuvers take place in the yard on the east side of the Academy." The guard points as we walk across the broad central square, our footsteps echoing hollowly in the silence. "The dormitories are in the southwest. Academic lessons take place in the keep, to the northwest." It's obvious which building he means—an immense castle with pointed spires blocking the stars directly behind us. The fortress on the hill that can be seen for miles, its flapping red standard my earlier guide.

Leading me into a square building with a small stone courtyard in its center, the guard takes the external whitewashed walkways to bring me up to the second story.

"Bedchamber 241," the guard says, unaware that my fae eyes let me read the lettering for myself. He hands me a key. "You share it with Arisha of Tallie. Tomorrow, you may collect your issued supplies and your allowance from the quartermaster. Most of our new students find the adjustment to the Academy's discipline difficult. For your sake, I suggest you adapt quickly. Treat the guards and instructors with the reverence you would offer your elders at home, and you will do well. You may be my superior in a ballroom, but here, at Great Falls, you are a student."

The last is said with no malice, and I thank the male—the man—demurely before ducking into the darkened room, a girl's soft snores the only sound to counter my pounding head. River, at least, has made it. As the bloody deputy headmaster. I rub my temple. It does fit, given his overprotective and in-constant-charge personality. The others I'll have to find in the morning. Along with the reason they all left me behind.

7

LERA

"*L*eralynn, wake up." A female voice urges me from sleep.

Blinking my eyes open, I find myself staring at a comely girl about my age, with frizzy brown hair and large eyes. For a few seconds, all I can do is stare at her rounded ear tips. *Arisha of Tallie,* my memory of the guard's words last night tells me. My roommate. I lift my still-aching head, the warming amulet reminding me that I'm a new student. A lady. Leralynn of Osprey, sent here to study with other prominent youths. For a moment, the story is so persuasive that my heart skips a beat as I scramble out of bed. I was late coming in last night, and if I am late again this morning—

Lera. I am Leralynn, a warrior of a fae quint on a crucial mission. And I need to find my mates.

Beyond Arisha, my gaze takes in the small white-walled room with high ceilings, as if the architect attempted to balance the tiny floor space by making the walls taller. Two narrow beds, two plain wooden dressers, and two tiny desks built to fold down from the wall make up the entirety of the furniture. The thick drapes covering the one tall window might have once been bright, but now are a heavy faded olive. Beside my bed, the contents of my saddlebags spill like wine over the floor, making it difficult to find a place to step. On Arisha's side of the room, pens, paper, and books are arranged in such perfect rows, I wonder if the young woman didn't use a ruler to place them.

"You may borrow one of my uniforms for the morning exercise if you'd like." Arisha shifts her feet impatiently, chewing on her lower lip. Freckles cross her sharp cheekbones, and, beneath her round glasses, the deep bags under her eyes speak to sleeplessness or stress—or both. She is already dressed in a pair of gray pants and a matching tunic with a red insignia that must be the school's crest, both a bit small on her. Her hands shake slightly as she wrestles her long hair into two uneven braids. "It will be a little loose on your thin frame, but better than…" She waves her hand at my travel clothes, which I'd not bothered removing before bed. "Whatever you decide, you should do so quickly. Master Coal and I have an understanding that I would rather not test."

I freeze, my fingers tightening over the gray tunic Arisha extends. "Coal?" I make myself move, changing into the offered clothes. *Coal. Coal. Coal.* "What understanding do you have with him exactly?"

"That I'm a waste of space and air that he should ignore when possible." Arisha frowns at one of her already unraveling braids. "I would like to give him every opportunity possible to continue ignoring me. Being late little helps."

Stars, Arisha truly thinks she met Coal months ago and has a whole history with the male. Autumn wasn't jesting about the power of the amulets. The complexity of magic required to build an entire intricate backstory in so many minds is enough to send a shiver down my spine.

I pull on Arisha's spare pants, using a cloth belt to keep them from falling.

She tosses me a stale roll, which I just manage to catch before it drops to the floor. "The instructors think training on an empty stomach teaches our bodies to burn fat instead of muscle and prepares us better for the 'trials of leadership.' So this is it until the midmorning meal."

"How long has, er, Master Coal, been teaching here?" I ask, shoving the roll into a pocket and hopping on one foot to get my boots back on as I follow Arisha out the door.

"Four or five months," Arisha says over her shoulder. "He came about the same time the deputy headmaster and one of the head medics did. The three of them served together on the far coast. No one in their right mind gets in Master Coal's or Commander River's way, but their medic friend is… attractive and kind, which has tripled the sick-call volume." I notice a faint blush going up Arisha's cheeks and have to swallow a curse. My males haven't just arrived—they've made an entrance.

"Is the—" I catch myself, tweaking my question before I can reveal more than I wish. "What's the medic's name?"

"Shade." Arisha stumbles as a pair of stunning women in our same drab gray uniforms brush none too gently past her. "And that would be Princess Katita and one of her favored-for-the-day ladies."

Before I can call Katita and her ilk out, the pair disappears into a sea of uniformed young cadets all flowing from their rooms to the outdoor walkways and steps. The din of conversation and boots clattering on wooden walkways mists the chilled air, my own breath turning to wisps of steam before me. Hurrying after Arisha—who is now explaining something I can't make myself pay mind to—I keep my gaze moving from face to face. I have to find the males. Quickly.

Quietly. Raising no suspicion. Plans order themselves in my mind, solidifying with each step. I'll see Coal shortly. A feigned injury can take me to Shade. The veil made River a deputy headmaster. Barging into his study might be hard to explain—but hopefully the male will find me. That—

"Leralynn!" Arisha's warning hits me too late, my distraction having walked me directly into a broad muscular back.

Dressed in the same grays as I, the back's owner turns slowly, his pine-and-citrus scent filling my nose. Amused emerald eyes look down at me from a height towering over all others, making my breath stop altogether. Thick red hair flips over a perfectly stunning, sharply angled face, one silver earring glinting.

Tye. My chest squeezes, the wave of relief washing over me so strong that I feel light-headed for a moment. I feel my hand close around Tye's wrist of its own volition. "You are here."

"Aye, lass," Tye says, glancing at where I'm still gripping his wrist. "The last I checked, I was in fact here. Are you somewhere else, then?"

Princess Katita and her friend now stop to chuckle, delicate hands covering painted lips.

I little care. Not now that I've found Tye. The half a day since I lost sight of the males is the longest we've been apart since we mated, and even with the bond itself muted in the mortal realm, the separation has left me breathless. Longing. It is a force of will to stop myself from leaping into Tye's arms, claiming his mouth before all the watching cadets.

As my eyes brush over Tye hungrily, I find myself unable to focus on his pointed ears and canines no matter how hard I try to look there, as if a great magnetic force repels my gaze. Beneath the loose folds of Tye's gray uniform, the outline of his lithe muscles are as familiar to me as his scent. As is everything about him—*almost* everything.

"Might I have my arm back now?" says Tye, something about his voice making my gaze snap up to meet his. And once I do, I understand what's off. The lively green eyes I know so well sparkle with no sign of recognition.

8

LERA

My attention sweeps to Tye's neck, the effort required to focus on where the amulet should be enough to make my head spin. When I finally manage to look, I see only the top of the male's shirt. No string. No wooden carving. Not even an impression of one beneath the cloth.

"Leralynn," Arisha hisses, pulling my hand off Tye's arm and tugging me along. "We're going to be late. Let's go."

I stumble, barely managing to stop myself from taking a nosedive down the steps. My gut clenches, the wrongness of Tye's unrecognizing gaze, his missing amulet, filling me with a new terror. Something happened in that aspen wood, something more ominous than a missed turn and misinterpreted change of course. Something that made the magic go terribly, terribly wrong.

"It's a pleasure to meet you, Leralynn," Tye calls after me, the amusement in his voice echoing off the now nearly empty dormitory walkways. Grabbing the railing, Tye vaults himself over it, jumping smoothly to the courtyard one story below.

Lifting his face, he pitches his voice back up toward me. "I've other parts you can grab as well, lass, if you are so inclined."

My skin blazes, the inferno growing with the chortles of the few stragglers around me. Numb horror spreads through my limbs as I follow Arisha into the vast central square. The pale dawn sky overhead washes everything in shades of blue and gray, and it's a relief when we cross out of shadow into the slowly warming sun.

"You are insane," Arisha mutters, releasing my arm.

"Do you know who that was?" I ask, my mind sorting through the fog for possible explanations for Tye's empty eyes and finding none, except that he'd perhaps been acting. Bluffing for the sake of our cover story. Yes—a convincing act. To avoid suspicion. It has to have been.

"Everyone knows Tyelor." Arisha sighs. "The man is Great Falls Academy's top athlete, here by special invitation and preparing for the continent's Prowess Trials. Swordplay, wrestling, acrobatics—you name it, Tyelor rules it. He rules every female's attention in the place too."

"Not every female's," I say, finally focusing on Arisha's annoyed expression. "You don't like him."

She shrugs. "I'm more keen on people who can work out a defensive strategy than ones who think their ability to wave about a pointy piece of metal—or other parts—is the stars' gift to humankind." Arisha's pace quickens across the square, her shoulders hunching. "If you think you can manage stairs without killing yourself, we should try to walk faster."

Crossing under a grand stone archway and entering the training yard, which is larger than anything I've seen before, I find the place divided into a dozen grass-covered corrals. Inside each enclosure, students go through the motions of swordplay and archery, wrestling and—in the two larger arenas—horsemanship. Instructors' calls and students' grunts of effort and pain fill the morning air.

"Look for the colored flags when you come here," Arisha says, pointing to the large triangular pennants waving beside each area. "The instructors choose what training area they need for the day and mark it with their flag. We are under Coal, who has the blue flag, which is—"

"There." My voice comes out in a low whisper as my gaze falls on Coal. With black pants hanging low on his lean hips, the warrior is bare to the waist, his deadly muscles sliding beneath his skin as he demonstrates a takedown. The tattoos spiraling down the groove of Coal's spine dance as if alive with each shift of his weight. The deadly precision of that beautiful body takes my breath even now—mine, and that of the five other female students who watch the demonstration from the sidelines with similarly still chests. "That is most certainly Coal."

"You are late," the male in question calls over his shoulder as Arisha and I approach the corral. Takedown complete, Coal's attention lingers on the other students as they pair off to practice it themselves. That done, the warrior leans sideways against the fence, his arms crossed over his chest as the morning sun sculpts the hard lines of his face to menacing perfection.

"Good morning," I say quietly, the sting of Tye's greeting still shooting down my nerves. My gut clenches as I await Coal's reaction, the screaming voice in the back of my mind a reminder of how wrong everything has gone.

Coal turns at the sound of my voice and rocks back on his heels, something unreadable in his shockingly blue gaze. "I realize you're new, but I imagine you did learn to tell time before stepping foot here?"

I tense. Wait. Hold his eyes, my mind pleading for some sign of recognition. Some signal that he knows me. Knows us.

Nothing. If my body responds to the familiar danger that always vibrates inside the warrior, Coal sees nothing before him but a fresh-faced cadet.

Ice grips me at the chill in his gaze. His utter indifference to my existence.

Dipping my eyes, I trail them along Coal's body. With his shirt off and torso bare, I should be able to see the veil amulet if I know what I'm looking for, if I can conquer my body's instinct to look away from the rune-carved disk. Starting at the center of the eight hard squares of Coal's abdomen, I move my eyes along the grooved midline of his body. Up between his wide pectorals. Out along the sharp collarbones—*bloody stars*, I've strayed off course.

Forcing my eyes back to Coal's midline, I trace the groove again, refusing to look away. My head pounds, the need to focus elsewhere so palpable that it makes breathing difficult. A ringing starts in my ears, the sound and pressure growing more painful with each fraction of an inch my gaze climbs.

I dig my nails into my palm. *Look up, Lera. Up. A little more.*

It takes me a moment to realize that I've reached my target because there, at the hollow of Coal's sternum where the amulet should be, nothing hangs at all. Instead, my aching eyes trace the outlines of a circular tattoo with an ornate pointed pattern, the exact size and design the amulet would have been. As if Coal's body somehow absorbed the magical artifact. My heart pounds, recalling the flat lay of Tye's shirt. *Stars.*

"Am I inconveniencing your daydreaming?" Coal's voice snaps like a whip, drawing my attention back to his face. Cold blue eyes weigh me—and find me wanting. Just like when he first saw me all those months ago in Zake's barn. "What is your name?"

Arisha curses under her breath, quietly enough that a human wouldn't have heard.

"Creative, though not physiologically possible, I believe," Coal tells Arisha, his brow cocking toward her quickly paling face. No wonder these students are terrified of River and Coal —when you're up against preternatural fae senses without knowing it, there's nowhere to hide. "Feel free to improve on that model as you take two laps around the Academy."

"That's over f-five miles," Arisha stutters.

"Fair point. Three laps." Coal's focus returns to me, his tone as hard as I've ever heard it. "I asked for your name, Cadet."

9

COAL

"Leralynn," the new student standing before Coal said, pronouncing the name as if it should mean something to him. In her early twenties, the young woman was stunning enough to stir Coal's cock, her shining auburn hair and large brown eyes reflecting the misty dawn rays. Ethereal, that was the only word for her. Even beneath an ill-fitting uniform she must have borrowed from Arisha, the swell of her breasts and the curve of her hips held the attention of every male in the training corral. Which had no right to bother Coal, though it did. Leralynn cleared her throat. "Or Lera. Or mortal."

"Mortal?" Coal echoed, the word singing to him even as the two dozen cadets of his training cadre laughed at the joke.

Lera wasn't laughing, though. She just stepped closer, the lilac scent of her making Coal's head swim. "It's a nickname a good friend once gave me."

Coal pushed back from the fence, stepping far enough away to let the chill air clear his senses. "Your friend isn't here.

Neither are your parents, your servants, your nursemaid, or anyone else who cares."

Hurt flashed across Lera's chocolate eyes. The young woman had plainly been expecting a different reception. All the new students—with their high-class upbringing and powerful family names—did. River thought shattering that particular illusion as quickly as possible was the humane approach. Coal little cared whether it was humane—he cared that it was efficient. In the five months since his assignment to Great Falls, half the students assigned to Coal's team had decided to pack up and go home within a week of arrival.

From her bewildered expression, Leralynn would be joining the departing ranks soon enough. With luck, she might complain about Coal before leaving. Make the headmaster finally decide that Coal was more trouble than he was worth. Then River would *have* to let him leave, go back to the far coast, where Coal could lick his wounds in private. If he was lucky, maybe find some new war to fight in—there was always one conflict or another with islanders. Coal had no business teaching—let alone teaching noble brats who were not much younger than his twenty-seven years, yet seemed to have lived not the quarter of the life he had.

Coal's attention returned to his newest headache, whose mere presence was already making half the male cadets in the corral trip over their own feet. Yes, the boys had not yet learned the dangers of women.

"Well, *mortal,* do you see the three dozen stones in that corner?" Coal jerked his chin toward a pile of rough, watermelon-sized boulders arranged into a neat pile. The limestone from which they'd been cracked had a chalklike feel, the grit having an uncanny way of rubbing skin and getting under clothes. "Move them to the next corner over. And then the next."

A muscle in Leralynn's jaw ticked.

Arisha moved slowly away from them in the corner of his vision.

Coal moved closer, invading Lera's space, seizing upon the embers of anger sparking in the girl's eyes at what she no doubt saw as unjust punishment. Anger was good. It made Coal's point for him. He wasn't her friend. Didn't want to be her friend. And given the painful effect Lera's mere presence was having on his body, the sooner she walked out of his world, the better. Coal clicked his tongue. "And once you do that, move them to the next. Do you think you can remember all that without a clerk's assistance?"

"I'll endeavor to keep track of so complex a routine," she said, her voice quiet but not weak. Despite barely reaching Coal's shoulder, Lera held her ground when larger men would have retreated, the heat of her body an answering blow to Coal's challenge. Small and fierce and somehow unafraid of him. "I'll do it all twice if you leave off Arisha. She was only late on my account."

Stars take him. "Make that offer *after* you finish the circuit," Coal said, returning to the other students, who'd opportunistically stopped drilling and now watched the show with unabashed curiosity. Or, in the males' case, watched Leralynn. A glare from Coal set that to rights before he tossed his voice over his shoulder. "If you finish in time to be of any use to your friend, that is."

Instead of an answer, Coal heard the scrape of stone on stone as the small cadet heaved the first burden into her arms. And then the second. The fifth. The tenth. By the time she'd moved the load one corner over, Coal knew he'd made a strategic error: making Lera haul stones about was a punishment, but implying that her speed would determine another's fate was a challenge. How the bloody hell was he to have guessed the small spitfire would rise to it?

Even with his back to her, pretending to watch the sparring pairs before him, Coal could hear Lera's labored breathing, see the tracks in the sand where her balance faltered as she hurried faster than was wise. *Stars,* she was going to injure herself if she kept it up. And there wasn't a bloody thing he could do about it now except to witness the gambit he himself had set into motion. This wasn't about the punishment, or even Lera's friend—not really. Coal had greeted Lera with an opening volley designed to drive her away, and the bloody woman was calling him on it. And winning. Two dozen students in the corral before him, and Coal couldn't get his attention off the one walking the perimeter fence—and doing so faster than a girl her size had any right to be.

Arisha of Tallie—who belonged in a sparring ring about as much as a tabby cat belonged in a choir—was just finishing the first of her three laps when Lera planted herself in front of Coal, standing so close that he took an involuntary step back. The girl's sweat carried a sweet lilac scent, tinged with a bit of a copper tang. Blood.

He tensed, the smell spurring his heart to a gallop that took all his self-control to rein in.

"I'm finished with the first circuit, sir." Leralynn told him, her brown eyes aflame. "If you allow Arisha to return to the corral, I'll get started with the second. And if you wish, the third after that."

Grasping Lera's slender wrist, Coal twisted it palm up. The calluses from what looked like weapons training were intact, but the skin on the sensitive middle of the hand was rubbed raw. Shallow but painful wounds that roused every protective instinct in Coal's body to the surface. Which made no sense. "Your sleeves are too long." Coal's voice was flat. "If you were smart, you'd have pushed them down to cover your hands and prevented this."

"I presumed the point of the exercise was to make me miserable, so thought I might as well be efficient about it." Lera's fingers curled over her palm. "Now, are you going to hold up your end of the deal…sir?"

Coal strode into Shade's infirmary office, slamming the door hard enough to make the wooden frame shake in protest. "I want out," Coal said without preamble, his blood simmering as it had since morning training. "I'm a soldier, not a bloody nursemaid for noble brats."

"Do you?" In his neat white shirt and leather vest, long black hair pulled back, Shade looked every inch the civilized officer—though Coal had fought beside Shade for enough years to know the man was a vicious warrior when the situation called for it. Still, Shade seemed as content here at the Academy as when he, Coal, and River served together at the coast, fighting the hordes of islanders wanting to gain a foothold on the continent.

"I was unaware that you ever *wanted* to be here," Shade said with a hint of amusement as he rose from behind his desk and walked around to perch himself on its edge. "So, you see how the absence of the desire now fails to make an impression on me."

"I'm not here to make an impression."

Shade's strange golden eyes strayed to the door, likely assuring the lock was engaged before speaking—this time in a low voice. Shade was a friend, yes, but also Coal's military superior, a fact that Coal sensed was about to be brought up. "You are here because you were one bad night away from doing something stupid," Shade murmured. "To put it bluntly, King Zenith invested too great a fortune in your training to let you get yourself killed in some suicidal outing. Until you've worked out…whatever is going on in there, Lieutenant, you aren't going anywhere." He gestured toward Coal's head as if it were a messy barracks.

"It's worked out." Coal crossed his arms. In the five months since Coal had come here—since Shade and River had forced him here—things had only worsened. The nightmares. The flashes of darkness and groundless fear. Images of a woman who was never real to begin with, yet whose loss bled him raw. Coal's spine stiffened. He was a soldier. He needed to fight, not sit shackled behind high walls. "I'm fine, Shade. What isn't fine is this made-up world of Great Falls Academy, where brats play at soldiers and generals, safely away from anything that might actually take their lives. I want no part of it."

"I see." Shade's words barely touched the air before the man was moving, his body low, his hands snatching at Coal's unprotected elbow.

Coal shifted his weight, his mind waking to the fight. Twisting away from Shade's opening attack, he crouched low, his breath even as his eyes took in the room. Lunging forward, his hands cut Shade's knees out from under him, sending the dark-haired warrior to the floor.

Shade fell smoothly, rolling over his shoulder to reclaim his footing. Chest rising with deep breaths, he bared his teeth, his feet light as he circled Coal. With a soft growl, the man lunged forward again, this time ducking under Coal's arm to grab his wrist. With a force few people had, Shade slammed Coal's arm against the wall, his strong grip a living restraint.

Coal's stomach twisted. The world rumbled in his ears.

Giving no reprieve, Shade captured Coal's other wrist, forcing both against Coal's sides.

The rumbling in Coal's ears turned to roaring. The air seemed to flash, like lightning striking through the night, and the stench of pain and fear and blood from a dank prison cell vibrated through each fiber of his body. His heart raced, beating so hard, his ribs felt the impact. His muscles tightened, powerful and ready, his eyes widening to take in the slowing world he was about to destroy.

Because he *would* destroy it.

Pressing his shoulder blades into the wall for purchase, Coal speared his heel into his assailant's chest so hard that he felt ribs crack.

His captor flew backward, crashing into his own desk and sliding to the floor. Wood splintered, black ink spilling across paper, mixing with the thin stream of red blood dripping from the bastard's cut brow. Shade's brow.

Coal swore. Dropping to one knee beside his friend, he slid a hand behind the warrior's back, easing him into a sitting position. "Are you insane?" Coal demanded, loosening the top of the man's jacket to help him breathe. "No. Don't move about."

Drawing a hissing breath, Shade wrapped his arm around his ribs, his yellow gaze piercing Coal's. Anyone less trained would have ended up with a broken neck, but Shade knew how to take a fall. Had known what was coming before he ever attacked.

"I will give you your medical clearance to leave when you can tell the difference between friend and foe—whether or not they are trying to restrain you." Shade's voice was tight with pain as he pressed his sleeve against the bleeding gash on his brow and frowned at the stain. "And River is fully with me on this. We've known each other for ten years, Coal. If you won't tell us what the hell those bastards who held you prisoner did to you, then find someone else to talk to. Until you figure this out, you are not going anywhere."

LERA

"Come. You'll feel better after you eat. Maybe." Shepherding me along, Arisha leads me into the dining hall, where high-backed cushioned chairs surround ornately carved wooden tables, each seating groups of four to eight quietly murmuring students. The shining marble floors reflect grand crystal candelabras hanging from the vaulted ceiling, the candles unlit in deference to the sun streaming in through tall, spotless windows. Fine woven runners in rich reds and blues mark the pathways between tables. The gray uniforms look as out of place here as ball gowns in a stable. "The dining hall is informal the first half of the day," Arisha explains, "but we dress up for dinner."

I nod, not trusting my voice. My breaths come heavy still, my muscles trembling from fatigue. My fae body will heal faster than a human's would, but I still hurt. The physical pain is the least of my worries just now, though. Like Tye, Coal didn't recognize me, didn't so much as glance my way the entire time I worked. Not an act. Where does that leave our mission, then? Do the males remember why we are at the Academy at all? Does *River,* our commander, remember?

Something went wrong after we parted ways on the forest path, and until I can get one of them alone, I have no way of knowing the extent of it. I shiver, remembering Coal's icy gaze. No connection, no attraction, not even a curiosity. As if what I believed were unbreakable bonds of love are nothing more than a trick of magic. A house of cards that, with that magic's disappearance, has simply collapsed.

Finding an empty table, Arisha motions for me to sit while she fetches two portions of hearty porridge and heels of steaming fresh bread, relief at training's end hanging around her like a cloud. Even after Coal allowed her to stop running, Arisha had done poorly in practice, tripping over her own feet so often that Coal finally set her aside to work basic punches against thin air. She'd fallen doing that too.

"Coal always goes hard on new people," Arisha says, pushing the bowl closer to me. "Don't take it personally. Though maybe negotiating with Coal on my behalf wasn't exactly the best strategic move."

I blink, forcing myself to concentrate on her words. "I was the one who made you late. You were kind to wait for me when I—when we met Tyelor this morning." I lean closer to the porridge, letting the warm scent ground me, and realize suddenly that I haven't eaten a real meal since our noon break yesterday. Somehow, that feels like days ago. A different lifetime in which my males surrounded me, jesting with each other, running a hand over my hair or lower back on their way past. My throat tightens. "Fair is fair."

"Not here." Arisha's freckled cheeks tighten. "In fact, once you know your way around better, you'd be better off not sitting with me at all. Everyone knows the physical training will force me out sooner or later, and you should be working toward better alliances."

"I'll make up my own mind if it's all the same to you," I tell Arisha, hissing as I pick up my spoon. The abrasions on my palms aren't deep, but they sting.

"Well, if I've not found my two new favorite lasses," Tye says, putting his tray down on the small table right after a heady citrus-and-pine scent fills my nose. Pulling a chair out for himself, he turns it around and straddles it in a smooth motion, his attention fully on Arisha. "I need a favor, braids."

The small kernel of hope that I dared feel dies in my chest.

"And at least half the students in Great Falls would happily trip over themselves to grant you your heart's desires," Arisha tells him, her too-keen eyes taking in my reaction. "So go bother them."

Tye flashes her a smile. "Aye, but see, it is the kind of favor *you* are best at—the mathematics kind. With numbers. And symbols. And counting."

"Counting? Well, I'd certainly not expect you to go beyond twenty on your own." Arisha tilts her head, her fingers worrying her left braid. The loose hair sticks out wildly enough to make the girl competitive for a scarecrow position. "What's in it for me?"

"Whatever you wish." Tye scoots his chair closer to her. "I can fetch your food while you work, massage your shoulders… get you a hair ribbon or ten."

Arisha moves her chair away. "I help you with your math homework. You help Leralynn with her hands." My eyes widen, but Arisha avoids my gaze, her attention now wholly on her food. "Given the amount of time you spend twirling around a stick for applause, you must know what to do with that." She waves in my direction.

"What happened?" Tye turns toward me, his long lashes and sharply angled face so painfully beautiful that I hate myself for my own heart's stutter. For how much my body longs for the warrior's touch, even knowing it's spurred by nothing but the rules of Arisha's transaction. *Stars.* I'm better than this. I hope I'm better than this.

"Coal happened." I pull my hands onto my lap. "And I don't need help. Thank you, though."

Reaching over the table with his long arms, Tye snatches my wrist impertinently. "Sorry, lass, but I'm not risking failing mathematics. They'll bar me from competing." Placing the back of my wrist onto the tabletop, the male opens my fingers gently, drawing a small breath as he assesses the damage with a knowing gaze. "Was it a rope?" Tye asks, the concern in his voice the first genuine thing I've heard since meeting him here.

"No."

Tye's emerald eyes flicker up to mine.

I study a rip in my sleeve.

"A secret. I like those." Dipping a corner of his linen napkin into a water glass, Tye dabs gently against the cuts, his grip on my wrist tightening when I try to pull away. "Hold on, lass. We need to wash the sand out before this turns from nuisance to corruption."

We. The word pierces me. Lifting my face, I find Tye absorbed in his work, those sharply angled cheekbones with their constellation of nearly invisible freckles tightened in concentration, one lock of red hair falling over his forehead, his hand as warm against the back of mine as if his fire magic had brushed the skin. I try not to soak him in too obviously, but it's desperately hard. Tye wets the napkin again, his rolled-up sleeves showing off his muscled arms.

I brace myself for the sting.

Tye pauses. This time, instead of bringing the cloth directly to my palm, he runs his thumb firmly over my forearm.

I gasp softly, my sore muscles singing at the exquisite pressure that radiates up my arm.

"Be good and I'll do that again," Tye murmurs, a corner of his mouth twitching.

"I—"

"Tyelor." The unexpected sound of River's voice makes my heart jump, then race like a rabbit.

Turning, I find River standing beside our table, the aura of command hanging about him with familiar ease. Back straight, River holds his hands behind him, his well-cut red coat buttoned high up his neck.

LERA

*A*risha and Tye rise at once, and by the time I follow their example a few moments later, the two are already bowing.

"Good morning, sir," Arisha and Tye say together, just as I mouth, *River.*

River's beautiful gray eyes slide over me with enough scrutiny to tighten my chest—and no familiarity. Although I was little expecting it by now, its absence still stings. "Your servant, ma'am," River says dryly. "I presume I've the pleasure of addressing Lady Leralynn of Osprey, who managed to break curfew last night and get on the wrong side of an instructor this morning?" River's keen gaze flickers over my hands, the distance between us widening with each passing breath. He's painfully handsome and somehow even taller and more imposing than I remember, as if we've spent years apart already.

"Yes," I answer, searching his eyes for something—anything.

A pause. Pregnant. Waiting.

"*Sir*," Tye murmurs to me.

Bloody stars. "Yes, sir," I tell River.

River nods. "Despite its grander-than-life reputation, Great Falls Academy is in truth a poor fit for a significant number of would-be students, Lady Leralynn." River's schooled gaze studies me with all the passion of a glass vase. "As such, I highly encourage anyone who finds our rules and customs unpalatable to depart sooner rather than later."

My throat closes, my mind trying and failing to overlay this official with the male who took me in my bedchamber two days ago. I reach inside myself on instinct, searching for the mating bond before remembering the amulets' effects on it. Amulets that all four of my males were wearing when I took mine off to gallop toward the odd call of magic. My mind races, wanting to follow this trail, but Arisha nudges me, and I realize with a start that I've never replied to River's... invitation to get out of his life.

Shoving all thought and feelings into the darkness of my mind, I raise my chin at the deputy headmaster, who wears a soldier's epaulets and a familiar face.

"Understood, sir." My voice is clear and uncowed, mirroring nothing of my soul. The voice I cultivated under Zake, where signs of weakness led to pain. "I will apply myself to learning swiftly."

River nods again, dismissing the new student as a nuisance while his attention shifts to Tye, whom he'd originally approached to see. The commander's already wide shoulders spread further, encroaching on the other's space without him ever taking a step. "A valuable medallion pendant has disappeared from my office, Tyelor," River says, his voice low. "Would you happen to know anything about it?"

Well, Autumn did say the veil amulets drew what they could from true history—and a good portion of Tye's was spent in and out of arrest. If I wasn't ready to scream in frustration, I might actually chuckle.

"I don't think so, sir." Tye cocks his head, feline impertinence in every lithe line of his beautiful body. "What did it look like?"

"A disk. The size of a small saucer. With designs inscribed."

Any trace of amusement drains from me. The key to Mystwood—that's what River describes. Our one and only way of getting home. Gone. And beyond believing it a valuable trinket, I don't think River even knows what he lost. The chill rushing over my skin turns to ice. The tear in the fabric, the threat to the mortal realm—none of it went away with my males' lost memories. And now I can't even travel back to summon aid.

"Hmm." Tye rocks back on his heels. "I've seen nothing of the sort, sir. But I will certainly keep my eyes open for it."

River steps forward, towering even over Tye. "If you locate it, please inform the culprit that thievery will not be tolerated at Great Falls. From anyone. No matter how many medals they've won. Have I made myself clear?"

Tye blinks, spreading his hands in innocence. "Of course, sir. As it shouldn't be."

River steps back, his eyes brushing me again, the smooth planes of his face impassive. Frowning, he focuses on my neck, as if he can see the veil amulet there. My breath halts, my body going still. *Do you see something, River? Do you remember who I am?*

The male crooks a finger at me.

I approach obediently, my heart beating a thready quick beat under his relentless gaze. *See me, River. Feel me.*

As I stop before him, River stretches his hand toward my neck. Toward—

"Jewelry is not permitted with gray uniforms," he says, and I realize his intention to pull the amulet off. My hands rise defensively, my head shaking in desperate protest that River ignores as his fingers wrap around the pendant and pull. The chain digs into the back of my neck as it breaks.

Holding my breath, I wait for the gasps and panic, the shock as my disguise comes crashing down around me, its careful preservation the only thing that's been preventing me from hauling my males out by the shirt collars and forcing them to remember me. But nothing comes. Blinking, I finally focus my eyes on exactly what River pulled from my neck and tossed like a bit of rubbish onto the tabletop. Not the veil amulet, but the intricate four-corded necklace he gifted me with the morning we left Lunos.

"It can cause injury during training," he says, already moving away. "You may wear jewelry only with formal dress."

I breath in the mix of relief and hurt, using the time it takes to sweep the broken gift into my pocket to reclaim my schooled face. "Did you take River's pendant?" I ask Tye once I'm certain the other male is well out of earshot. Tye—*my* Tye —very well might have, for the amusement of it if nothing else. But the male before me knows nothing of his own roguish history in Lunos.

Tye grins. "Actually, I've no notion what River was talking about. But if I find it, I've some idea how much it's worth now, aye?"

WE RETURN to Coal for more training after breakfast and dive into the academic components of Great Falls' famous education in the afternoon. This opens another gaping problem. Raised as a stable hand, I learned my letters from a kind older servant who took me under her wing. The difference between basic reading and strategic analysis, however, is as vast as the rift between realms. The veil amulet might have convinced the teachers I belong in their class, but it can't compensate for the fact that I understand nothing of what's placed before me. Especially when I'm busy trying to work a way out of this mess.

Pulling a shawl tight around my ornate silver dress—Arisha prompted me to change for dinner after classes ended, having the decency to only raise a single brow when I pulled out one of Autumn's ridiculously royal creations—I step into the library where Arisha, Tye, and I are to meet up for study that I'll understand none of. The deeply carved wooden doors open into a great round room with a domed red-and-gold ceiling, the walls lined so high up with shelves of books that ladders stand beside them to help pull down the volumes. The trove of information surrounding me hums with the reminder of what I'm missing. How much I don't know about what happened to my males—and need to figure out. Quickly.

I realize my hands are shaking and sink into the first high-backed chair I find, grateful to have arrived early. It's the first quiet moment I've had to think since waking up here at dawn. My mouth is dry, my heart beating a thin pattering rhythm against my ribs, my stomach hollow despite the lavish spread of healthy food at dinner. Leafy salads and roasted root vegetables and poached chicken breasts. Even the perfectly seasoned risotto tastes like dust in my mouth. Bracing my elbows on the table before me, I cradle my aching head and force myself to sort through the disaster again.

The males and I were approaching Academy grounds… The images swim in my head.

No. I approached alone, clutching the Academy invitation that freed me from Lord Zake of Osprey, who took me in as his ward.

No. No, that isn't right.

There is no Osprey.

Of course there is, I spent my childhood there.

The ache in my head turns to painful pounding with each beat of my heart.

I was traveling in the forest.

No, on the main road of course. Like a proper lady.

No.

"Are you quite all right?" asks a male voice a few feet away. Blinking up, I find a man in dark olive robes rising from behind the library's main desk. In his late fifties, the librarian has a well-tutored voice, light brown hair peppered with gray, and thick glasses. Leaning on a cane to assist his stiff left leg, he makes his way toward my table, his eyes examining me with uncomfortable intensity as he touches my shoulder. "You appear pale, my lady. And new."

I shift away and the man's hand drops from my shoulder, the loss of contact burning my flesh in reminder of my males' absence. *Stars,* I'm like a stray dog desperate for touch. "I'm well. Just a bit overwhelmed." I stand, starting for the door. "Excuse me."

My mind swims again. *I can't leave—I need to study, lest the Academy sends me back to Lord Zake in disgrace.* No.

"Wait." The man takes a step toward me. "My name is Gavriel. I'm the Academy's librarian. What is your name?"

"Lady Leralynn of Osprey," I mutter.

Gavriel sighs, running his hand through his hair the same way that…that someone I once knew did when anxious. "I believe you need to take the veil off for a spell."

"Your pardon?" I ask over the pounding in my skull. My hands touch my face, finding only skin. "What veil?"

Gavriel curses and limps around me, his cane making an efficient *tick tick tick* against the marble floor. Stopping behind me, he brushes the back of my neck, a small click of a lock sounding before I can pull away.

The pounding in my head stops at once, my thoughts clearing as I feel the amulet slipping down into my hand, the intricately carved runes on its wooden face as cold as ice.

"There we are." Gavriel limps quickly to the library door, sliding the latch closed. "Feeling better?"

1 2

———

LERA

"Who are you?" My voice skitters off the rounded library walls.

"Gavriel," he repeats simply, inclining his head to me as he pulls a chair out for himself and sits, massaging his knee. "Currently the librarian at Great Falls."

"And at other times?" I press.

"A cardinal of the Sentinel Guild, keeping watch over the mortal realm."

I sink slowly into my chair, my hand clutching the veil amulet. *Stars.* With everything that's happened, I'd forgotten to remove it as Autumn instructed—with near disastrous results. Now, without the magical artifact hanging around my neck, the headache and confusion are easing quickly—though even that little helps comprehend Gavriel's presence. I focus on his ears, expecting my gaze to slip away as it does with the males, but find no problem looking at him.

"I am human," Gavriel confirms. "And you are fae."

I swallow. "But the veil amulet had no effect on you."

"It had full effect, or I'd have found you earlier."

79

"But—"

"I've been expecting you, Leralynn. And I had to trust my deductions over what my own eyes and mind insisted I was seeing. As I've been trained to do." Gavriel pulls a pendant from beneath his robes, showing it off as if the symbol of pen and shield should mean something to me. Seeing that it doesn't, he sighs and tucks the disk away. "Perhaps I should start at the beginning. After the ancients separated the mortal lands from Lunos, the humans feared that with our limited life span, the truth would morph and wither. The Sentinel Guild guards the history, studies the present, and stands watch should the divide ever be breached—for good or ill."

"By *stands watch* you mean—" I say.

Gavriel nods. "We keep the knowledge alive."

I rub my face. "In other words, you are a walking reference text of events so long past that no one else gives a damn about them anymore?" I wince. "My apologies. I could have worded that better."

Gavriel adjusts his glasses. "Yes. And... yes." He motions to a thick volume resting on the edge of his desk, and I oblige the silent request, bringing the book over to him. "The twist to your humor being that my guild's work has proven correct—as evidenced by my having anticipated your coming. And yes, I will explain that in a moment as well."

He flips through the book, his attention on the pages. "Have you heard the legend about fae coming through from the other lands to take a worthy warrior and grant him eternal life?"

"I have. Zake, the lord I used to be indentured to, told it often—mostly because he believed himself to be the chosen one. The man was so stars bent on it that he built a whole estate at Mystwood's edge, waiting for immortality to summon him." I wrap my arms around myself, the memories pricking like tiny needles. "The irony was that fae warriors *did* show up at Zake's estate, except for a different reason."

"The Sentinel's Guild would take issue with your word choice, Leralynn," Gavriel says.

"Which word?"

"Irony." He turns the book he's holding around, the pictures showing a human turning fae in stages, ears rising, body and hair lengthening, a sword held high in her hands. The next image over shows the same grand hero protecting a village from shadowed hordes. "We prefer prophecy."

I stare at Gavriel, waiting for the laugh, but the man is serious. "You think that I—" I shake my head. "The fae didn't summon me to Lunos to gift me with immortal life, Gavriel. That was more an accidental by-product of my death."

"And yet here you are." The man opens his hands, his brown eyes round with excitement. "Born in the mortal world, summoned to Lunos, returning as an immortal warrior yourself—right when and where beasts of wrongness and corruption have begun raising their heads." Gavriel closes the book. "That is why I took the position at Great Falls, if you were wondering. After hearing of fae taking a mortal near Mystwood, I sought out reports of unusual incidents—which Great Falls has seen a bit of in the past months. My prediction was that you'd return as an immortal warrior right in the center of the fray. I was not wrong. A battle is coming, and you are here to defend our kind, Leralynn. With me here to guide you through it, the best I am able."

I'm speechless for a moment, unsure whether to laugh hysterically or scream. "Bloody stars, Gavriel. You are as insane as Zake." My headache creeps back even without the amulet, and I squeeze my temples to avoid shaking him. "Listen to me. I'm not a lone hero returned to battle beasts untold. I'm here as part of a five-warrior quint ordered to find and seal a crack in the wards protecting the mortal realm from magic."

For the first time since walking into the library, I see Gavriel's scholarly face rippling with confusion. "Five-warrior quint? No. No, that can't be right." He huffs. "That wasn't in the prophecy. These texts have been studied and deciphered by the kingdom's greatest minds. The Protector comes alone."

"Then we both agree I'm not the Protector you are waiting for." I force my voice under control and lean toward him with the most polite demeanor I can manage. "But if you could see your way to using all those centuries of knowledge to help me find a way out of the mess I'm actually in, I'd be most obliged. Yesterday, River, Coal, Shade, Tye, and I were approaching the Academy when I heard a static-like noise. I took off my amulet to investigate, but my horse tripped over what seemed to be an old rune-covered tablet. There was a flash, and I was unconscious for some time. When I finally made my way to the Academy, I discovered that the males now actually believe the veil amulet's legends. I need to get their memories back. Can you help?"

Gavriel stares at me, his mouth working without sound.

I wait, holding his gaze and my breath.

After a few heartbeats, the man shakes himself and pulls a sheet of handwritten notes from inside his breast pocket. "There have been reports of wild animal assaults from some of Great Falls's farms, but what I've been able to glean suggests beasts from another realm," Gavriel says as if I'd not spoken at all. "Skysis—"

"Sclices."

"Ah, sclices. I will make the correction. I believe sclices to be the culprits and have outlined the details here. This should be our first line of attack." He slides the sheet over to me and takes off his glasses, polishing them intently on his wool robe.

"Since the prophecy mentions nothing of companions, there is no cause to focus there."

"Wait, what?" I blink. Rub my eyes. Blink again. "Gavriel… I little care what the prophecy says. I care about reversing what happened to my quint so we can continue with our very *real* and very *urgent* mission." A mission, I realize, which my males remember no more than they recall the veil amulets or sclices or anything else they've encountered over centuries in Lunos. "Do you…do you understand what I'm trying to say at all?"

His jaw tightens. "If your companions were important, the prophecy would have mentioned them. And given the rather prominent Academy personnel you are naming, it is entirely possible that their role in this affair is to be played out from their current personas. We need to focus on protecting the mortal realm. Nothing else."

"I don't think there is a *we*, then." Rising to my feet, I clip the veil amulet back onto my neck and start for the door.

"There is something else you should know," Gavriel calls after me. "Your old master has been stirring up fuss about fae, accusing the immortals of everything from replacing healthy babes with ill ones to killing livestock, and worse. It's taken hold—hate, I fear, is rather easy to spread."

"I grew up next to Mystwood," I say without turning. "Tales of murderous fae are nothing new to me."

"No." Gavriel's voice sharpens. "I speak not of legends and children's tales of far-off beasts. Zake and his inquisitors are arresting people on charges of being fae blood carriers and sympathizers. By the time they are done questioning or cleansing or whatever name they give torture nowadays, there is usually little left but a confession. And execution."

I shake my head. "There are no fae in the mortal lands, bar the five of us. And we came just a day ago."

"I'm certain the families of five hundred of Zake's victims will be pleased to hear that," says Gavriel.

"Why are you telling me this?" I ask, ice gripping my chest as tightly as I grip the doorknob.

"So you know what is likely to happen if you yank off your amulet in front of the Academy's deputy headmaster, as I believe you might consider doing. Either that, or accuse River, Coal, Shade, Tye, or anyone else of fae craft."

LERA

I rush out of the library into the long, torch-lit hallway so quickly that I crash into Tye for the second time that day. The male's pine-and-citrus scent alerts me to his identity a moment before his firm, warm hands steady my elbows. I resist the urge to press into his hard chest, though every instinct in my body tells me I belong there.

"Are you all right?" Arisha asks with wide blue eyes, holding her armful of books closer to her chest. "Is there something in there?"

"Yes. Stupid ideas," I mutter, though not quietly enough to get past Tye's keen hearing.

Throwing his head back, the male laughs, the sound rich and easy. Releasing me much earlier than I wish, he sticks his hands into his pockets, the movement shifting his vest to reveal an embroidered shirt beneath the velvet. The rich blue-and-gold crest of the Prowess Trials—the Alliance's grand competition of strength and agility—winks at me from the fabric. In Lunos, Tye was once heading for authentic glory, until a jealous prince forced him to abandon the life dream. Now it seems the amulet is giving Tye another chance.

"How old are you, Tye?" I blurt, speaking over whatever Tye or Arisha were about to say next.

He blinks once. "Twenty-two."

Bloody hell take me. "What do you think of fae?" I press on, little caring for how odd the question sounds. My heart beats fast and shallow against my ribs. I need to know whether Gavriel's assessment of the danger is true. And I need to know quickly.

Tye cocks his right brow, his wickedly handsome face and green eyes taking on a mischievous tinge. "I think anyone immortal likely has access to old expensive things. And I think I can make good use of such items. Is there one sitting in the library?"

"Tyelor," Arisha hisses at him. "That is not amusing."

"You only think so because you can't see your own face just now." Tye opens his eyes wide in a fair imitation of Arisha before returning his gaze to me, the humor fading. "Word about fae is that a small gang of the bastards came through Mystwood and kidnapped a virgin last year—and more have crept in since to do murder and worse. Does no good gossip reach Osprey?"

"You don't actually believe that, do you?" I ask. "About fae being evil, I mean, not gossip's travel patterns."

"Don't know either way, and it doesn't matter. Braids here is right." Tye tugs on Arisha's hair, making the woman scowl. "Talking about fae craft is a great way to end up on an inquisitor's table having your joints measured for length. And whispering of it on Academy grounds—even theoretically—is a sure way to end up in River's study." Tye takes a step toward me, his voice dropping dramatically. "Which means you are a dangerous woman already."

You have no idea.

"Are you two going to study or exchange taunts?" Arisha demands, tucking her braids out of harm's reach.

I pull my shawl tighter around my shoulders. "Neither for me, I'm afraid. It's been a bit of a trying first day, and I'm turning in early. Please enjoy mathematics without my company." I hurry down the broad stone steps outside before either can ask questions, pausing only to call over my shoulder, "If you are such an impressive athlete, Tye, you could carry Arisha's books, you know."

"The lass won't let me," Tye calls after me. "Apparently, I'm not to be trusted with such precious artifacts."

The light notes of Tye's voice haunt me all the way back to my bedchamber, where I shut the door and slide my back down it until I'm sitting on the cold floor. My hands tremble, and I force myself to take deep, even breaths the way Coal—my Coal—would have told me to do now. This whole mess isn't prophecy. It's a mistake. An accident. A by-product of a magical relic shattering beneath a running horse's hooves.

No, not *shattered*. I jerk to my feet, my mind racing. The relic was never shattered, just cracked. The pieces might still be reassembled into a whole. If I can find my way back to where it all happened before weather covers the tracks or wrecks the softer insides of the tablet.

Crossing the room, I survey the settling evening through my large window. I'll have to wait until darkness before standing a chance of going over the Academy wall undetected. Whether the night's full moon and my immortal eyes will prove enough to let me follow my own tracks back to the forked road where it all started remains to be seen. At worst, I'll have to wait out in the woods until sunrise. Either way, it's a plan. After a day stuck in my disguise, going through the motions, it's action. And that makes me feel better.

I change from my dress into a dark suit of soft leather I'd brought from Lunos, getting myself ready and under the covers before Arisha returns to the darkened room. The woman whispers my name and, upon discovering me seemingly asleep, makes quick and quiet work of getting into bed herself. A quarter hour later, her soft steady breathing fills the bedchamber.

I hope you are a heavy sleeper, Arisha, I mouth shortly after the Academy's bell tolls ten-o'clock curfew. Swinging myself out of bed, I sheathe my blade down the length of my spine and tuck Shade's mittens into my belt. Using a few drops of oil from the lock-picking kit, I lubricate the window hinges before swinging them open into the cold crisp night.

The fifteen-foot drop to the ground makes my stomach tighten, but there is little help for it since the door leads to the central square courtyard, where a pair of the Academy's guardsmen stand watch. Plus, having seen Tye make a similar jump this morning for the sheer showiness of it, I know it can be done. Not letting myself fret over it further, I throw my legs over the window ledge, dangle in the air, and let go.

My legs flex, taking my weight as I land on the soft earth and curse. The jump didn't break my legs, but I did nearly twist an ankle. A fae body is a nice thing, but without the centuries of training the males have, it will be a long time yet before I can use its full ability. Coal had been working with me on that before we left. *Coal.* My heart squeezes.

Drawing a few deep breaths, I turn about to examine my surroundings. The backdrop of trees stares back at me, the Academy eerily quiet in the darkness. Closing my eyes, I press into a great oak's shadow and listen. It truly isn't fair how much I can hear the humans, their measured steps along the cobblestone paths on the other side of the dormitory, their softly exchanged reports. Curt, professional words of a well-trained guard force.

Great Falls Academy is not taking any chances with security. *River* is not taking any chances. Except for the one he knows nothing about.

Taking a breath, I move deeper into the buffer of wilderness separating the Academy's core complex from the protective wall around it, a moat of oaks and pines concealing the tall stone eyesore from sight. I marked one of those oaks earlier, with its sturdy branches and close-to-the-wall location, as my exit point. Silvery moonlight slants down through the branches, giving me just enough light. Not an easy climb, but doable. And certainly better than trying to talk my way past the guards at the gate. Finding the tree, I rub my hands over the wide trunk.

"I wouldn't do that." The self-satisfied voice purrs so close to my ear that my heart jumps inside my ribs. Tye may not know he's fae, but he certainly kept both his instincts and feline impertinence when the veil settled over him. "You'll get yourself caught faster than you can say 'get lost, Tyelor gorgeous.'"

Heart still pounding, I twist to find Tye leaning against the tree next to mine, his muscled arms crossed over his leather-clad chest. Emerald eyes glowing in the moonlight slide up over my hips and breasts before finally settling on my face, the predatory glint in them so familiar that it hurts, for there is no recognition lurking behind it.

"What are you doing here?" I demand.

"Saving you from a fairly severe thrashing, by the looks of it." Tye jerks his chin from the tree to the wall. "Do you imagine you're the first to discover this oak's convenient location? There's going to be a guard near here any moment. If you want to get over the wall—and I am rather curious as to what you think you're going to find there—you'll have to work a little harder for it."

"And you've an idea of a better path?" I ask. Whether the veil imparted Tye with such knowledge or the rogue's trained eye deduced it on instinct, I trust the male's criminal-mindedness over my own any day.

"Aye." Tye stretches lazily, pausing in midmotion, his head cocking attentively to one side. When I open my mouth to ask what he's marking, Tye clamps his palm over it, his other arm jerking me against his chest. "Shhhh. Behind us." Tye's lips are so close to my ear, the whispered words tickle, his warmth and breathing steady against my back. "I told you the guards patrol this all the time. This way."

RIVER

River laid the latest grim report on Headmaster Sage's desk and stepped back, putting his hands into the small of his back. Great Falls Academy held to the military protocol and, like River himself, Headmaster Sage was a lifelong soldier. That was where the similarity ended. With thin shoulders, a gleaming bald pate, and pointed features that seemed stuck in a permanent pinch, Sage led his troops from behind paper and ink. "That is the fifth unexplained attack in a week, sir, and three dead," River said, inclining his head. "Should we send the students home until—"

"Of course not. If you've lost your mind, sir, please be good enough to inform me in writing." Leaning back in his chair, Sage studied the reports, his sour expression hardening.

River knew what the smaller man was reading. Assault after assault, with culprits named as everything from wild animals to bandits to fae spirits. So far, all the misadventures remained outside the Academy walls, the attacks occurring on the farms and the small town near the estate. But it kept happening.

Sage shook his head, stacking the reports into a perfectly neat pile to match all the other neat piles in his office. Even the logs in the crackling fireplace had been laid out in strict parallels. "The Academy's stronghold has stood for two hundred years. Shutting our doors will destroy everything King Zenith has worked for."

As well as destroy Sage's career. But that little needed to be said.

"With due respect, sir," River said, his voice a calm contrast to Sage's heated tone. "If we lose a student to whatever wild beasts are hunting these grounds, the Academy's reputation would suffer a worse blow."

"I was under the impression that student safety was the reason I brought you here to begin with, Captain River. I have already issued instructions prohibiting the cadets from leaving Academy walls. Am I to understand that you find yourself unable to keep them to such basic discipline?" The man flicked the air with his hand. "If so, I urge you to make an example of one, and the rest will lie as quiet as the sheep they are."

Not the description River would have applied to any of the Academy students, but there was nothing to be gained by arguing that point. More importantly, River wished to give Sage no reason to demonstrate his methods. In a microcosm of two hundred would-be generals, keeping a bit firmly in the cadets' mouths was paramount; abusing them under the flag of the Academy's authority was an entirely different matter. Sage would toe the line with Zenith's daughter Katita and the other royalty, but the offspring of lesser nobles would have no such protection.

Pulling out a handkerchief, Sage coughed wetly.

"Meanwhile, see if you can't find the town's wandering monster. Once you get your hands dirty, I predict you'll discover these menacing assaults coming from no more than an overactive wolf or two. If not for this bloody chill, I'd take care of it myself."

Striding out of Sage's office into the keep's long torch-lit corridor, River called on one of the pages to find Coal and Shade—the only two men he intended to take on the night's outing. Sage might not have intended for him to go tonight, but River wouldn't wait another minute with the safety of Great Falls at risk. The page, a small lad nicknamed Rabbit, paled at once, giving River a dubious look over a promise that Coal would not smite him on sight.

Coal had that effect on people, River thought, heading down a long spiraling staircase. On most people. Though Coal's latest charge, Leralynn of Osprey, appeared to have missed the announcement. The young woman would no doubt discover her oversight—to her peril.

River paused, gripping the railing as sudden nausea rolled over him. The new cadet looked so like River's late wife that he'd nearly grabbed her. Eyes the color of liquid chocolate, lush auburn hair, a self-assured confidence teetering on impertinence that no doubt got her in trouble more often than not. After a quick glance to ensure he was, in fact, alone on the stairs, River let himself sag against the rail for a moment as he rubbed his face. He'd been the one to gift Diana with the mare that threw her to her death. River, who had vowed to protect her with his life, had failed.

The bitter irony of it all was that River had accepted the position at Great Falls to get away from memories of Diana, and here was her ghost walking back into his life.

. . .

Two hours later, with the Academy bedded down for the night, River led Coal and Shade out of the compound's main gate. Dressed in his signature black, Coal was a specter against the night, only his blond hair pulled up into a warrior's bun providing any relief from the darkness. A darkness that the warrior's eyes echoed too—had ever since he escaped captivity. What exactly happened to Coal when the islanders took him during that ill-fated scouting trip two years ago, River didn't know. Not even a direct order to speak of it had worked, and River knew better than to try again.

The Academy's guards cadre were competent enough, but nothing equated to the battlefield experience River shared with the two warriors. Plus, whatever was truly terrorizing the town and farms, Sage wanted the details kept quiet. River had to agree with that. If the Academy was to remain open as usual, then they needed to control the gossip.

Beside Coal, Shade moved with a predatory lupine grace that made him one of the most dangerous warriors on a battlefield—though the man's heart lay in healing, not killing. The assignment to Great Falls was supposed to help fill that need, and here River was, dragging him right back out into patrol. "If you've other obligations this evening—" River cut himself off at Shade's curt shake of the head.

"Nothing worth missing a hunt over." The warrior's yellow eyes shone. Good. Shade checked the blade sheathed down the length of his spine. "Where do you want me?"

Surveying the moonlit forest, River considered the question. "All the assaults have happened at night, so I believe we are dealing with something nocturnal. We split to circle the wall first, ensure no immediate threat, then reconnect to head toward the farmland and set up on the livestock."

Shade nodded once, melting silently into the woods. Sometimes River wondered if the male wasn't part wolf himself for how he prowled through the forest, the smells and darkness of night seeming to free something inside him.

"If you're this worried, why not send the students home for cause?" Coal asked, moving off in the opposite direction of Shade. "Say they couldn't master the curriculum."

"Politics." River shook his head, his gaze moving as he fell in step beside Coal. "Explaining why we forced one kingdom's subject out over another will look biased no matter what. All expulsions must be self-selected."

Coal snorted. "Give me a name of anyone you want sent home and I'll have her signing paperwork by day's end."

"Her?" River knew he should stop talking, but his treacherous mouth defied him. "Would you be thinking of your new student in particular?"

Coal's eyes remained on the woods. "I was not. But if you mean Leralynn of Osprey, she'll pack her bags quickly. I know the type." Coal shifted, drawing a boot dagger into his free hand. "Center of the world, expecting recognition the instant they draw breath in a room—and damn well getting it from every male within range." The last came as a quiet afterthought that made River's jaw tighten in the darkness.

15

LERA

With his hand on the small of my back, Tye moves on silent feet along the woods lining the wall, keeping to the darkest patches as we stray farther and farther from the barracks. Try as I may to follow the turns and twists, the grounds—already unfamiliar in daylight—are utterly unidentifiable dressed in cast shadows. The grass is dry with cold, crackling softly around my boots, and the cool air is sharp with the smell of earth and pine. After a quarter hour's stealth, the male motions for me to stop and crouches next to a set of hedges that look no different from the dozens of others. A few heartbeats later, his hand brushes dirt away from a trapdoor, which opens obediently on well-oiled hinges.

I stare into liquid darkness beneath us. "An underground passage?"

Tye nods, swinging himself down into the abyss without ceremony. When I let myself dangle off the edge to follow him down, I discover my legs are unable to touch the ground. I clench my teeth. Tye jumped from the second story for the enjoyment of it this morning, so his easy descent tells me nothing about the floor I cannot see. The ankle I nearly twisted getting out of my window whines with fear. I draw a shaking breath, my hands aching from the strain as I try to talk myself into letting go.

Firm hands grip my calves, pulling in clear command. Tye's spotting touch echoes through me, the relief so palpable that I let my grip slide on sheer trust. The instant I do, my body drops into the male's waiting arms, which close around me protectively.

For a moment, I stay there, my face pressed into Tye's shoulder, drinking in his warmth and fresh scent. The steady rise and fall of his broad, muscled chest is soothing enough to stop time itself, returning me back to a world where the male held me readily with heart and soul. It's so familiar here, I can almost forget for a moment that everything's changed.

Unbidden, the desire to tell Tye everything fills my lungs. *You are fae, Tye. My mate. And though you remember nothing of it and think you've a life here, it's all different.* I bite my lip. Would I believe such a tale? No. No one sane would. Gavriel's warning of what fae craft accusations lead to nowadays sends a chill down my neck. This disaster with the veil amulets needs actions, not words. It needs a magical tablet to be found and fixed.

Setting me on my feet, Tye steps away and pulls down on a rope. The trap door closes obediently above us. "It's an escape tunnel," he says, leading the way forward along the rough stone. "Not very posh, but it will get us to the other side of the wall. Keep your hand on the rock to steady your bearing."

I obey, stepping gingerly, my immortal eyes making out no more than an occasional glimpse of a wall—a human would see not even that.

"The guards don't monitor this?" My foot steps on what

feels like a dead rat lying in the middle of the path. I inhale sharply before moving on.

"We're passing near the main gates now, actually," Tye whispers. "There is a place in the guardhouse where they can see any light passing through here. So long as we light no candle or lantern, the risk is minimal." Tye's silhouette seems to glance over his shoulder. "But minimal isn't the same as zero, pretty lass. Are you still certain that whatever it is you want to do is worth angering our lords and masters? Speaking of that, what are we doing exactly?"

"*We* aren't doing anything." My hand presses hard into the rock as I quicken my step enough to overtake the male. "I'll take it from here. You need to go back to the Academy, Tye."

Tye steps along with me. "I've been told I'm good company."

"I've been told that getting tossed into a lake will teach me to swim—that didn't make it true." I stop, turning toward him. "Why are you helping me? In fact, how did you find me near that oak to begin with?"

Tye chuckles. "You had the look of someone about to make a jailbreak. As to why I came—I'm trying to impress you, of course." He stretches. "And because it seems an entertaining way to spend the night."

"And if we are caught?"

"Then the night will quickly become less entertaining." He motions toward the passage. "Come along, mischief. You won't find the exit without me."

Fair point. Quitting arguing lest I win, I follow Tye along the uneven dips and rises until he finally blocks my path with his arm. Ordering me to stay put, the male feels along the wall until finally tugging on something I can't see. A moment later, a rope ladder unfurls beside us. Why couldn't the veil amulet have endowed me with this knowledge?

Sending me up ahead of him, Tye brings up the rear until we emerge into the wilderness. Fresh air fills my nose and lungs, washing away the stench of mold and dung my fae senses absorbed too clearly in the passage. Against the starlit sky, Tye's silhouette has a soft, preternatural glow that turns his lithe movements into dance-like perfection. Now, like me, the male stands with his face tipped up, drawing gulps of crisp air. "Where to now?"

16

LERA

"That somewhat depends on where we are," I mutter, turning about to get my bearings. The forbidding tower of the Academy's keep, the jagged mountain range, the sloping forested ridge, all stand mocking sentinel against the night. Clear, yet telling me nothing. When I approached the Academy, the damn stone relic was rather proactive in attracting my attention, but my secret hopes that its shards might oblige me with the same courtesy are fading quickly. Which means I am going to be looking for my own tracks in the forest after all. A fool's errand at night. My feet trip over a root I'd failed to notice, the loud crackle of dry leaves and branches as I fumble for balance a mockery in itself.

Stars. A heaviness settles on my chest, the weight of it making it hard to inhale. What the bloody hell was I thinking coming out here? Dragging Tye right along into trouble with me? Tye, who thinks he is human and me no more than a conquest. A distraction. My fingers grip my shirt hem as I turn about, the forest alive with an owl's ghostly hoots and a wolf's too-close howl. Just like Shade, except not. A tremor runs through me.

Everything is *just like* but not. What if this is the reality, and the soul-gripping connection I thought I had with the males was never anything but a trick of magic? If we were truly meant for each other, would they not have noted me? Felt something? Anything? The wind blows into my face, its icy fingers racing down my skin. If this is the truth of it without magic helping us, then breaking the amulets' hold heralds nothing but pretty lies. My throat closes, my eyes stinging, though I don't let the tears fall.

"Lass?" Tye's hands settle on my shoulders, turning me toward him.

I swallow, suddenly unsure what to do. What to say. Five. There are supposed to be five of us. And now there aren't. And it hurts like a knife slicing across my soul.

"Five what?" Tye asks, and I realize I've spoken the word aloud. "What are you searching for, Lera?"

"Tracks," I say numbly. "I dropped something on my way. I'd hoped to find it."

"At night?"

"I couldn't exactly walk out during daylight, now could I?"

Tye's answering chuckle vibrates through me, a rumble that starts in his chest and makes my bones tremble. Alone in the darkness with nothing but the sounds of the forest around us, the deep loneliness I've somehow held at bay before now slams into me with a bitter vengeance. Before I can draw my next breath, Tye pulls me in against his shoulder, his arms wrapping me tightly, his heart a steady beat beneath his breast. His fresh scent is a balm to my senses, his muscles surrounding me like steel wrapped in velvet.

The phantom limb of magic that I awoke with in this new fae body stirs in its shackles, unable to move.

I want him. Every fiber in my body wants to be pressed against his, even with the mating bond muted. I may not be his female right now, but he is my male. And I'm too lonely, too tired, to care about the former.

My hand fists in Tye's shirt, pulling the male toward me roughly, my lips covering his with desperate need. As the warrior's taste fills me, his achingly familiar mouth hot against mine, my body wakens, begging for more. Real or not.

Tye's hands grip either side of my face, pulling me away gently even as his sudden hardness throbs against my belly. His breath comes hard, his green eyes gleaming in the moonlight. "Not that I mind, lass, but I think you do. Or will come morning."

My heart pounds against my ribs, the sound echoing in my ears. "Come morning, I'll deny it ever happened," I say, my breath ragged. Needy. Maybe I'm not Tye's conquest, but he is mine. A notch on *my* damn belt. My teeth grind together, my hands digging into his shoulders. "Don't go getting attached, pretty lad."

A tiny predatory growl escapes Tye's lips, his emerald eyes flashing in the moonlight. "Oh, we'll see about the morning, lass. I'm told I can be *very* memorable." The male's mouth is descending upon mine even as he bites off his own words, his body pushing me back back back until I feel a tree trunk digging into my shoulders.

Tye's kiss deepens, his lips and tongue plundering my mouth with hot savageness. Heat ripples through my core, my legs and arms and abdomen tingling with energy as pressure builds high between my thighs. My sex pulses hungrily, blindly. More. I want more. The void inside me howls, screaming for Tye's cock while I clench and clench around nothing.

With a growl, I shove into Tye, my strength too great to be mortal even in this world's shackles. A lesser male would have swayed from the assault, but Tye, Tye only lifts his face away from mine as his body absorbs everything I can throw and doesn't give an inch. Heartbeat after heartbeat, he stands his ground, looming over me while his broad shoulders block out the moonlight. He stands, taking it all—until he moves.

Grabbing my wrists, he pins them above my head, his knee forcing my thighs apart. Deprived of means to squeeze my legs, the pressure along my sex turns unbearable. I struggle futilely against his hold, each failed attempt to escape only feeding the merciless ache inside me.

A flash of Tye's teeth, of the canines I can't see, and a sharp sting sinks into the tender spot where my neck and shoulder meet. The pain of the claiming shoots down my body, turning to exquisite heat.

Tye licks the bite, the tiny laps of his tongue starkly soft, as exotic as ice in the eye of a flame. I writhe, but the iron bands of his hands at my wrists let me do nothing but feel every unbearable zing. My body trembles, the surrender and storm of sensation battering me from all sides. The world about me narrows to the dampness soaking my underthings, to the tingling heat that brings me to my toes with desperation.

Tye shifts my wrists until he controls both my arms with one hand, his other sliding along my shoulder, my breast, my waist and *down down down*.

RIVER

$\mathcal{C}$oal tapped his ear, signaling to River.

River paused, cocking his head in search of the sound that Coal had marked. A wolf howled. An owl hooted nearby, a pair of squirrels who should be sleeping scattering along the trees instead. As if something—someone—was disturbing their slumber. Someone whose heavy breathing River could now make out.

A small movement of River's hand had Coal walking again, the warrior's steps silent on the cold earth. A predator stalking prey. River's steady heartbeat kept its rhythm even as his mind raced. Whatever the foe, it was too close to the Academy. Had to be put down. Now. Tonight. With Shade's help if possible, but not at the risk of letting it escape. River's blade whispered free of its sheath.

The sounds of panting breath increased, branches snapping beneath feet that belonged to neither River nor Coal. Close enough to the Academy's wall that a stone's throw would reach it. Stopping with his back pressed against a wide oak that was the last point of concealment between them and the target, River shared a readying glance with Coal.

The warrior nodded.

River's hand lifted and closed into a fist in the moonlight. *Go. Go. Go.*

Twisting around the trunk at the same time as Coal, River brought his sword into ready guard just as the foliage opened to—

Tyelor of Blair, pinning Leralynn of Osprey to a bloody oak, the man's hand so deeply inside the woman's tight pants that his fingers couldn't help but be stroking inside her hot folds even now.

River's chest tightened, heat simmering in his blood and filling his lungs, his face, his hands. Leralynn's auburn hair was loose but for a single braid on the left side, swinging like a mesmerizing pendulum with the couple's movement. The moonlight showed the naked skin of her exposed throat as she tilted up her head to meet Tye's kiss, her undulating body giving so generously of itself that a tremor ran along River's skin, making his cock twitch at the thought.

The furnace inside River blazed hotter with each of Lera's soft gasps, and when her face turned slightly, she reminded him so much of Diana that River had to bite back a roar. The damn woman was out in the wilderness, beyond the Academy's protective walls, here where three people had died in as many nights. That alone made River's arms long to shake her. Except his arms wanted to do so much more than just shake the woman. The scent of her arousal spun River's head, the glistening wetness on Tye's fingers as his hand slowly withdrew and slid up her torso toward her heavy breasts as tantalizing as chilled wine in a desert's midst. An ache he had no right to feel for a student gripped River's groin so fiercely that no shifting would be enough to relieve the sudden horrid tightness in his britches.

"What the bloody hell are you two doing?" River's voice was ice. Too controlled for his racing heart, so polar to the inferno inside him that it was a wonder the two didn't meet in an eruption of steam.

Lera gasped, tearing her mouth away from Tye's.

Tye cursed, his green-eyed gaze moving between River and Coal in a too-experienced assessment of the situation even as he pushed Leralynn behind him. As if his back would protect the woman from the deserved wrath.

Leralynn's eyes widened as she met River's, her skin blanching beautifully. When she turned, River caught sight of the sword hilt rising above her shoulder. She'd not come here just for the...for companionship, then. River didn't know whether that made him feel better or worse.

Not that it mattered. Leralynn was done. Sage might not allow students to be shown the door outright, but by the time River was through with her, she'd be running for the exit. Which would be best for all involved.

LERA

I gasp. My body, trembling in anticipation of the release Tye's deft fingers teased to the surface so skillfully, recoils at the abrupt change.

River's ire saturates the air, overpowering the forest's fresh scent. Sheer masculine dominance in each contour of his muscular body, his movements vibrate with a restrained violence that—despite my wishes—stokes my anxiety and arousal in equal measure. I focus on the chill breeze to clear my foggy mind. River is angry, yes, but it is a kind of fury I'd imagine the male reserves for an invading host from the dark realm, not a stray student snogging in the darkness. As it is, the intensity in River's gray gaze is so potent, his eyes seem to glow with it.

A few paces away, Coal stands with his arms crossed over his chest.

I've been here before, between an angry River and glaring Coal, and a contrite Tye. But as familiar as it is—as they are—the alien coldness in their eyes is a harsh reality.

Tye shifts his weight, placing himself in the line of fire

between River and me, but I need not look at River again to know there will be no reprieve. For whatever reason, the male's attention is locked on me alone, and only I can decide whether to answer the challenge or crumple beneath it.

My chin rises. My breaths, rapid after Tye's deft touch, escape in small puffs of steam. Meeting River's eyes, I match him glare for glare as his command of the forested alcove, the Academy, the very air around us ripples out with absolute certainty. His command of everything—except me.

Crossing the two paces between us, River pushes Tye aside to grab my chin between thumb and forefinger. The movement sings with the self-confidence of the king River doesn't remember he is. The veil amulet might confuse the memories, but it plainly leaves the essence of soul and experience intact. Except River's soul now finds mine a stranger.

I pull back.

"Stand still, Cadet." River injects the entire ocean of difference between our statuses into those three words. "I inquired what you are doing here—in explicit violation of the rules—one day after your arrival."

"I brought her here, sir," Tye drawls with just enough impertinence to give River no choice but to turn some of his wrath toward the male. Once assured of River's attention, Tye pulls his shoulders back farther, raising his head in a gesture that exposes his neck more than offers a challenge. "Leralynn is an attractive woman, and I had hoped the spice of...the forbidden forest might give me the advantage I need to secure her affections. Or at least her consent."

"It is fortunate that that spice also enticed the young woman in question to bring a sword." Stepping out of the woods, Shade surveys the four of us. The male's yellow eyes are so familiar that I can't help but hold my breath in anticipation of recognition, of his long arms wrapping around my body, cocooning me in their tender warmth.

A kernel of hope rises inside me. We are a quint, strongest when together. Now that the five of us are so close…

Shade's yellow eyes trace the outline of my body before focusing on my face. His full lips open. Shut. Shaking himself, he drags his gaze back toward River. "I think I found at least one of our wild beasts. And before you ask, there won't be time to get Tyelor and his…companion…back behind the wall. The wind's been carrying our scent to it, not the other way around. Anyone with a weapon should pull it now."

I draw my sword. In my side vision, Coal nods approvingly, reaching down into his boot to toss a knife to Tye—the only one of us still unarmed. I feel the twin to Coal's knife in my own boot, my hands aching to draw it. But I fight better with one weapon, and whatever is coming already has Shade bringing his blade to ready guard.

The trees rustle, and a familiar snort-like breathing now reaches my ears. A few moments later, not even our upwind position can mask the stench-filled calling card of the dark realm's rodent—not that the males remember how to interpret the smell. I brace myself for the sclices, but when three dark shapes leap at us from the darkness, I find myself unable to focus, my gaze sliding off the shapes as if trying to grip grease.

Tye stumbles beside me, blood flowing from his shoulder as he shoves a shape away. A heartbeat later, a blow I don't see coming knocks me flat onto the earth, droplets of yellow saliva streaking across my face.

I kick away the shape I can't focus on. It yields. The sclice is lighter than I'm used to. Certainly smaller than the one who tagged my ribs back in Slait. For a heartbeat, I see the rodent before me—a scrawny elongated hog beast with a too-large lower jaw even by sclice standards. Then the heartbeat is gone, my gaze skidding away from the dark shape as the amulet around my neck heats, scalding my skin.

Stars. I freeze halfway to my feet. The veil amulet. The bloody amulet that I can't take off in front of anyone here, lest they haul me to a prison cell or worse. Leralynn of Osprey, the human, does not see the sclices—but Lera of Lunos sees them just fine.

1 9

———

LERA

*R*iver grabs my waist, pushing me behind him as he crouches into a fighting stance.

"Don't trust your eyes," Coal orders, his voice low and level and so calm that I'd never think him playing with death if I wasn't looking at it now. His eyes closed, cheekbones and jaw sharp in the moonlight, Coal dances with his sword, the pattern making the most of his prowess and immortal senses. "The beasts play tricks with the darkness."

The beasts play tricks with your mind.

Still in front of me, River crouches, his head cocked in concentration before he strikes with his sword and dark blood spills onto the ground, the stench of it enough to make me gag. Now that I know what I should be looking at, I can make out the shapes again. Three snarling sclices with vertical-slitted eyes and back-hinged knees and too-long front limbs—all familiar, yet off. The one River just wounded is too tall but scrawny, while the one about to fall to Coal's sword has so many fangs that its mouth looks to be permanently hinged open. My head pulses with the effort of watching them against the insistence of my amulet that I look away. The moment I relax my concentration, my gaze slips. It is as if these perverted versions of sclices have a crude veil of their own and the only reason my fae self can see them is because I already know what they are.

Branches crack behind me, the sounds as loud as thunder in the darkness. I jerk around so quickly that the earth sways, my mind groping for the slipping focus, without which I see nothing of the sclices. *Too long.* I've waited too long to strike, making myself vulnerable. I give up straining my mind in favor of swinging my sword in a full wide circle.

I hit only air.

My stomach squeezes, my hands white-knuckled around my sword. The sclice is close. So very close. My heart races. I swing again. Blindly. Wildly. Losing my footing for lack of contact.

As I stumble, a hog's rancid breath brushes the back of my neck.

Before I can scream, a great wolf leaps from the woods, his yellow eyes flashing as he throws himself onto the shape behind me. Gray fur and darkness roll, dragging one another back into the forest's shadows.

"Shade!" I call after him, my voice cracking from my too-dry mouth.

A few paces off, Coal grunts with satisfaction as his sword finds its mark and a sclice tumbles to the ground, its body and dull dead eyes suddenly visible. "What the bloody hell is this?" Coal rolls the corpse over with his foot.

"Something damned by the fae," says River.

I cringe—and not just from River's words. Sclices are ugly enough, but deformed ones are worse still. Now that I can see it clearly, the beast's corrupt mouth takes up half its face, the saliva rolling free from the hideous maw. From beneath the short fur hide, the sclice's skin protrudes in a mosaic of moles, one so large, it looks like a warped snowflake.

I turn away from the corpse, my chest tight as I take in the settled silence. With the dead body at Coal's feet, I hear no more movement. The males, their swords at the ready, disperse toward the edges of the clearing to check for additional intruders, their beautiful faces tight with concentration. Feeling. Listening. Scenting—for whatever good that will do with the whole place reeking of sewage.

I shake myself, a tingle along my spine screaming that the males are wrong. I saw three of the beasts, which means one is still *here*. Staying still. Lying in ambush. Forcing my breath and heart to slow, I survey the battleground, my mind on nothing but the truth of the sclice's existence. *I am Lera of Lunos. I am not human.* The amulet burns against my skin, the headache returning. *I am Lera of Lunos. I—*I gasp as red-slitted eyes crouched low beneath a bush not a pace away meet mine.

Thick-as-tree-trunk limbs, a melon-sized snout, teeth made to shred meat. *Bloody stars.*

The discovered sclice roars, rushing me just as I raise my sword. Dark blood sprays the air.

"Not bad for a wee lass," Tye mutters at the edge of my hearing.

"Not bad for a damn soldier," Coal echoes, with equal quiet. "But could be better."

My arms tremble from the strain. Even with my blade solidly striking flesh, the sheer size and force of the beast brings me to my knees. My breath catches, my lungs too tight to draw air.

The wounded sclice rears to its full height looming over me, clawed limbs ready to tear.

Everything inside me screams to roll away, to sprint, to run run run. I force my hands to stay on the sword. With my heart and breath speeding, it won't be long until I can't focus enough to see the sclice anymore—and the males are blind to it utterly. I have to stay, to drive the sword firmly into the beast's flesh. Not a killing blow—I've struck the thing's thigh—but a way to mark the sclice's location for the others. Give my males a chance.

The raised claws lower. My ribs scream in anticipated pain of another sclice attack, my body readying itself for the blow. With all the muscle I've ever gained, I force the blade in in in.

Something rips me away just before the sclice's nails rake the space where my head was. Iron-hard arms, pounding heart, a scent of fury and woods. The male gripping me twists in the air, taking the brunt of our fall against a wedge of stump and stones.

"Have you no sense?" River shouts into my face, his eyes surveying me desperately. Pushing off the ground, he hauls me upright, the hands he had around my waist now gripping my shoulders. "You could have died just now, Leralynn." He shakes me, his eyes flashing. "Do you understand?"

"Yes," I breathe. In my side vision, I see Coal and Tye's twin assaults converging on the sword I've left in the sclice—the blade now appearing to fly about in the darkness. A heartbeat later, the outline of a too-large sclice drops to the ground, becoming more and more visible as dark liquid drains from its severed neck. Coal spares me a brief nod of approval before cleaning off his blade.

Safe. We are all safe. Relief slams into me so powerfully that I stumble, only River's grip on my shoulders holding me up. River. Right. I look back into his ice-gray eyes, recalling the question. "Yes, sir."

He lets me go too quickly, hollering for Shade as he surveys the new kill.

"I'm here." Shade—once again in his fae form—steps out

of the woods where his wolf disappeared minutes earlier, breathing hard. I wonder what would have happened if the males saw Shade shift before their very eyes—and whether it is better or worse that they didn't. Of the four, Shade and Tye are the only shifters, though Tye's relationship with his tiger is very tenuous still. If *that* shift happened in the mortal world, all hell would break lose.

My attention focuses on Shade, my heart squeezing at the beautiful sight of him, his swinging black hair, damp with sweat, his arms rippling with corded muscle. Shade exchanges curt nods with Coal—who is now clearing the perimeter— before jogging to River. "I took one down, whatever it was. How did you make out?"

I step forward despite myself, my soul calling toward the shifter. "The wolf—"

Tye gives me an odd look.

"Wolf?" Shade glances my way, his yellow eyes slightly unfocused, as if struggling to orient. "No. Whatever it was, it was no wolf."

My breath stops. Shade thinks I'm asking about the sclice he killed. Shade doesn't know he shifted. Doesn't realize his wolf was involved in the tussle. Neither does *anyone*, it seems. Surely they'd remember… Unless the veil covered up the too-close shift by distracting the males' attention from the wolf altogether. Given that the animal was among us for mere heartbeats, it's possible. I swallow. Given what's already happened with the amulet's powerful magic, anything is bloody possible.

"No, that is certainly not a wolf," Coal says, jerking his head toward the sclice corpses. "I've no notion what it is, but 'deranged hog' seems descriptive enough."

"Are you all right, lass?" Tye's voice brushes the top of my head, and I realize the male has come up behind me, his feet as silent as a tiger's. Warm callused hands brush along my shoulders and arms, the touch so familiar, I want to burrow in Tye's chest.

"It appears we found your mystery beasts, River," Shade mutters nearby, his face pulled back in a grimace. "So the night wasn't wasted, at least."

I close my eyes. Not *River's* mystery beast—the Academy's. This perverted trio of sclices had been killing for a week before we stepped foot on Great Falls grounds, and would have gone on doing so if not for us. *Us*—the quint. Whether the males know it or not, we are where we are supposed to be.

Tye's cheek presses against my hair. "Did you know you smell of lilac?" he drawls softly.

"Your shoulder—" I open my eyes, remembering the blood from the initial contact, and reach for the male.

"Shade." River's ice-cold voice cuts between us before I can touch Tye, the command in it instantly summoning everyone's attention. "Please examine Tyelor while Coal escorts Leralynn back to the Academy and places her chambers under guard. I will deal with them both tomorrow."

As Coal's callused fingers encircle my arm firmly, his familiar metallic scent surrounding me, I give one last glance at the shattered clearing, three precious males cleaning up with the calm practicality of seasoned warriors. And then, with a small shift of his face toward me, all I can see are River's furious gray eyes. Lingering in my mind long after the night swallows them.

~

PART II: CRIME AND PUNISHMENT

1

RIVER

River's hands closed on the window frame of his high tower office, the grip tight enough to blanch his knuckles. He hadn't slept. Had given up on even trying to do so, for each time he'd dared to close his eyes, he could see nothing but Leralynn.

Leralynn standing tall in the moonlight, her curves silhouetted against the sky. Leralynn meeting his eyes in a way that drowned out the rest of the world. Leralynn kissing Tye, pressing into an oak beside the very wall that students were forbidden to touch. River could still smell the woman's arousal, see her hips undulating hungrily against Tye's hand, her need and pleasure stirring River's own body into rebellion.

Stars. Taking a shuddering breath, River focused his attention on the window. Outside, the vast courtyard was near empty. The students had liberty for the week's end, and despite dawn's arrival hours ago, the frostbitten grass and swept cobblestones saw no foot traffic except Tye jogging to his athletic training earlier. Normal. Ordinary. And after the strange beasts they finally put down last night, the Academy would stay as such.

River winced. Thinking of the night was a mistake, for the memories had started rolling over him again. Leralynn, as fearless as any warrior, her presence—her courage—so much greater than her size as she plunged her sword into the beast that no one could see. There was a moment there when River couldn't understand why she wasn't pulling back. And then it hit him, together with a wave of terror that slowed time. The woman was trying to mark the beast's location for the others, even if it would cost her life to do so. It was the kind of courageous and reckless and intelligent thing that Diana would have done.

A fine rattle drew River's attention to his hands, which had started to shake from their grip on the window ledge. Last night had been close. Too close. A heartbeat more and the world might have lost the fire that was Leralynn. Just as the world had lost Diana. River's throat closed. Yes, that was the other reason he dared not shut his eyes again.

After months of seeing nothing but his late wife's face, last night River saw only Lera's. He couldn't even draw Diana's features in his mind without them warping to Leralynn's long auburn hair and warm chocolate eyes, her internal glow that drew him in like a moth to the proverbial flame.

A rap sounded against his door.

"Come," River called, turning his back to the window as he straightened his crisp red-and-gold tunic, rolling his shoulders into a posture befitting a commander.

"Sir." Dressed in his signature black leather, blond hair pulled back tight, Coal strode into the office on silent feet and crossed his arms in silent endurance of River's intrusive gaze. The man looked terrible—not that anyone beside River or Shade would notice the haunted shimmer behind the warrior's icy blue eyes. Whatever had happened to Coal in captivity, it was still eroding him from the inside. The Academy was supposed to provide a place for him to put down those demons, but things were getting worse instead. As if a piece of Coal's soul had been torn away and now the rest of him leaked out through the wound.

The analogy struck too close to what River himself felt.

"Lieutenant." River nodded his greeting to the warrior.

"It's frosty in here," Coal said, looking around at River's office with its stone walls and dark wood accents. "Are the visiting cadets not cowing quickly enough, or is it for personal masochism?"

It was drafty, River would admit, mountain air blowing through the old caulking, frost edging each windowpane. He'd not bothered to light the fireplace yet today, his mind on other things.

River straightened a stack of papers on his desk, ignoring the question. "Any more on last night's invisible hogs?"

"I surveyed the whole perimeter this morning and found no signs of additional pack mates," Coal said crisply. "I think we put this lot down for good, sir."

Of course Coal had been out already. And, doubtlessly, alone. Maybe he and Leralynn were kindred spirits, both unable to walk past danger without sticking their noses in.

"I've also given the descriptions to Master Gavriel." Crossing his arms, Coal leaned against the wall. "The librarian will look through his books to see if he can shed light on what the beasts were."

"Good. The man's intelligent and discreet—a rare combination." River ached to rub his hands over his face, but locked them behind his back instead. There had been another execution in Grayson, the closest large town, last night—a laundress accused of using fae craft to make garments sicken their owners, or some similar ghastly nonsense. "Remind the students that anyone discussing the fae will find himself in my study. As much as I dislike banning a discussion topic, the last thing we need is for one kingdom's nobles to start accusing another. Especially when last night proved that something unnatural is truly afoot."

"And what of Tyelor and Leralynn? Shall I tell them they imagined the whole incident?" Coal raised a brow.

Leralynn. As if the woman's name itself carried a curse, River's heart stuttered the moment he heard it. *Leralynn. Leralynn.* River tightened his jaw. "Those two are another problem altogether."

"The pair handled themselves adequately," Coal said, picking up a glass paperweight on River's desk, eyeing it skeptically and putting it back down again. It was the highest praise River had ever heard from the warrior. Which was probably why the man suddenly needed something to do with his hands.

"I don't care how they handled themselves," River snapped. "Leralynn came a hair's breadth from death last night—because she decided that the rules all cadets live under don't apply to her. A student who cannot be bothered to respect the Academy's structure on her first damn day. I've said it before and I will again—we've too many young nobles who do not belong, and the faster we can set them straight, the better for all involved." The words came out hotter than River wished, but Coal gave no sign of having noticed— though he doubtlessly had. Nothing got past the man. River had learned that long ago.

A pregnant silence hung in the air, then Coal shrugged. "And Tyelor?"

"Tyelor is an upperclassman and a known quantity," River said, reclaiming his equilibrium as they entered familiar ground. With the young man's athletic background and natural knack for combat training, River put Tye in the same category of warrior as himself, Coal, and Shade—something River would not say for anyone else in Great Falls. River trusted Tye with little else, but he did trust the man to defend himself. "I'm still of a mind that Tyelor can be turned into a halfway-responsible human being if given limits. I will deal with him this afternoon."

"Understood." Coal's intelligent blue gaze pierced River. "*Only* Tyelor?"

"Yes." River walked to his desk and settled into the large leather chair. He had never delegated responsibility in his life, but this… River needed to hand this one off lest he do something he would regret. "I am leaving Leralynn's punishment to you. I trust you to make it commensurate with the severity of her trespasses last night."

No questions from Coal. No cocked brow of surprise or a questioning glance as the warrior nodded, pushed away from the wall, and strode to the door.

River's chest tightened, his heart pounding his ribs as he raised his voice once more. "Coal."

Hand already on the door handle, the warrior paused but did not turn—for which River was grateful.

"I'd like Leralynn of Osprey gone from Great Falls," River said.

2

———————————

LERA

*T*ink.

Rubbing my eyes, I sit up in bed, the small room of the Great Falls Academy dormitory blinking back at me. The sunlight streaming through the large window illuminates the tall pale white walls, bits of dust playing in the strong rays. Having only returned from my unfortunate run-in with sclices—and perhaps equally unfortunate run-in with River and Coal—in the middle of the night, I've only had four hours sleep. Several paces away, Arisha is already swinging her legs toward the floor, her messy braids swaying against her chest as she swivels her head in search of the noise's source.

Tink. Tink.

"I think it's coming from the window." My voice is groggy. Today's liberty day was supposed to allow for a bit of a lie-in, but something—or someone—seems to have other ideas. The noise comes again. Yes, definitely the window. Like a bird's beak hitting glass, except I see no bird anywhere.

Tink. Tink. Tink.

Stuffing her feet into slippers, Arisha puts on her glasses and shuffles to the window, her heavy cotton nightgown swaying about her ankles. Grasping hold of the shutters, she swings the panes open, jumping aside with a yelp as a pebble intended for the glass knocks into her shoulder instead. A heartbeat later, Tye swings himself into our room, his emerald eyes sparkling with self-satisfied amusement while Arisha sputters. He flicks a lock of red hair out of his face, looking painfully handsome and unfairly well rested. In some semblance of justice, the cleared lock of hair flops right back over the male's green eyes.

"You… You!" Rushing back to her bed, Arisha pulls a sheet over herself, her face suddenly paler than normal underneath her scattering of freckles. She points a finger at Tye, her mouth opening and closing as if searching for new words. "You—"

"Aye. Me. I think we've established that part quite solidly, lass." Tye's long arm reaches for the window, shutting it to cut off the chill wind. Through Tye's wide collar, I see the bandage crossing his shoulder as he stretches and suppresses a wince. I'd forgotten he took a sclice claw in last night's battle. He is dressed in a modified version of our training grays, his tunic sleeveless and wrapped tightly around his muscular abdomen, his jacket hanging loose. Tye's wide shoulders and taut waist draw a clean triangle, darker patches of sweat glistening against the light fabric. A scent of soap beneath the sweat underscores his masculine scent, mixing with the pine and citrus that is always Tye.

Catching me watching him, Tye grins with feline impertinence, his soft growl reminding me exactly of how he'd tasted against the forest's moonlight, how my body roused to the feel of his deft fingers sliding along my skin. Slipping deeper. My sex clenches at the very memory, and Tye's grin widens. Yes, the bastard isn't even trying to pretend he doesn't smell my arousal. Tye may think himself human, but his fae senses are picking up all the details.

I get up, crossing my arms. Unlike Arisha, my nightshirt is a thin slip of red silk that falls to midthigh, but I'll be damned if I let Tye make me scramble for clothing in my own bedchamber. "Is there a reason you are in our room?"

Tye's eyes glide over my thighs and hips, catching appreciatively on my suddenly heavy breasts, on my nipples peaking in the cool air. A heartbeat later, he shifts his legs uncomfortably, the bulge there twitching.

"I hope it hurts. A lot," I murmur so quietly that only Tye's fae ears have a chance of picking up the words.

The male snorts.

"H-how did…" Arisha, still stuttering, points to the window. "That is fifteen feet off the ground."

"He climbs well," I tell the girl over my shoulder while my gaze narrows on the male. "But yes, after Tye tells us *why* he's graced us with his presence, he can explain whether the door somehow offended him."

"I'm delivering a message from the deputy headmaster." With my bed vacated, Tye makes himself at ease on it, pressing his back against the wall while stretching out his long legs. His mussed red hair looks nearly aflame in the room's golden morning light. After giving me one more slow caress with his gaze, Tye's eyes stray to Arisha, who has somehow managed to tangle herself in the bedsheet she is using for cover. And who knows nothing about the night's escapade.

Right. I grope for some plausible excuse to speak to Tye alone and come up empty-handed. *You could have waited, you ass.*

"I know Lera snuck outside last night." Arisha rolls her large blue eyes at us both. "I now imagine she was with you, Tyelor, and that the pair of you were caught by none other than River himself. The next time you need to make a stealthy exit, please wake me up so I can close the window before the room freezes."

"You left the window open?" Tye covers his face with a large palm. "What kind of hooligan are you?"

"A cranky one." I sigh, recalling River's fury over finding Tye and me on the other side of the wall and his ominous promise to deal with us. I don't recall ever facing the full force of the male's cold ire, and I little like it. "I've also the sense that my day is about to get worse."

Tye nods, the humor from his face fading. "I'm to report to River at two this afternoon, while you are to join Coal in the training corrals. I imagine they think making us wait will play nicely on our anxiety." The tightness in Tye's voice says there might be good reason to be anxious. He sits up, resting his corded forearms on his thighs. His biceps shift and ripple under his bare skin, making it impossible to look away even if I wanted to. "Now, listen to me, lass. And listen carefully. Coal is going to ask you what the bloody hell you thought you were doing outside the wall last night. When he does, you will tell him that you were just following me. I convinced you that I know the best place to stargaze, and before you knew it, I was helping you over the wall. Are you following?"

Keep the secret passage a secret and let Tye take the blame.

"We went over the wall at *my* behest," I say, holding his emerald gaze. Then the rest of Tye's words finally register, and I throw up my arms. "And why would I follow you to view stars, which I can see just fine by tipping my head up?"

A quick flash of a smile. "Because you were so struck by my enchanting personality that you were willing to go with me under any pretense."

Bastard. "And I brought a sword along because…?"

The grin widens, white teeth flashing in a way that steals

my breath, "Because despite being struck by my irresistible personality, you are also smart."

"I *am* smart," I tell him dryly, swallowing against the sudden cavity in my chest. I have to remind myself that, in spite of appearances, Tye's casual familiarity is simply a function of his personality, not a true kinship. This Tye doesn't know me—not really—and the sting of that keeps taking me by surprise, rising in sudden sharp waves. "And I also don't let my friends take the blame for my choices. You followed me over the wall, not the other way around. If you'd like our stories to match, I recommend you stick to that one."

Tye's humor disappears, the beautiful angles of his face going from mischievous to hard in an instant. "Trust me, lass. I've been down this road before. Do what I say."

I raise my chin.

Tye curses, turning to Arisha, who is still clutching her sheet, brown hair frizzing around her sharp cheekbones. "Can you talk some sense into the lass? Explain how she's just arrived, which paints a bloody bull's-eye on her back."

"River and Coal do make a habit of encouraging newer cadets to depart," Arisha says with a wince. Now standing beside her clothing chest, she appears to be having trouble working out a way to rummage through it without releasing her sheet. "It's their solution to the fact that, for political reasons, the headmaster won't allow any expulsions."

Hopping off my bed, Tye strips out of his jacket and lays it over Arisha's shoulders, the large man's garment easily falling below her backside. "Don't get excited, braids. I'm not looking." That done, Tye turns his back to my roommate and studies me unabashedly as I lay out my own clothing, a new drab gray uniform that fits me only marginally better than yesterday's did. Other students will be able to wear whatever they want on their liberty day, but I'm heading into the opposite of liberty.

"I imagine killing and maiming students carries little political good will either, so no matter what Coal has in mind, I'll survive it with my limbs intact." I hold my hand up, cutting off Tye's protest. The necessary secrecy and tale the veil amulets spin can force me to do many things—but I will not allow it to make me shrink away from my males.

I only hope that whatever Coal has planned leaves me with enough energy to go right back over the wall tonight. Between the soft interior of the cracked tablet and the fleeting nature of tracks in spring soil, I've little time to find and reassemble the magic-charged rune before the weather takes it. And after that, once the males have their memories back, we can get back to working out what allowed those morphed sclices into the human realm to begin with—with River back in charge.

I put my hands at the hem of my nightgown and am about to pull it up, so used to disrobing casually around my males, when I catch myself with a flush. Another small stab of pain. I can't let Tye's easy way confuse my senses.

I look from my clothes to Tye, who is still standing with his back to Arisha, eyeing me with a coy kind of mischief, as if the quieter he is, the greater chance I'll have of forgetting he's there. "Are you going to watch me dress?"

"I could help you," Tye drawls. "Though in full disclosure, I'm somewhat better at the *dis*robing part when it comes to females."

"Get out." I point to the window. "Now."

3

———

LERA

Gavriel is so excited to hear the details of last night's sclices when I visit him in the grand library, I can't help thinking of Autumn, who takes a child's delight in any and all information. Then I look down at the neat rows of pens, inks, and books guarding the man's desk, and the difference between him and chaos-thriving Autumn becomes so stark that my eyes threaten to sting. I focus on the rough sketches of the mole-covered beasts the librarian and I are working on.

"Fascinating," Gavriel says, writing notes as quickly as his hand can dip pen into ink, his gray-streaked brown hair flopping over his forehead. "Would you say these sclices were bigger or smaller than average? Was their stench closer to that of vegetable rot or was it more a latrine-like scent? It may behoove us to have you walk past both the compost and refuse piles for an accurate comparison."

I'm all right, Gavriel, thank you for asking. Tye took a nasty slice on his shoulder, though; River is furious with me; Coal intends to make me regret ever stepping foot here; and Shade shifted without any knowledge of it. "They just stank. As for size, it was more that they were disproportional to their own bodies. Like the sclice version of a five-legged cat or something." I rub my face. The grand round room of the library, with its soaring red-and-gold dome, cheery warmth, and ever-present scent of paper and binding, has a surreal type of comfort. "How could Shade not realize that he shifts?"

"Hmm?" Gavriel works out quick arithmetic that I can't follow on the corner of his parchment, then adds measurement estimates to his notes, which he tosses sand over while speaking. "Oh. Shade. I imagine the veil affects only the fae in him, not the animal. So the instant he shifts back, the veil spins a plausible explanation for missed time." The man trails off, tapping his hand against the drawing. "Can you describe the mole pattern again? How many moles would you estimate there were?"

My jaw clenches. "I was fighting for my life. I wasn't counting bloody moles."

"No, of course not. That's only to be expected this early on." Gavriel smiles in what I think he thinks is reasonable encouragement. "We can work on training your attention to such details."

We can work on my not breaking your neck. I take a deep breath. Gavriel is the only one I can talk to about my reality, my mission. And that means taking his educated idiocy together with what insights and company he offers. I motion toward the stack of books detailing various runes. "Have you found anything more on the origins of the tablet I broke on the way here?"

"I'm afraid I've had no success in that as yet." The apology in Gavriel's tone is sincere, which does make it difficult to hate him just now. The man takes off his glasses, wiping them on his thick olive robe. "I know you are eager to reassemble it, but I can't recommend toying with magic like that without understanding the ramifications. For all we know—"

"For all we know, River, Coal, Tye, and Shade are in danger of losing themselves forever if I don't fix this quickly." My hands curl around the table's edge, my jaw tightening. This has to work. There is nothing else. I've nothing else.

Gavriel sighs. "I realize you little want to hear this, Leralynn, but it is possible the males are exactly where they are supposed to be."

"You're right." I rise, sliding my chair back so hard that it topples. Comparing Gavriel to Autumn is like holding a lantern beside the sun. "I don't want to hear it." I spread my hands on the table, leaning forward into Gavriel's space. "If you want the mortal world to survive, you need River, not me, to lead the charge. He's the only one in this realm with a full understanding of the Citadel's reports and the only one with a plan in place for how to approach it. The centuries he's spent leading the fight against rogue magic don't hurt either. Except right now, River is a bloody deputy headmaster of an isolated school. My quint commander doesn't know his own sister's name, let alone that he holds all of humanity's fate on his shoulders."

The doorbells chime a ridiculously happy tune as I pull the library door open and slam it behind me. *Bells on a library door?* Gavriel's strangeness rears its head in new ways each time I meet him. A quick glance at the sun says I've an hour to eat something before Coal takes his turn at making my life miserable. After that… After that, all bets are off.

I WALK onto the training grounds a few minutes before the

Academy's bell tower strikes two in the afternoon, the place deserted except for a single blue standard flapping at the far training court. In the emptiness of a liberty day, the Academy's towering stone walls and broad cobblestoned courtyards take on an echoing eeriness. The ominous gray-skied murk of the afternoon doesn't help. Corral after corral of neatly raked sand greet me as I pass, my attention on the lone shirtless figure fighting ghosts in the farthest of the rings. The dull *thud thud thud* of Coal's training sword hitting rope-wrapped posts echoes through the yard, my immortal eyes tracking the warrior's deadly dance from a hundred paces away.

High strike, low, middle parry, step. High parry, roll over the shoulder, middle strike. Repeat. I know this pattern as well as Coal does, just as I know he hates it. The thin sheen of sweat covering his bare muscled back says he's been here for some time—as surely as the two broken practice swords lying in a pile of discarded shards. In the odd overcast light, the long tattoo twisting down Coal's spine and his many scars draw little attention to themselves, though I doubt I'll ever not see them on him.

My chest tightens. Stepping up to the fence enclosing the training corral, I brace my forearms against the wood, watching the wooden post shudder and rock beneath the mighty blows, Coal's sword a blur as he dances across the sand. Even in the mortal realm, Coal's strange inward-facing magic saturates his body, honing it for survival. Perhaps I shouldn't be surprised. Coal's magic had flourished even during the centuries he spent as a slave in the dark realm of Mors. The male may not manipulate the elements like River and Tye or mend broken bones like Shade, but between his own training and the strength, speed, and faster healing his strange magic grants him, Coal is one of the greatest warriors the realms have ever seen.

High. Low. Middle. Step. Strike.

Coal's practice blade shatters, and I wince for both the abused wood and the warrior's shoulder that took the impact. Coal's metallic scent reaches me with the shifting wind. Tossing the broken blade into a pile with the two others, the warrior turns to look at me, his blue eyes harsh. Unreadable.

I search the male's face for clues of what he makes of last night's outing, the sculpted angles of his set jaw and cheekbones, but there is no information to be had on that front. Coal is too good at hiding his thoughts. After years as a Mors slave, he has to be. I wonder how his human persona is accounting for the nightmares—which, if I'm reading the tightness in his shoulders correctly, the male is having again. In spades.

Taking two new practice blades from a rack Coal has already pulled out, I vault over the chest-high wooden fence. A trick Tye taught me, just as Coal worked on my riding and combat. Landing softly, I toss one of the blades to him, rotating the other to get its full feel.

"This isn't why you are here." Coal's hand closes over the practice blade, the wood already an extension of his body.

"I'm aware." I settle into my fighting stance, my feet finding purchase in the sand as I bring my blade to ready guard, watching Coal over the sword's dull tip. "But this is why you are here. And I'm early."

Coal cocks his head, watching me curiously while tossing the practice blade from one hand to the other.

I hold my breath. *Talk to me, Coal. With your sword if not your words.*

He snorts, the blade in his hand now swinging a wide, contemplative circle. "You *are* aware of what's to happen this afternoon, right?" he asks, his low, gravelly voice tinged with curiosity—and annoyance at my nonchalance. He wants me intimidated before my punishment even starts, and I won't give him the satisfaction. "Moving stones yesterday was only a taste. Wasting energy before it even begins isn't the wisest decision I've seen made."

I don't answer. In the past year, Coal and the other males have trained me, pushed me beyond my imagined limits, cheered as I conquered each challenge, no matter how many tries and screams and bruises it took to get there. They never punished me, though—and the chasm of that difference suddenly shakes the very foundation beneath me.

I swallow, telling myself I'm making a mountain from a molehill. From the perspective of a military unit, River has enforced discipline for centuries. *Stars,* Tye alone has stories upon stories of being punished, and I've seen Coal take his share from River. It never changed them from the brothers they are. This, even under the veil that makes us strangers, will change nothing either. It can't. And as for Coal, I trust he'll stop short of doing true damage.

Realizing that Coal is watching me, waiting for an answer I've not voiced, I clear my throat.

"We'll call this a warm-up," Coal says, saving me from the need to find words by swinging his blade for my shoulder. Hard.

4

LERA

I snap off a parry, managing to deflect Coal's blow only by virtue of having expected it after so many times facing the warrior across the sands. The flicker of surprise in the male's blue eyes brushes against my skin, intensifying as I adjust my footing in an experienced wager that Coal's next assault will come from above. Then an ankle sweep. Then—

I fall backward, my ankle kicked swiftly from beneath my body, the sand rising in a small amused puff. Knowing what Coal will do offers only so much protection against stopping it. Rolling backward over my shoulder, I return to my feet, my attention tightening on the male's movements. The slight, intrigue-touched gaze as he circles, the flex of his sharply carved jaw, the crests of his hips shifting over the waistline of black fighting leathers. His scalpel-precise strike at my ribs.

My sword snaps down as I step, parry, strike, my breath quickening with each movement. The rhythmic *clack, clack, clack* of our swords vibrates across the empty ground in a hypnotic chorus that fills an aching void inside me. *Clack, clack,*

clack. My heart keeps time with the strikes and parries, the perfectly packed sand beneath my boots a familiar echo.

My breath catches as Coal's blade shifts to his weak hand, a brush of pleasure rippling down my spine. The warrior isn't just toying with me, but training. Honing his own skills as he dances, each swing and lunge and slice carrying enough force to crack bones. Trusting me not to get dead. Not to be frightened into dropping my guard.

The harsh lines of his beautiful face are set in concentration, his metallic musk washing over me, weaving an illusion of usual quint training. *Focus, Lera. Shade can't just heal a limp anymore.*

I shift my weight again, circling Coal, my eyes intent on his hips and shoulders. The immortal's ethereal movements flow with perfection, thin whips of steam rising from the sheen of sweat that accentuates each muscle. The tension of his pectoral as he winds up his assault, the ripple in his biceps as he executes. Never stopping. Never letting me stop either.

Awake. Alive. My body blazes with heat despite the crisp spring air, my breath coming fast, the growing ache in my lungs a distant distraction.

Clack. Clack. Clack.

"Good to see Lieutenant Coal taking out the trash." A musical female voice I've heard before sounds from the edge of my vision, followed by a beat of silence before coming again. "How long do you wager it will take, Tyelor? I'll put a kiss down on an hour. Name your time and your wager."

My gaze shifts, cutting across Tye's muscular forearms as he leans on the fence, Princess Katita standing beside him. Her white-blond hair and brilliant teal eyes mark her immediately, even from the corner of the eye. She's that striking—and that invasive of any space she stands in.

Coal lunges in, his blade rapping painfully against my left

ribs, then twists to capture my sword arm. The eerie gray light sculpts his lines, giving his skin a new golden hue that highlights his harsh blue eyes. Eyes that hold neither compassion nor quarter. The blazing heat of him wraps around me, his chest expanding with even breaths that make him bigger still. Claiming all my attention with a warrior's ruthless skill, until I dare not mind my stinging left side, much less anything beyond the world of us.

I gasp for air, Coal's metallic scent filling my nose. My world.

Stepping away for sword room, Coal loops his practice sword back in a deadly arc that aims for my head.

I swing my sword high to meet his blow, the clash of wood filling the air. Rippling through my arms, my spine, my thighs. With our blades now crossed, I shove my whole body against the contact, forcing Coal's own sword closer to his throat. One inch. Two. Salt streaks down my face, stinging my eyes. My lungs burn, my muscles screaming with the effort of it. Shaking.

Coal cocks a brow, the first sign he's given of having an opinion on anything I do. Even if that opinion calls me three times the fool for getting into a battle of strength. Letting my own momentum shift my balance, Coal steps aside before hooking my blade and ripping it from my grip.

The slick hilt slips from my grip a moment before Coal's leg hooks mine. I fall backward, landing hard on the sand just as my weapon did a moment ago. Breath halts in my lungs, the dull thud of impact filling my ears even as I force my body to keep moving and roll to my feet. *Get up. Get up. Get up.*

Grains of sand grate against my tongue as I reclaim my fighting stance and kick Coal's chest, my foot meeting a rock-hard body that refuses to yield.

Tossing his own sword aside, Coal crouches, circling me

with a predatory calm. His breathing is steady, his muscles moving not a hair more than needed. Flexing his knees to lower his level, the male launches at me from the side, collapsing both of my legs from under me as he straddles my chest. The hot weight of him squeezes my lungs, his hands forcing my wrists up over my head, grating my knuckles into the gritty dirt.

I curse.

Coal forces my wrists up higher, lowering his glistening body toward mine, his battle-honed pectorals heaving with harsh breaths, his metallic scent filling my nose. The air between us crackles with heat and strain. My already speeding heart lurches into an outright gallop, something primal inside me waking to rage against the restraint. Instinct has me reaching for my magic, roaring at finding it shackled. The mortal world's bonds tighten over the cords of power so hard, it hurts.

Anger and fury lash through me, feeding off each other as I thrash between the twin holds of Coal's iron hands and this world's chokehold on my magic. The hobbled power inside me bangs futilely against its restraints. My body arches, the violence inside me exploding, rattling my bones. Hurting. Hurting. Hurting.

So much violence. So much darkness. So much pain.

Too much to all be mine. *Stars.* One of the first discoveries we'd made in Lunos—when I awoke in the throes of *Coal's* nightmare—was that during times of intense sensation, Coal's strange magic has a way of bridging the gap between us. Of letting my body temporarily strengthen from the male's power.

Coal's nightmares do the trick. Bedding does it better.

My vision narrows on nothing but Coal's face, so close to my own that the steam of our breaths mixes together. His eyes, focused on nothing but me, are tight. Tiny specks of purple fight their way to sparkle amidst brilliant blue. Yes, Coal's strange magic is roaring as loudly as my own, my weaver's body picking up the echo even here, on mortal soil.

I snarl, the carnal sound still new despite the six months that have passed since my brush with death forged my human self into this immortal form, the magic linking me forever with four fae warriors.

Magic. Yes. What if that's all it was? What if, without it, we're nothing but five fae warriors who once fought beside each other? My throat closes, but I force air through it nonetheless.

Coal releases me as I banish the thought to a place deep inside me, his eyes unreadable as he dusts himself free of sand. Free of me.

The fence where Katita and Tye had stopped is now empty once more.

"Maybe we scared them off," I mutter, realizing I'd spoken aloud when Coal's brow rises in question. I shake my head quickly.

For a moment, I swear the corner of Coal's mouth twitches. "If you are adequately warmed up," he says, recovering and putting away the fallen weapon, "it's time for us to get started."

5

―――――

COAL

ulling on his discarded black tunic, Coal turned away from the woman whose lilac scent made his head swim. Leralynn had fought admirably the previous night, but their match in the sparring ring just now had felt like something else altogether. A musical symphony that pierced so deeply into Coal's core that his heart still pounded against his ribs. And his heart wasn't the only thing pounding painfully.

With sweat slicking her creamy skin, Lera's face glowed ethereally despite the darkening sky, her auburn hair falling in a cascade of shining locks. The short pause since the match ended had already tightened her nipples to hard points that lifted her shirt, making it impossible to avoid noting the soul-wrenching breasts she seemed unaware she possessed.

Coal, however, was rather aware of the objects in question. Very inconveniently aware. Just as he'd been aware of her tight thighs and hips, the tantalizing curve of her shoulder meeting her neck that taunted something primal inside him. Made him want to *bite*, stars take him.

None of which was either logical or acceptable. Or welcome.

Leralynn was a cadet. A student—an infuriatingly stubborn student who seemed to have been born without self-preservation instincts. If Sage, the Academy's headmaster, could hear Coal's thoughts, he'd string him up on a whipping post. And would be right, for once in his life.

Swallowing, Coal hopped the training yard fence and led Lera out at a brisk run, the graying sky a perfect harmony to his racing pulse. With luck, it might start raining. Icy hail would be even better, especially if it could pour right into his leathers and put down his painfully throbbing hardness.

Reaching the edge of the corrals, Coal turned toward the tall perimeter wall, crossing the great stone courtyard at a jog. Their footsteps echoed through the empty space, the only sound but for the clank of a metalsmith's iron and a lone hawk high overhead. He'd intended to stay inside Academy grounds, but the place suddenly felt too small. Too much like a cage. Plus, Leralynn didn't deserve to be gawked at.

It had taken all of Coal's will to halt himself from shoving Tye and Katita right into the sand and keeping them there until the pair couldn't look at Lera again without twitching in pained memory. Like the lust, the protectiveness had come out of nowhere, gripping Coal's chest like a band of iron, making it hard to breath. Hard to think.

Which Coal needed to start doing. And fast.

Stopping before the infamous tree that Lera no doubt used to get herself over the wall last night, Coal made short work of pulling himself up and jumping the two-pace gap to the wall. No need to explain more than that. Actually, there was little need to explain anything with Lera, not when she understood him without words. And, somehow, Coal understood her. *Why,* he had no idea—and no intention of trying to figure out. That could only lead to trouble, and trouble was exactly what he'd come to the Academy to avoid.

Sparring had been a mistake. Fortunately for all involved, the mistake wouldn't have a chance to repeat itself since the girl would be packing up soon enough. River seldom asked for a favor, and if the commander wanted Lera gone, then Coal would make it so. And would keep the girl at arm's length until then.

Landing on the soft-packed earth beyond the wall, Coal spared a backward glance to ensure his charge was still there.

She was. And her damn eyes were alight with...with excitement at the turn of events.

Coal growled under his breath and picked up the pace, choosing a trail uphill through the dense mountain forest. The rough, rocky terrain and whipping pine needles set an appropriately ominous atmosphere for the rest of the afternoon. Lifting his face toward the chill wind, Coal savored its nip along his skin, his body merging with the forest-covered hills. For a moment, he pretended he was alone, that the tantalizing lilac scent the breeze carried came from nothing but oddly placed flowers. That River never ordered him to drive Lera out of Great Falls. That his world made some bloody sense.

None of it was true.

Especially the part about the world making sense. Running a step behind him—probably because the trail was too narrow to let her pull ahead—Leralynn looked downright *pleased.* As if an uphill trek through puddles and branches and bugs was exactly the way she'd wanted to spend her day of liberty. Her gaze never stopped surveying the terrain, especially each time they came to an overlook where sheep pastures and forested trails drew a mosaic across the countryside, with the steep gray mountain faces as a dramatic backdrop. *Stars,* despite a pace that would have had anyone but Shade or Tye emptying their stomach three times by now, Lera seemed utterly unaware that she was supposed to feel anxious and miserable at all.

Cresting a hill, Coal spied a patch of thick mud. Dropping them both for push-ups in the middle of the cold goo, Coal felt a prick of satisfaction when a small flash of irritation finally flittered across Lera's face. "Two dozen," Coal said. "All the way dow—"

Coal shut his mouth. Leralynn was already dipping into the freezing mud with each descent, the tightness around her jaw confirming that grit and moisture were seeping effectively into her gray uniform. Her head swiveled each time she straightened her arms. Not just surveying her surroundings but…watching for something. Or searching for it. Coal's gaze tightened.

"Another dozen," Coal ordered a heartbeat after the set was finished, waiting just long enough to let a false sense of relief fill Lera before snatching it away.

At least that had been Coal's intention—and a failed one judging by an utter lack of surprise in the girl's face. As if she'd known exactly what he'd do. Just as she had when the two sparred that afternoon. Yes, Leralynn was a decent fighter —but not so good as to block Coal's opening volley the way she had. Not without somehow knowing to expect it. Knowing *him.*

A shiver that had nothing to do with the mud and cold ran down Coal's spine, a memory echoing through his skull.

Coal's hands were shackled, his shoulders screaming from the strain. The taste of blood and fear choked him, blood from his last beating crusting along his skin. The islanders who'd held him for the past year never intended to let him leave. Never let him take his life either, no matter how he tried.

A noise scraped against Coal's hearing. He shifted, the sores beneath his shackles sending lightning bolts of agony down his skin, choking him.

"You aren't alone." A feminine voice sounded behind him, soft steps circling until a young woman with intelligent brown eyes came to stand before him. She was small, barely reaching Coal's shoulder, yet she filled his world with a lilac scent that drowned out all else. One of the islanders he'd not seen before.

"Let me out." Coal's quiet words ripped from his raw throat, the sound of his own plea tightening his chest.

The woman bit her lip, her eyes glistening. "I can't," she whispered. "I can't take your pain either. But I can be here. So you aren't alone."

Coal shook himself, trying to shed the memory of the mirage. Of whatever that woman had been. She'd done as she promised, staying with him whenever his captors let him be, mending his soul piece by piece even while his captors bled his body. But when River and Shade finally broke Coal free, he'd found no trace of her. Not in the prison. Not in the silent night. Not anywhere.

Later, at the docks, Coal learned that a woman matching her description had purchased passage on a ship two days earlier. Had left. Without saying a word.

Coal shook himself. A small woman with auburn hair and intelligent brown eyes—just like Lera. No wonder his body was playing games with him.

Beside Coal, Lera had finished the second set of push-ups and was awaiting further orders. Saying nothing, Coal got to his feet and set them running again. Up a hill. Down. Pushing through pine branches and climbing hand and foot over tumbles of lichen-covered boulders. Back up. Up higher still, Leralynn's breaths became ragged as the already gray sky darkened further. Sooner or later, Coal was going to get that rain he wanted.

They had just crested another hill when the young

woman's forever watchful eyes froze on a spot some yards to their right and widened, her hand bracing on her thigh. Following her gaze, Coal tried to mark what might have caught Lera's attention but found nothing—just a forested slope leading up to a sharp ridge across from them, cloaked in a wide grove of trembling green aspens. Coal jerked his chin toward the decline. "Move."

"Wait," Lera said, her breath more strained than Coal had expected, her pulse beating so hard that he could see it in the soft side of her neck. "One moment, sir. Please."

"No."

Lera didn't move.

Coal gripped her upper arm, dragging her back into a run.

Lera took a single step before tripping over another, her hand clutching her side. The strained breath grew rapid, her slender shoulders trembling with a distress that made Coal freeze—despite this having been the goal of the excursion. *Bloody hell,* he was turning into mother Shade.

Lera swayed slightly.

"Leralynn?" Dropping to one knee beside her, Coal surveyed the girl's face.

Color high but decent, eyes sharp, lips pink. He had to be missing something—she was strong, one of only a handful of people who'd been able to keep up with him. If she crashed this suddenly, *something* had happened.

"Talk to me, Lera," Coal ordered, his eyes intent on hers.

Twisting away from his gaze, Lera bent double, dry-heaving into the earth. "Please," she whimpered between bouts of coughing, her body trembling like a newborn foal's. "Can't. Just. One. Breath."

Coal's gaze narrowed. Where the hell did that one-word speech come from? She'd said "One moment, sir," easily enough—why would she find it harder to speak now? Coal's attention shifted to Lera's chest, its rise and fall steady enough.

Something cold slithered through Coal's core. In all his years as a soldier, Coal had pushed himself and others enough to learn the breaking points. Knew enough to stop pushing a hair before such a point was reached.

And he sure as hell knew when someone was lying.

A simmer of heat started in Coal's blood, spreading like a crack in a glass through every fiber of his body. His jaw tightened, his fists clenching in a fury to rival the coming rain. Leralynn was *lying* to him. Playing him. As she had all damn day—sparring with him, forcing his guard down with every parry and thrust, all but goading him into taking their run farther. Until now. The girl was no more at endurance's end than she'd been minutes earlier, her elaborate show merely a way to buy time while she marked the land as carefully as a cartographer.

Yes, she'd found something. Perhaps the very something that had her climbing over the wall last night, a sword at her back.

Coal followed her gaze, still seeing nothing of particular interest except perhaps a set of switchback tracks. No, Coal didn't know what the bloody hell Lera sought, but he knew when he was being toyed with. And that Lera was doing it dug so painfully into him that bile rose up Coal's throat.

"What's wrong?" Coal demanded, his voice low. One last chance for Lera to give him the truth.

"Can't. Breathe."

Coal's jaw tightened, the chill in him turning into crackling ice. An idiot. He'd been an idiot, while River has seen the woman for what she was. The first time since the western isles that he'd loosened a part of himself with anyone but River and Shade, and this was what he got.

Deceit. Like that of another woman who'd once brushed Coal's soul.

Something inside Coal snapped, as clear and loud as a branch beneath a careless boot.

Grabbing Lera's nape, Coal forced her to her feet, the woman's stagger damn believable except for the spice of excitement, not misery, spicing her lilac scent. When she tried to mutter something Coal couldn't bear hearing, he tightened his grip to the edge of pain. If Leralynn wanted to play games, he would ensure there was no need for feigning distress.

6

LERA

I found it, I found it, I found it.

As Coal pushes me on, I mark every landmark in sight, the path back to the shattered tablet—only one steep gulley away—dimming all the world to irrelevance. My heart pounds, the tendrils of hope sending new energy through my body.

Even as Coal leads me back into the thicker part of the forest, away from that clicking aspen grove shimmering on the next hillside over, I keep the image in my mind, tracing our route to get back to the tracks. With the weather threatening to turn, I'll have to go out tonight. Even if it means swallowing my pride now.

"On your back. Legs six inches up." Coal's icy voice hauls me back to reality. Face unreadable, the male points to a shallow, fast-running stream—an offshoot of the Great Falls waterfall a mile off. The riffle is just over a pace wide, small stones agitating the rushing water to a white foam.

I wave away the buzzing mayflies, trying to make sense of the order.

Instead of explaining, Coal sweeps the back of my knee, only his quick grip on my tunic stopping me from cracking my head open as I fall into the stream. The freezing water is upon me at once, clawing my lungs and face and thighs. Taking my breath. My muscles seize, the shock of it jerking me up, only to have Coal shove me right back into the water.

I fight to draw air, freezing liquid rushing over me, jetting into my mouth and nose and ears. I spit, my heels pounding the stream as Coal holds me down, my head downstream of my body. The water turns to needles, my constricted lungs screaming. I gasp for air, able to draw none into my shaking body. When I finally do, it flows together with the rushing stream.

I choke, my heart pounding, driving panic though my blood. Bile and spit and water climb up my throat. My thrashing limbs make turning my head into an unbearable effort, even when Coal's hand lifts from my chest to let me retch.

"Are you—" My tongue is too thick for my mouth, the words possible only from fury alone. "Are you insane?"

Coal crouches beside my head, his beautiful, chiseled face as hard as I've ever seen it, the graying sky reflecting in his blue eyes. "Do I have your attention now?" he asks, his low voice a deadly rumble. "On your back. Feet six inches off the earth. I don't give a damn what you do with your head, but if you get up before I tell you to, you'll be doing this with my hand pressed down on your sternum."

My mind spins, finding no logic. No footing.

Swallowing my curses together with rushing water, I hold Coal's gaze as I surrender to whatever this is. Lie in the stream. Keep my legs up as water weights down my boots. Try to keep from choking on the rushing stream.

Ten seconds. Thirty. A minute. Until not even anger can

warm me, despair rushing in to fill the void. My body numbs, my muscles shaking against the hard rushing stream. I can't do it. It isn't bloody fair, and I can't do it. And—my head goes under, the water rushing gleefully into my mouth. Deeper. Into my throat and up my nose, pounding against my clamped vocal cords.

Terror rushes through me, the world darkening around the edges. My lungs hurt, my body desperate for air that's somewhere. Not here. Not anywhere. I feel my limbs flailing against the rushing water, the muscles stiff and desperate and unable to find purchase. To remember what to do. Faster. I need to move faster. No time. No time. No—

Coal jerks me up by my tunic, and I fall to my hands and knees, my own coughs tearing through my chest.

"That's right, Leralynn of Osprey." The male's soft voice is as cold as the stream. "You don't deserve this. You need Great Falls no more than you need manure stuck to your boot soles."

I blink, lifting my pounding head to meet Coal's eyes, my sluggish mind struggling to understand. "You want me to leave? Is that what this is all about?"

Coal leans his face so close to mine that drops of water from my shivering body land on his chest, his familiar metallic scent filled with a bitter tang of fury. "Yes," he says, a muscle ticking along his jaw. "And I'm not the only one."

I recoil as if struck, the words hurting more than the cold, cold stream. "You'll have to keep waiting."

The ticking muscle in Coal's jaw quickens, but he says nothing. His icy blue eyes crackle in the thunder-charged air, something in him about to break as surely as a gathering storm.

Overhead, a fleeing hawk swoops close, the forest around us silent in anticipation.

Coal wants me gone. And not just him. Heat rushes through me despite the chill, my chattering teeth gritting. The mask I've seen River don so many times slips over my face as I grip the stones on either side of the stream and lower myself right back into the water.

Whatever happens, Coal won't get the satisfaction of seeing me surrender.

7

ARISHA

wo scoops grain, one scoop sweet for three dozen of the horses, for four weeks with each feed sack holding—no, wait, with the spring weather breaking, fresh grass might come soon. Arisha crossed off the calculation. Would the extra green grass mean the horses needed less grain, or would the extra running they did on soft ground lead to them needing more?

"Should we tell her?"

"That would be a full-time job, Nolan, and I need to watch Tyelor's training. He needs someone to keep him honest."

Arisha buried her head deeper into her book, ignoring Princess Katita and her royal cousins. *One and a half scoop of*—something rough hit Arisha between the eyes, sending her sprawling onto the ground. Glaring up, Arisha saw the tree she'd just walked into. A few paces away, the group of royals broke into ill-concealed chortles. Brilliant. That was the third —no, fourth—time this month alone she'd walked into something. Was someone moving the damn trees and building in the middle of the night? At least when the stunning

Leralynn stumbled into something, the something inevitably turned out to be Great Falls' top athlete.

One who Princess Katita believed to be her property.

Scowling, Arisha gathered her books and hurried into the sanctuary of the library. She needed to alphabetize the books. Or count them. Or maybe regroup everything by time period instead. Anything to keep her mind off whatever torment Master Coal was inflicting on Lera. The girl was brave and kind and as unaware of her own mortality as a fourteen-year-old boy. Pitted against Coal's creative sadism, the combination could end in nothing but utter disaster.

The chime of newly attached doorbells startled Arisha free of her thoughts. "Uncle Gavriel?" she called, stepping into the great circle of the library's entrance hall. The librarian's desk where Gavriel usually sat was empty, though the sound of a cane tapping the polished marble floor echoed from somewhere in the room. "Uncle?"

"Arisha." Stepping out from behind the far stacks, Gavriel limped toward her with more energy than she'd seen in him lately. The extra glint in his brown eyes was downright contagious. "Are you quite all right, my dear?"

"Yes." Arisha picked a stray leaf from her braid and adjusted her glasses. "You, however, look like a cat with a bowl of cream." Despite being alone in the library, Arisha dropped her voice. "Has the Guild welcomed you back?" Gavriel's vocal disagreements on both the interpretation of the fae prophecies and the Guild's rules surrounding them had gotten the man put out the door a year ago. Gavriel, being Gavriel, immediately got himself hired into Great Falls Academy, negotiating a spot for his niece along the way.

"Not quite, but they will." Gavriel set his books on a table and went to pull out the pot of tea and platter of sweets he always kept for Arisha's visit. Sugar-powdered scones with raisins, by the smell of them. "They truly will have no choice but to acknowledge my theories."

With a sigh, Arisha neatened Gavriel's books into an ordered stack and glanced at his newly placed door chimes. Gavriel wanted to know if anyone invaded his space, which meant he was planning to be more reckless than usual. "You've discovered new evidence?"

"Better." The man returned to the table, handing Arisha a tea tray. "I've proven my theory correct. I found the Protector."

The tea tray slipped from Arisha's hands, Gavriel rescuing the pot before it could spill. Arisha's heart quickened. After a lifetime's work with no acknowledgment, her uncle deserved a bit of recognition. "Are you certain? Where is he?"

"She. And right here in Great Falls Academy, just as I predicted." Gavriel winced. "She isn't what I expected, I grant you. A bit rough around the edges and not quite ready to accept her role, but I will work with her through it."

A familiar thick dread settled on Arisha's tongue. There he went again, the reason Uncle Gavriel was cut off from his life's work to begin with. "What do you mean *work* with her? The Sentinel Guild is very clear—watch, record, don't intervene. Prophecies tend to go awry when people start sticking their tongues and pens in them. I believe you taught me that."

Gavriel adjusted his glasses. "This is different, Arisha. And vital. The danger arrived in advance of the Protector, and she… I fear that left to her own devices, she is going to be chasing young men instead of saving the mortal realm. Sometimes prophecies need a bit of guidance, eh?" He poured Arisha a cup of tea. "The Guild will come around once they see."

"Are you going to tell me who it is?" Arisha asked, letting

out a heavy breath. She'd seen Gavriel here before and knew when there was no talking reason into the man. The best she could do was manage the damage and ensure his noble intentions did not dig a grave for him.

Despite the empty library, Gavriel dropped his voice before speaking. "Leralynn of Osprey. She wears a veil amulet, of course, but it is her."

"Leralynn?" Arisha blinked. "Are there two Leralynns?"

"We've started off on a very productive foot already," Gavriel continued. "The Great Falls area has been under siege from the nastiest of creatures—Sky…no, Sclices. I explained to Leralynn yesterday—"

"Leralynn of Osprey?" Arisha's fingers curled around her paper, crumpling the calculations. The kind, beautiful Lera who couldn't keep her nose out of a hornet's nest was an *immortal fae warrior?* No. Arisha had always imagined the Protector to look and act more like Deputy Headmaster River or maybe Master Coal. A small smile touched Arisha's face. *Coal.* Who was likely trying to run an immortal fae into the ground right now. Serves the bastard right.

Arisha's smile faded as the rest of Gavriel's sentence registered. "What do you mean, you *explained* to Leralynn? The Sentinel Guild watches. We don't interfere. Tell me you didn't actually speak to her about… Stars. Uncle." Arisha's stomach clenched, her heartbeat quickening. The Guild's vow of noninterference was vital, lest the whole mortal realm turned to war over winning the immortal warrior to their side of the truth. Arisha wasn't yet a full Sentinel, but even she knew that. Leralynn—Arisha's mind still spun with notions— had to be free to make her own choices. Arisha's eyes widened. "Please tell me you had nothing to do with Lera's sneaking out and going over the wall last night?"

Instead of blushing, Gavriel set up taller. "Indeed. I was

pleased to learn she took my word to heart, and we had a very productive discussion this morning about the creatures she encountered."

"Yes, well, Lera got caught," Arisha told Gavriel, her voice hard. "Master Coal is punishing her as we speak—at River's orders. I little need to tell you what those two do to new cadets."

"Hmm." Gabriel made a sound that was more intrigue than repentance. "That may work out in our favor quite nicely, in truth. And by *our* favor, I mean the entire human race's."

Arisha's brows narrowed. "Because the Protector needs extra experience in misery?"

"Because Leralynn must get those young men out of her thoughts so she can focus on the task at hand," Gavriel said, leaning forward. "The girl insists that Tye, Coal, River, and Shade are all fae as well, the five being part of a Lunos *quint* together. Mates, in fact. According to Leralynn, a magical artifact she broke caused the men—males—to absorb the properties of the veil amulets they wore. The four believe themselves human."

"Coal. River. Tye. Shade." Arisha felt like a damn parrot, her understanding of the world spinning on its head. Her already fast pulse jumped again. Those names... They were an integral part of the Academy. An *influential* part, whose actions could have a ripple effect through the entire Continental Alliance. *Stars,* River and Coal were in direct line of command of King Zenith's daughter. And here Gavriel was, trying to put a bit into Lera's mouth—which would inevitably affect her mates' actions too. Did Gavriel not understand he'd be put to death for this? No, of course he didn't. Uncle Gavriel was brilliant and kind and as disconnected from reality as his books.

Taking off his glasses, Gavriel wiped them on the corner of his robe. "I confess that Lera's excursion last night *might* have been motivated by a desire to find the broken artifact as much as my explicit instruction on a Protector's duties, but it's better to stay optimistic, don't you think?"

"Optimistic?!" Arisha checked her voice. "You are trying to direct the Protector to do your bidding, and your *optimistic* version of events is that she obeys you blindly and stops fighting for her mates' memories?"

"Lera is very young and easily distracted by amorous escapades," Gavriel said defensively. "I've no nefarious agenda. I just wish to help her grow in her destiny and save as many lives along the way as possible."

"No, Uncle. You want to help Lera grow into your vision of her destiny." Arisha stood, her heart pounding against her ribs as she started to collect her books, her thoughts spinning too wildly to keep up with. Moving Gavriel's papers aside, Arisha felt her hand brush against an odd disc, its runes unfamiliar but plainly fae made. She frowned, recalling River's complaint of a missing pendant, and felt a cold shiver run down her spine. "What is that, Uncle Gavriel?"

8

LERA

I can't breathe. The icy water running over my face never stops, never lets up no matter how much I spit it out. I'm cold and I'm wet, and it feels like I've been so for days and years. The coarse wet fabric of my uniform rakes over my skin each time I move, sending shots of pain where it rubs over abrasions left by the branches we'd run through. At least the pain breaks up the freezing numbness.

Through it all, Coal's blue eyes watch me with unwavering intensity, his whole body repeating a single word: *leave.*

"No." I shout it into his face at first. And when I've no more energy to spare for that, I shout it in silence.

No.

Go to hell, or bring hell here.

I'm bloody staying.

When, some eons into the torment, I first hear a wolf's howl, I think the noise is inside my mind. An exhausted wet body playing tricks on its sluggish mind. When the howl calls a third time, the familiar notes—along with Coal's hands hauling me to the bank—shake me from my trance. The return to awareness is so harsh, I can't hold back a choking sob that Coal pretends he doesn't see.

"A stroke of fortune," Coal says, his voice as cold as ever. "We're going back indoors for now."

I blink at him. I didn't quit. Why—

"A storm is coming." Coal points to the sky in answer to my silent question.

He's right, I realize, still not moving. Sometime in the past hour, the wind has picked up and now screams through the pine branches, the gray skies already leaking rain. The *plop plop plop* of fat drops hitting the stream sends a stab of fear through me, though I can't quite understand why.

"Leralynn." Coal's chiseled face and blond hair fill my vision. A moment later, he grabs my shoulder, shaking me roughly. "Leralynn!"

I blink at him.

Coal's gaze surveys me once, then stays on my eyes. When he speaks, his voice is as certain and commanding as the storm itself. "Listen to me. Can you walk?"

A wind-curled swirl of spray from the stream hits my face. *Wind. Rain. Storm.* It finally hits me then, the reason why the rain sent the shock of fear through me. Soon, maybe already, the tablet and my tracks—my only hopes of getting the males' memories back—will be gone. Washed away.

"No," I whisper. My halting breath and racing heart now have nothing to do with the chill. I struggle to my knees, my numb hands giving way, though Coal stops me from falling. Even as he does, I seek my landmarks. Plot my course.

"On your feet, Cadet." Coal wraps his warm, muscled arm around me. "I will help you."

No. I push away from him, landing myself right back in the stream.

Coal curses. Reaches for me again.

This time, I move with greater purpose, pulling myself to the other side of the water. "Don't touch me." I intend my words to sound strong, but they come out in a rough-edged croak. "Don't. Touch. Me."

A wolf calls again.

A flicker of something crosses Coal's face, and he pulls his hands back slowly, showing me his empty palms. Even as he does, his gaze assesses me the way one might consider tackling a rabid dog. Another moment and Coal will do just that.

I can't let that happen.

Scrambling to my feet, I break into a run, racing the coming storm back toward my nearly two-day-old tracks. My numb feet pound the soft ground, sliding on uneven earth and tripping over rocks. A harsh wind blows with enough force to make the fallen leaves and twigs rise into the air, hitting my face, the shock of it making me sway. Losing time I do not have.

"Leralynn, stop!" Coal's bellow races up from behind, the voice so close that I can feel it. Then Coal is on me, tackling me to the ground, twisting my shoulders to force my gaze to meet his. Impatience, fury, and something more—fear. His chest heaves, pressing into mine, trapping me. "You are not thinking straight. Follow me. *Now*."

"Let me go," I holler at him, my voice rising with true fear. I can't do this. Can't pretend a day longer that I'm human, can't face the males through the veil's perverse looking glass. And each second Coal holds me, he further seals that horrid fate. "Let me go!"

Coal drags me to my feet, holding me roughly. "This isn't a negotiation, Cadet. You want to stay at Great Falls, you take my damn hand and come."

My mind goes silent, the ultimatum so clear that my

response comes with no thought. I can't outfight Coal. And I can't let him slow me down a moment longer.

"I quit!" I shout into the male's face, loud enough to be heard over the wind. "I'm done with your runs, your punishment, your half drowning me. I'm not an Academy student as of this moment, so get your damn hands off me. Now."

Coal freezes, face pale. And then he does as I demanded. Icy air rushes in to take his place.

I run the instant he lets me go, before I can let loneliness rush in with the cold air, before I can second-guess myself. I sprint. My clumsy body focuses on nothing but the mountain slope, now hazy through wet, windy air. Droplets of rain bounce off leaves and pine needles, striking them like tiny never-ending drums. Branches bend in the wind to clash against their neighbors and hiss and snap their displeasure. Everywhere I look, the forest is different from the way it was, the trees bending and shifting through misty gray sheets of rain, clutches of dirt and spray flying through the air. The smell of wet earth and damp bark saturate the air so thickly, I scent nothing else.

Fat raindrops pelt my face, fueling each of my strides. Through it all, my gaze focuses on nothing but the lone set of tracks that is miraculously still there, winding through the trees. The slight change in the pattern Sprite's one shoeless hoof left is no longer visible, but I know the tracks as mine and thank the stars that Coal's bloody stream was not so far as to make me lose the sacred route.

Coal. I stumble as the image of him flashes in my mind, turning my stomach. Even when the reconnected rune restores the quints' memories, I'm not sure I'll ever look at him—at the male who wanted me gone—the same way again. An uncontrolled shudder races through my body, spreading panic. For a heartbeat, my face is beneath the surface again, freezing water rushing into my mouth and nose. Closing my lungs. Choking off my air. I gasp, my eyes wide and heart hammering my ribs.

I force a breath down my throat, fighting off the dizziness I've no time for. With the growing rain, there will soon be little left to follow on the steep sloped earth. Faster. I have to move faster, rush straight down the slope that I used switchbacks to climb. I do. I run, allowing no thoughts, no memories of Coal's ice-filled eyes. No—

My boot lands on something soft, the steep ground suddenly slipping from under me.

I fall onto my side, the slope dragging me down with the mud. The breath I fought so hard to draw now grips my chest, gravity seizing me. Pulling me into a tumbling roll down the slope. Rocks scrape my skin, my numb fingers unable to grasp anything to stop the slide.

Down, down, down.

My side, my belly, my head, all take turns against the ground. I bounce off the first tree I hit, the second sending me on my way with a bruise. The third finally stops me, my back striking the trunk so hard that the world blinks. Lightning cracks the air just as my wits clear, thunder following a breath later. The rain pelting my face churns into a downpour, mud and earth running in streams down the slope, taking me with them when I dare try to rise.

This time, I ride the landslide on my back, the wind hiding my scream. I'm aware and yet can do nothing to halt the speeding motion, my hands and feet finding no purchase, for the side of the mountain is riding down right along with me. By the time we stop at the slope's bottom, the rain is a thick curtain that lets me see nothing beyond my own fingertips.

Lighting cracks again, felling a large tree not twenty paces away. Felling the last of my hopes with it. I've lost the tracks. Lost my males. Lost myself. Forever.

Wrapping my arms around my knees, I cry, shaking as badly as the branches.

9

COAL

"*I quit,*" Leralynn had shouted into his face, her voice conquering the wind to impale him. For a heartbeat, Coal had stood frozen. He'd gotten what he'd come out here for, and yet the victory felt so vile, he couldn't force his body to move. So he didn't. He stood there, holding on to Lera as if she'd not spoken, as if he'd misheard.

Lera's tantalizing face came close to him, her brown eyes hard and shockingly luminescent against her pale skin, her gray uniform plastered to every inch of her body. Her words struck his chest like rocks. *"I'm not an Academy student as of this moment, so get your damn hands off me. Now."*

The instant he did so, Lera turned and ran, the fat drops of rain splattering against her footprints. And now she was gone, the storm drowning out any sound, any trace of her.

Coal's chest tightened. Twisting around, he buried his fist into a tree with enough force to make his knuckles sing. And then he did it again. And again, until the droplets of rain washing down the bark ran laced with red. As if the tree itself was bleeding.

The dark afternoon sky flashed with lightning, followed by the thunder's roll. The sharp flash of deadly light grounded into a tree far below, the cracking, smoking trunk setting each of Coal's senses to alert.

"Leralynn!' Coal's voice rose in a bellow that the forest swallowed like a bit of debris. "Lera!"

No answer.

Coal swore. The weather was turning foul faster than he'd expected, and from the wind and smell, it would worsen still. A full-on storm, with Leralynn alone in the thick of it. Rain struck Coal's face with a vengeance, the droplets morphing from sharp needles to thick globs.

Turning, Coal took quick bearings of the forest and sprinted in the direction Lera had disappeared, his ears straining but hearing nothing except the rushing stream and rain drenching the leaves. "Lera!" he shouted again and again, the words echoing mockingly and receiving no answer. No Lera. And with the growing storm, no footprints either.

Coal's heart stuttered, then tripped into a gallop, a fear-filled heat spreading through his blood. Where the bloody hell could Lera have gone? He couldn't see her. Couldn't smell her. Couldn't hear her. The girl *couldn't* have gone far, not exhausted as she was. Ten steps, perhaps. Twenty considering her stubbornness. Any other cadet would be huddled beneath the first kind-looking bush, sobbing and rocking herself.

Lera was most certainly not any other cadet. She was a warrior in her own right, too stubborn and proud to step away. To ask for help. To show weakness. Coal should never have left her, no matter what she'd demanded. No matter whether she was under the Academy's control or not, whether he had the right to bodily drag her off or not.

Coal had gone too far. When he'd realized Lera was playing him, the punishment had stopped being about River's orders and become personal. Because Coal had been stupid enough to trust the girl. Because Lera had looked so much like the woman who'd brushed his soul and left. Because Coal was an irresponsible bastard who'd never deserved River's confidence.

Coal's only job now was to get the girl back to the Academy alive. And if she complained, River could whip him for kidnapping for all he cared.

"Leralynn!" Coal twisted around, surveying the drenched woods again and again and again, searching amidst the shades of gray, between the gleaming green leaves. Water smashed his mouth each time he opened it to call her name.

No answer but the pounding rain. No smell but that of wet earth and the tang of lightning.

Coal's muscles tightened, the frustration and fury pressing so hard against his lungs and chest that it was a miracle the bones didn't crack. A growl that sounded anything but human escaped his chest as he sank his knuckles into another tree, the exploding pain in his fist a momentary relief from the roaring inside his blood.

Coal twisted about, unable to stop, to think.

Where would the girl have gone? Where, where, where? Coal's heart pounded in rhythm to the rain. He raced along the stream searching for any clues as to Lera's course. She'd have surely run—though stars knew how she *could* run—as far away from where Coal stood as possible. But that still left too much ground. Upstream or down? Toward the Academy or away? The overlook that had drawn her attention, perhaps, or —Coal's foot slipped on wet earth, his breath catching as he reclaimed his balance and looked down.

The slope down was wet and steep enough to have almost taken him along. If Lera had been here... Now that he looked closer, Coal marked a distinct trail cutting down the slope. Not the narrow streaks of sliding feet, but a wide swath of disturbed mud that a body sliding down would leave. Five paces lower, a tree held a scrap of gray cloth, stuck on a sharp, broken-off branch.

Coal had let Lera leave, and she'd fallen.

Thunder cracked as if in mockery. *Yes,* the skies said. *It was you. You. You.*

LERA

It's sometime later—minutes, perhaps, or maybe days—when a set of sharp teeth closing around my upper arm draws my face from my knees. The rain has slowed from a torrential storm to a heavy downpour, though my sluggish mind can't work out whether this fact is of any importance. I'm almost surprised to see that I'm still here, huddled against the base of a tree, branches whipping overhead. Surprised to note that none of them have cracked my skull.

The teeth release and bite again, this time harder.

Turning my head, I find a drenched gray wolf with a black muzzle and intense yellow eyes. My throat closes, my hand reaching out with desperation even as I fear I'm stretching toward a mirage. Wet, warm fur closes the distance to me, a large lupine tongue lapping the dirt and rain and tears off my face.

Wrapping my arms around Shade's wolf, I bury my face in the animal's neck, breathing the earthy scent of him. "I knew it was you last night," I say finally into the wolf's fur. "Can you shift?" *Can you shift now?*

Yellow eyes blink with recognition but little comprehension. Taking my hand between his teeth, the wolf pulls me toward a massive cluster of tumbled boulders. When I don't budge, the wolf growls his annoyance and lets go of my arm. His narrowed gaze leaves me with no doubt that he is preparing to resink his teeth into me and is hesitating only while deciding on his choice of target.

"Wait!" I find my limbs with difficulty, my gaze never leaving Shade for fear he too will disappear. "One blink for yes, two for no. Can you shift at will?"

The wolf growls. Snaps his teeth impatiently.

"Can you understand my speech?" My chest is tight. "One blink or—" The wolf turns his head, his eyes following an errant squirrel. I curse under my breath. What exactly Shade's wolf understands has been a subject of speculation even in Lunos and now seems even less promising. By the time the wolf's attention returns to me, the animal is shifting impatiently on his paws, his glistening teeth on snapping display.

"Don't you dare bite just for the fun of it," I mutter, using a nearby tree to climb to my feet. Shade may not understand my words directly, but the wolf has made his plans for his teeth all too clear.

The wolf snorts. Turning, he raises his tail and trots off, turning his head once to ensure I'm following.

Half walking, half crawling, I pull myself after Shade's wolf, who, fortunately, leads me only twenty paces off to a small protective cave between three of the massive boulders. Blinking at the pit in the cave's floor, I realize the wolf has already dug out the bottom to clear away the worst of the wet mud and create an extra barrier from the wind. Climbing inside, I curl around my wolf, his thick fur and lupine breath warming my shaking core.

COAL

A wolf's howl raked across Coal's soul, a sound that should have had Coal reaching for a weapon but spurred him into a run instead. He was at the bottom of the hill Lera had slid down, the slope so long and steep that Coal had to switchback down it to avoid cracking his head. To his left, the forest continued in a shivering cluster of aspen and pine. To his right, a rock formation held up the base of another rolling hill.

"Leralynn," Coal hollered, his throat raw. "Where are you?"

The wolf howled again, as if in clear answer. The sound came from the base of that rock formation on Coal's right, where a dark entrance to a cave that a smart animal might claim could be seen. This time, Coal did draw his boot knife as he closed the distance, his breath misting in the cold air.

A scraping echoed from the cave's mouth.

Then something that sounded like a *shush*.

An indignant feminine yelp.

Before Coal could fully process the significance of the sound, a gray wolf streaked out from under the rocks, its teeth bare and ears laid flat as it headed right for Coal. A ripple of something Coal couldn't explain raced through him, a perverse instinct that had him throwing away the knife instead of holding it toward the predator. Predictably, the idiotic move was a mistake. In the next heartbeat, the wolf hit Coal's chest, knocking him flat into the earth.

Coal fell hard, a stone digging into his shoulders. His heart pounded, his mind unable to focus as a deadly maw hovered above his face. The wolf's saliva dripped down, landing with the rain on Coal's cheeks, the predator's yellow eyes burning into him.

Darkness flashed before Coal's eyes, the great weight atop his chest an echo of the islanders' shackles. Coal's heart tripped, hesitating for a moment before sprinting so quickly that Coal could feel it against his neck. *The stench of rot and blood filled Coal's nose, his mouth thick with a pain that was not yet here, but would come.*

GHHHHHHHRRRRRRR

The wolf's low growl came again, rising from deep in its chest while hackles rose in a thick gray ridge along its back. The animal's breath was so close now that Coal felt it along his skin.

Coal's hand closed around a stone, but just as he readied to smash the animal's skull, the significance of the feminine voice finally penetrated. Lera. It *was* Lera. Alive. And here. Somehow—though stars only knew what made Coal certain of it—the wolf was protecting, not harming, the girl.

Muscles shaking with effort, Coal opened his hand and let the stone roll free.

Unimpressed, the wolf pulled his lips back from glistening canines and snapped them inches from Coal's face.

Coal lifted his chin, exposing his neck to the predator as he met the animal's bright golden eyes. Daring him to finish it. Asking him to.

A heartbeat passed, marked with the wolf's panting breath, the great lupine muscles as taut and trembling as Coal's own. A second beat. A third.

"Come on, you flea sack," Coal growled, flashing his own teeth. "Finish it."

The wolf snorted and bent on his front paws, his shoulder

blades rising. Then, pushing away from Coal's shoulders, he streaked off into the forest.

Heart still pounding, Coal jumped to his feet, his gaze darting in confusion as he sheathed his knife into his boot. His mind raced with his pulse. He was alive. Whether this was a good thing, he didn't know.

"Are you all right?" Lera's voice gripped Coal's throat, turning him toward the rocks. The girl was pale and wet in the mouth of the cave, shaking in her torn gray uniform, her hand gripping the rock with bone-white knuckles—which told him she was a breath away from collapsing.

"Leralynn." The world narrowed to the girl standing in the cave's mouth. With the next breath, Coal was moving, launching himself to grab Lera before she disappeared again. Catching hold of her, Coal shoved both of them into the cave, his fingers digging into Lera's arms so hard that he was bound to leave bruises. But he couldn't let go, or spare a thought for why.

LERA

*L*unging forward, Coal grabs the tops of my arms, fingers digging into my wet tunic and the flesh beneath. His nostrils flare, his shoulders rising and falling with quick breaths. Before I can respond, he shoves us into the cave, his powerful thighs flexing fluidly. In the shadows and damp, his blond hair is dark, blue eyes flashing with icy flame. The water running down his face makes the perfect chiseled lines of it only more beautiful. More deadly. More arrogant. When Coal's predatory gaze finds mine, heat rushes through my core.

"Are you damn insane?" Coal shouts into my face, the fear and fury rolling off him so thick that it settles like copper on my tongue. "You could have died."

My heart stops, my body freezing like a trapped rabbit. I can't face him. Not now. Not like this. The path to the rune-inscribed tablet is *gone*, and with it, my hope of reversing the males' memories. This Coal who is now shaking my shoulders knows me as little as I know him—or the *him* he thinks he is—

the void between us as vast as any realm. A fury to echo Coal's surges through me. Fear. Hate.

I hate Coal for letting me leave. Hate him for following. Hate him for forcing me into that stream. For making my heart beat harder just with his mere proximity, the intense gaze of his blue eyes.

"Are you listening to me, damn you?" Coal's face is inches from mine, every ounce of intensity focused on me alone. Without even the sky to dilute the force of Coal's attention, I feel as though a thousand tiny claws grip every part of my body.

My thighs tighten. So do my fists.

Coal grabs my right wrist just before my knuckles can hit his jaw. Forcing my arm back and against the stone, he captures my left hand as well. "In case you've more brilliant ideas."

I pull against the restraints, their lack of give somehow reassuring. As if I matter enough to bother holding. My chest tightens, my throat thick. "What are you doing here?" I demand. "You wanted me gone, didn't you?"

Coal's jaw tenses.

"Then you win," I shout, throwing my weight against his hold. Again. *Again.* The male's grip doesn't waver. My heart quickens, pounding harder and faster until I'm certain it will bruise my ribs. "What more do you want from me?" I shout into the male's face.

Coal leans farther into my space, violence shimmering beneath his skin. With wet black clothes clinging to his body, his every lithe muscle is on display as surely as if he were naked, power coming off him in dizzying waves. It's as if the very elements of weather that turned me into a drowned rat have enhanced the male. When Coal speaks, his breath is so close and hot that it runs tingling wisps over my skin. "The truth. What the hell were you buying yourself time to do on that overlook? What's the bloody game you're playing at?"

"Nothing." My voice is hoarse, broken.

Coal growls. "Stop. Lying." He shakes me again, hard. "You're hiding something, Cadet."

"I told you, I'm not a cad—"

Coal pulls me even closer, his grip on my wrists white-hot steel.

Too close. He's too close, the heat and power of his body washing over me, waking too many senses. My blood quickens, my muscles fighting his unyielding hold even as unwelcome wetness slickens my folds. I can't think, not with Coal's body an inch from mine, his eyes pinning me as surely as his hands hold my wrists. Worse still, the magic inside me thrashes against the shackles of the mortal world, pulling so hard that it hurts. As a human, I felt the male's power wash over me like a great wave, sweeping away every hold and shield. As a fae, the sensation is tenfold. A hundred. For the power comes not just from Coal, but from my own rebellious body that can't be this close to the male, this insanely tangled with him, without rousing.

Coal doesn't know he's my mate, but my damn body does. And it cares little for anything else. Not that Coal is all but a stranger now. Or that he'd forced me into an icy stream until my lungs howled and my very blood slowed. My male—my precious, violent, terrible male—is still mine. With a snap that's as vicious as a whip's crack along my core, a cord of power inside me snaps free and rises to the challenge of Coal's body. My own budding magic, perhaps, or an echo of Coal's, or something else entirely. I don't know. Don't care. For it fills my every fiber with an ache that wants what it can't have. My words fight their way through a storm just to escape, my sharp canines bared. "Go. To. Hell."

The male growls, and there is nothing human, nothing mortal in the primal power of the low sound, which rumbles through his whole chest. The vibrations rake through me, lighting each ridge inside my soul. Inside my channel. My need.

My sex clenches over the emptiness inside it, each unfilled throb sending a fresh wave of anguish through me. The shivering in my body morphs to a tremble that has nothing to do with the cold.

With a strength that is too great to be my own, I rip free of Coal's hold, my elbow cracking into his ribs with enough force to send a distant echo of pain through me.

Coal grunts, the surprise in his eyes flashing once before transforming to an inferno. Grabbing my shoulders, he throws me onto the ground, heedless of the stones. Heedless of anything. When his hands grab the top of my shirt and rip the fabric in a single vicious pull, the bite of cloth only drives the roaring need inside me higher and higher. The amulet bounces along my skin, shivering with a magic that Coal can't see.

Blood pounds in my ears and clenching sex until I want nothing but to feel Coal inside me. Filling me. Pressure builds with each second that I'm denied his cock, fueling the raging storm inside me. And yet, yet, the male still hovers above me, his arms trembling beneath his wavering control.

"No." He shakes his head as if fending off dizziness, his voice escaping a stranglehold. "I don't bed cadets."

Hooking my arm under Coal, I knock his body into the side wall with more strength than a human female should have. The male's eyes widen as his back strikes stone, the fire in them flashing all the way down to my screaming sex. Arrows of gripping need shoot through the insides of my thighs, my legs, my damn toes.

I tear open Coal's fly with the same ease with which he's destroyed my shirt, my strength—and somehow, his strength—twining through my muscle fibers.

Coal's cock is so hard as it springs free of its confines that it jabs my abdomen. The male's control snaps with a grunt as he binds me with his powerful legs. This time when Coal throws me down, I'm on my belly, the scent of wet earth and Coal's metallic tang filling my nose. A jerk at my hips bares me fully, my wet skin tightening as cool air brushes along it, the hot wetness coating my folds so at odds with the chill that I can feel the steam rising into the damp air.

I buck, seeking Coal's cock in blind need.

The male grips my hips roughly, his knees pushing apart my thighs just before he thrusts in all the way to the hilt.

I gasp. My slick channel captures Coal greedily, only to clench in fury as he pulls back, the pulsing tip of his cock just filling my entrance.

Coal's breath is ragged. He waits, torn between his need and his stars-damned principles.

I little care. Whipping my head around, I skim my teeth into Coal's forearm, my canines breaking skin.

He roars. Jerking his arm away, he slams it down between my shoulder blades, flattening me against the ground so hard that my ribs compress all the air from my lungs. Forcing my thighs even farther apart, Coal thrusts into me again and again, and this time, this time it is the full great length of him over and over and over.

1 2

COAL

*L*era's blazing sex clenched around Coal's throbbing shaft. His blood pounded. Simmered. The scent of Lera's arousal was strong enough to make Coal's head swim, her body radiating a glorious strength that called to something deep inside him.

The woman on the islands who'd pieced together his soul before shattering it all over again. Yes, that was what his damn body was rousing to. Lera looked too much like her—that was all. That was it. It had to be, because Leralynn was *a student.* A student he'd just met, splayed open beneath him, taking his cock like it was meant to be inside her. And Coal couldn't make himself care. Couldn't control himself, couldn't do anything but throw all caution and every ounce of good sense to the storm.

Coal pulled back, thrusting again into her blazing wetness. Lera's sex grabbed on to him greedily, merciless to the agonizing pulsing of his rock-hard cock. She moaned, making him bite back a roar as he slammed into her harder. Her bared backside was tight with muscle, the auburn locks of hair showing between her legs thick and wet. Coal craved to taste her. Bite her. Have her.

Despite Coal's hold on her back, the woman's taut curved bottom rose to meet his thrusts, until the smack of his hips against hers echoed wetly through the cave. *Again. Again. Again.* Each penetration driving deeper and raking like fire over Coal's skin. Coal's breaths came in ragged pants, the naked muscles of Lera's back bunching in a beautiful response.

Leralynn's moans turned to screams with each thrust, her mounting pleasure driving Coal on. Her voice was tantalizing as a siren's call, cutting to his core.

Beyond the cave, the woods howled with the last vestiges of the storm, the branches cracking beneath the force of the wind as it conquered the forest. Yes, that was what Coal wanted. Needed. Craved with an urge so primal that his mind could not follow. Coal would conquer Lera's body like that storm took the forest. He would make her scream with pleasure and need and desperation.

Three more thrusts, each hard enough to make Lera jerk, and Coal pulled back enough to lift his hips, flipping Lera over onto her back. The woman's hair fell in pools of auburn, her blazing eyes such a rich chocolate that she seemed more than human. Her lush breasts trembled from the motion, the large nipples bunching as hard as Coal's twitching cock, until he was suddenly unsure which of them would be doing the damn conquering.

He pulled off his wet shirt in one rough motion, suddenly resentful of anything separating his skin from hers. Lera's nails raked up his back in appreciation, leaving trails of heat along his tightly bunched muscles.

Whatever control he still possessed vanished. With a growl, Coal drove into her again, watching her face as her eyes widened and glazed, her lush lips parting in a moan. Coal's mouth was closing over Lera's before the sound was finished, claiming her as deeply above as he was below. Her mouth was sweet and hot, her tongue tangling with his, drawing him in deeper.

Thrust. Thrust. Thrust. Each plunge into Lera's gripping sex only made Coal's need for her stronger, the force with which he drove into her somehow flowing both ways. It was as if this woman was inside him just as much as he was inside her, her power pounding against the shields protecting Coal's soul. Chipping at them bit by thrusting bit.

A shudder ran through Coal, only the press of Lera's nails against his skin keeping him in the present.

Stars take him. Coal intended to consume Lera, and yet, as he reached for her breast, he feared it was she who was going to unravel him into ribbons.

13

LERA

Coal's hand closes over my right breast, a moment of pain turning into molten heat that flows directly to my apex, intensifying each sensation. His kiss deepens to a demand. My legs wrap around his muscled hips, the large head of his cock scraping against every ridge inside me as he thrusts.

"Ahhhhhh!" The sound escapes me when Coal's lips pull away. I feel an abyss closing around me, Coal's cock taking me higher and higher until I know I will never survive the fall. His heaving chest and shoulders move over me, a breathtaking map of scars and twitching muscles and tight, glistening skin.

His teeth flash, his mouth closing over my nipple. His lips are hot around my skin, the bit of stubble grown after the morning shave scraping against sensitive flesh. Down below, my sex pulsates, each beat sending a wave of aching pleasure through my body. When Coal sucks on his captured nipple, the fresh wave of pleasure shakes my spine, and I clamp my teeth together to keep from begging for release.

I won't plead. Not to Coal. Not ever.

I rake my nails over his back instead, his taut, naked backside, pulling him in deeper and marking him as mine. Coal's head jerks up, his blazing blue eyes sparking with specks of purple. When my nails dig deeper, Coal drops his hand to stroke over my swollen apex in brutal reprisal.

My body explodes, the waves of convulsions hitting one after the other, each making the rising sensations that much more unbearable. I scream, arching to the cave's ceiling, then scream again as Coal's warmth spills into me, completing my utter defeat.

For a heartbeat, neither of us moves. His warm weight is so reassuring atop me that I never want the moment to end. When Coal finally pulls away, my world is still rippling from a climax so high that it has left me dizzy. Unable to think. To move.

I blink, uncertain where I am, my immortal body feeling each sensation—from the chill air to the rocks poking my back to my still-throbbing sex—with equal intensity. An overwhelming bouquet.

"Leralynn." Coal's voice is gut-wrenchingly raw. Low.

I turn my head to find the male on his knees beside me, his piercing blue eyes wide, his powerful chest rising and falling with desperate gasps. The purple specks in his eyes are gone, and the tightly bound blond hair now hangs in loose strands that brush his wet shoulders. Rubbing his face, Coal moves as far from me as the cave allows, and the loss of his closeness drives a spike of ice into me.

"I-I was out of line," he says. Still on his knees, Coal's back is straight, his head bent in utter devastation. On his thighs, his hands dig into the leathers we never fully got rid of.

Right. In Coal's world, he hasn't coupled with his mate— he's rutted with a student he was supposed to have been disciplining. Driving out of the Academy.

I swallow. A bitterness fills my mouth, sending a chill slithering across my skin. I knew the truth going in. Wanted him on a level too primal to resist. And now the bill is coming due.

Sitting up, I wrap the remains of my wet shirt around my shoulders. "Yes, you were. Not here, but back at that stream. I'd say you were so damn out of line, you crossed the bloody border to Lunos."

Coal's brow rises, right along with perfect stubborn chin. "Did you imagine you'd *enjoy* your punishment?"

My body, which I thought unable to do much of anything just now, rouses. "That wasn't punishment, you bastard. That was—"

"Yes?" Coal leans forward, his powerful forearms braced on his thighs. No apology, no regret in his now-hard face. "Tell me what you thought that was."

I open my mouth and close it without speaking. Coal did try quite a few options to inspire misery first and, in the end, did no damage. Left no scars like the ones Zake's belt would have. Zake had taken pleasure from hearing of my nightmares, seeing me tremble at the sight of his leather. Coal held me down with his words, not his hands. Had watched. Had pulled me out of the water when my own stubborn mind refused. But it was still horrible. Worse than horrible. "It doesn't matter. You wanted me to quit, and you have your wish. So you need not feel 'out of line' for anything." Turning away, I go about gathering what remains of my clothes for inspection. "I'm not an Academy cadet, and you aren't my instructor. Nothing of consequence happened here today."

Coal's eyes bore into my back. I know he knows my words for a lie. Coal felt something—and not just in his cock.

My chest tightens, and I turn away, forcing my attention to working out the logistics of covering myself with the remains of my pants and shirt while I return to the Academy to take the rest of my things. Because I know now—I will be leaving.

At the stream, I'd thrown the words at Coal to get him to back away, believing the point would turn moot once the rune restored the males' memories. But without the tablet, I've exhausted my options here and will have to search elsewhere. The realization sends dread spiraling through me, and grief at the thought of leaving my males. But I'm the last remaining member of the quint who knows the quint even exists—this is what any one of them would do in my place.

Behind me, Coal's efficient rustling motions are too loud for the dark void in my mind.

"Who hurt you?"

"What?" I refuse to turn toward him, lest his familiar lithe body pulls my heart back toward it. "What are you talking about?"

A calloused finger traces my back, refusing to stop when I tense beneath his touch along my scars. Ah. That. I open my mouth to respond and feel the amulet around my neck warm in reminder. Leralynn of Osprey was raised in a mansion, not a stable. "The lord who took me in as his ward required strict discipline."

A low quiet growl that a human may not have heard escapes Coal's throat.

I pull away, his touch on my skin feeling too good. "Where did you get yours?"

Silence. I turn, holding my torn shirt to cover my breasts, and find Coal's hard face, defined cheekbones, and jaw sculpted into unyielding stone. The same face he doubtlessly uses to keep anyone stupid enough to ask that question from ever asking again.

I lift a brow. *You started it.*

A muscle tics in Coal's jaw, his silence simmering. I sigh,

shrugging a now too-cold shoulder. I know more about Coal's slavery in the dark realm than he does just now, our odd magical connection having shoved his memories and nightmares into my consciousness more than once. I wonder what his new fogged mind makes of those dreams. If he still has them at all. Perhaps it's better that he not tell me, for the way things are between us now, I've no way of salving the wounds the words would open.

I turn away again, wrapping the remains of my shirt around me like a wet towel. At least the pants are more or less salvageable.

"I was captured by the islanders while fighting on the coast. They kept me prisoner for some time. Most of the scars I imagine you refer to are from my time there." Coal's low voice moves around me until the male crouches inches from my face. His gaze surveys my body with a soldier's experienced evaluation, lingering on pale, goose-bumped skin and shaking muscles. Whatever the afternoon's sparring and stream and storm hadn't already taken from me, our little bout of physicality did, the small burst of Coal's shared strength now fading.

Taking off his shirt, Coal pulls it over my head in lieu of my rag.

"I don't need your help," I say, going to pull it back.

Coal's hard grip captures my elbow. "I didn't ask. I brought you out of the Academy walls this afternoon, and it is my responsibility to take you back. What you do afterward is your own business. Can you walk?"

"I will walk."

"That's not what I asked," says Coal.

I sigh and rub my face, the fatigue washing over me so sudden and strong that I realize I'm swaying only when the male's strong arms steady me. I swallow, too exhausted to fight. "What if I told you there was a fae-made artifact that I passed on the way to the Academy?" I say, studying my hands as I speak. "And that I wanted to retrace my trail to find it before the rain washed away the path."

Coal curses. Colorfully. Despite my sagging muscles, he grabs my shoulders and shakes me hard, forcing me to look into his face. "If you told me something that stupid, I'd tell you that Grayson—the nearest town to Great Falls—just executed two of its people on charges of fae craft. And then I would shove you right back into the stream until you set your head on straight. So it is fortunate that you intend to say nothing of that sort."

"I was jesting," I whisper quickly, and Coal lets me go as if he held heated stone. He makes quick work of pulling his blond hair back into a low bun and somehow, within five seconds, even shirtless, he looks as confident and put-together as he did this afternoon. Rubbing my arms, I push myself up to my feet. Once standing, I pause with my hand on the rock, my one last final card to play. Not because it's smart, but because I have to know and may get no chance after this. "Can you do one thing for me?" I ask, my shoulders tensing as he grunts in tentative consideration. "Touch your ear."

"My own ear?"

"Yes," I snap, watching his face, my chest still, my pulse pounding. "Your own ear. Touch it."

Giving me a worried look, Coal reaches for his right ear, his fingers skimming the bottom.

"The top of your ear."

"That was the top," says Coal.

Damn it. "Here—" Scooting forward, I take Coal's rough hand and set it to the tip of the pointed ear I know is there, though my eyes slide off it each time I try to look. Beneath my touch, I feel Coal's finger slide along the elongated slope until—

Coal screams, the pain in his voice ripping my chest. When I pull away, the male is rocking with his head between his hands, his body shaking as I've never seen. His glazed blue eyes see nothing.

"Coal!" I take the male's bare shoulder, now blazing hot as if with fever. "Coal. What's wrong?"

The warrior blinks, his eyes returning to focus. To confusion. The rocking stops, and he frowns at my touch. "What did you want me to do?"

My mouth is dry as I pull back, shaking my head. "N-Nothing. I changed my mind." The words come in a horrified whisper. The veil magic isn't just convincing my males of the illusion, it is fighting to keep that reality. Like the pressure I felt when I forced myself to see the sclice last night—except, by the sound of Coal's scream, many times worse. I recall Autumn's warning about the importance of removing the amulets at least once a day. With the magic absorbed, the males cannot do that. And their bodies are adjusting the best they can.

Whatever solid ground I still felt beneath me falls away.

14

LERA

Coal and I don't speak as we make our way back to the Academy, the earlier storm having calmed to a chill wet evening wind. Coal walks a step behind me, as if afraid I might fall or bolt or else melt to the ground in a pile of injured regret. The male's misplaced guilt over what we did grows more palpable with each step closer to the school's high stone wall, just as the wet, slippery earth confirms what I already knew about the state of Sprite's and my tracks.

My cold, numb body is a match to my equally numb mind. The litany of hard facts marches through my thoughts, interspersed with the memory of Coal's scream when he touched his ear, making me flinch each time. I can't stay at the Academy, where I am creating more problems than I'm solving—wreaking havoc with the males instead of helping them, threatening their disguises, confusing their senses. My tracks have washed away, and even if they hadn't—even if I could find my way back to that clearing in the woods and that shattered tablet—the clay was already well on its way to disintegrating even before the rain. The veil's hold is overwhelmingly complete.

I kick a stone, watching it plop along the mud. Not even a satisfying thud at the end.

We came here to discover the nature of magic leaking into the mortal world and instead became victims of it. Centuries of vital information and reports are now locked deep in River's mind, which means I'm no closer to saving the mortal realm here than I would be anywhere else. Without River's direction and knowledge, I've no notion of how to even start looking for the rip, and I certainly can't do it while working *against* my males.

Autumn may be able to guide me through seeking out the rip—she may even have a way of reversing the veil—but that comes down to crossing Mystwood.

Without River's passage key, which he announced stolen from him only yesterday, doing so would be suicidal. Maybe I'll go find the Sentinel Guild, see if they've a key squirreled away somewhere, or else brave Mystwood without it. With the magic acting the way it shouldn't, maybe I'll survive the passage—and at least dying in Mystwood forest would be swift, whereas watching my males not know me—not need me —hurts all the time.

So Guild or Autumn? Roam the mortal realm in relative safety to reach a possibly useless destination, or risk Mystwood to get to a more likely solution? I click my tongue, the proverbial dice spinning inside my mind to land with my friend's face up. Autumn it is. The four males at the Academy, whether they know who they are or not, don't need me to hold up the walls against whatever rodents come their way. They need me to help them regain themselves. And at present, I'm only making things worse.

It seems Gavriel had one thing right—the prophecy

mentions no companions for the human turned fae, and here I am with none.

"I want you in the baths," Coal says as we return to Academy grounds the same way we left—over the wall. It's the most direct route from our forest path, though this time, my muscles shake numbly as I climb the high stone and shinny down the rustling tree. In the evening's dimness, the human guards take Coal's short grunt as all the reason they need to find employment elsewhere. "Then the infirmary."

"I want it to be summer with flying squirrels," I mutter over my shoulder. Sleep. I want sleep. Then I'll ride out in the morning.

Coal quickens his pace, cutting off my path. Against the darkening sky, his silhouette rises like a powerful beast, his light hair at odds with the settling blackness. The grass out here beyond the inner walls is damp with dew and sparkling in the dying light. The Academy and its keep tower before us, torches and lanterns already lit in its many windows. Students settling into their last evening of freedom for the week. "I wasn't making a suggestion."

"No?" I raise my face to meet his, quelling the insane urge to kiss him and punch him, both—neither of which would help me just now. "I forget the term for when someone with zero authority tells someone who doesn't give a damn what he wants her to do."

"The term is *now*," River says, stepping out of the shadows.

My breath freezes in my lungs. It's the first time I've seen him since last night's battle—since that promise of retribution in his cold gray eyes. If anything, he's more dominating, more breathtaking than ever, his close-cropped dark hair framing a strong, perfectly sculpted face. A king's face, though he doesn't know it. His back is almost painfully straight, his broad chest covered in creaseless red wool. A chest I used to have unlimited leave to caress, to press my face into. I swallow a hard breath, a tiny squeak escaping my throat.

Apparently, the guard at the wall didn't just melt out of the way, he went squealing to the keep tower. Head turning slowly, River sweeps Coal and me with his gaze, his nostrils flaring delicately. Taking in our mixed scents. Putting pieces together until his face is carved of cold marble.

Coal's movements are so subtle, I can barely see the shift of muscles as he straightens before his commander, lifting his chin just enough to bare his neck to River. Not surrender, but a show of fealty. A promise to accept any sentence River might pass. My chest clenches.

"That *now* applies to both of you," River says. "Infirmary. Go." Turning on his heel, River strides away, his final words coming over his shoulder. "I will have clothes for you both sent there and will join you shortly."

Coal's shoulders stiffen, and I swallow a sigh. Little as I want to see anyone just now, I'm not going to let Coal face River's wrath on his own. Even if it means facing Shade's unrecognizing yellow eyes again, when I'd been hoping to leave with the memory of his wolf safely in my mind.

15

LERA

half hour later, I sit wrapped in a woolen blanket on a worktable in Shade's infirmary, the air around me filled with sharp-smelling salves—some of which are still tingling along the gashes on my back. Having smelled the situation of Coal and me with as much efficiency as River had earlier, Shade sent Coal into the other room before efficiently stripping me down to my undergarments with as little interest as if he were taking a saddle off a horse.

Now, Shade is quiet as he works, his healer's hands sliding across my chilled muscles. It's an effort of will to stop myself from sinking into Shade's warm, callused palms. From nuzzling against his broad chest or velvety neck.

Shade's long black hair is pulled back in a neat ponytail, his soft gray sweater covered beneath a starched white healer's overcoat—the Academy's red-and-gold crest stark against the fabric. Yes, the shifter is as stunning and clinically steady around my body as ever, but without a trace of the deep feeling I'm used to—the kind bedside manner a far cry from true affection. My stomach clenches. Some part of me has always known losing Shade would be the hardest. I just didn't know it would leave me this hollow.

"—urine?"

I blink, realizing Shade had asked something. "Your pardon?"

"I asked whether you saw any blood in your urine when you used the chamber pot earlier," Shade repeats.

My face blazes. "No."

"Are you taking a tonic to avoid pregnancy?"

Oh, stars take me. I'm not, but my fae body hasn't yet matured enough to start monthly bleeds. "Yes."

"The tonics do not prevent the spread of sickness," Shade tells me with a nonchalance of someone ensuring understanding of an arithmetic problem. "That is something to be conscious of if you take multiple partners."

One more word and I swear my heated skin alone will set the infirmary on fire. I focus my thoughts on icy hail and frigid streams.

Shade puts a finger beneath my chin, forcing my face to his. "I expect an acknowledgment of understanding when I explain something important. If I cannot trust you to give me honest verbal answers, I will rely on a more thorough physical examination for the information I need." His voice is kind despite his stern words. "That wasn't a threat, just reality."

I like you better as a wolf. "Understood," I tell Shade quickly. "I'm aware bedding carries more risks than pregnancy and am careful. Is that acceptable?"

"And the tonic you lied about?"

I really like you better as a wolf. "I've not started bleeding. And yes, I am aware it is unusual. It is what it is. And… And no, I'm not bleeding now if you're about to ask."

Shade nods as if finding nothing odd about the conversation and thankfully stops talking. His clean earthy scent surrounds me, and I let my eyes close for one blissful moment, his hands inspecting an abrasion on my collarbone, pretending this is just another moment back in Lunos.

"I've no notion how you managed to return with only a few deep gashes and fatigue, but beside a whimperworthy muscle ache in the morning, you should be all right." Shade's voice is as warm as the crackling fire, but the professional distance in it stings more than the medicine he spreads.

I give him a tight smile. Mating with Coal had sped up the healing of my already quicker-to-heal body, though the crash from that boost is already on the horizon. My Shade would have known that. Would have yelled at Coal and me both for being reckless.

Moving to stand before me, Shade finds my gaze. "How are you feeling, cub?" he asks.

"I—" My heart stutters, the hope from that one word racing though my blood. I survey the male before me anew, taking in his wet hair and tired eyes. Shade's wolf was gone for hours in a storm. Surely the male realizes his own absence, feels the fatigue of muscles from running across rough terrain. Might he now recall more than that? I force myself to breathe. "What did you call me?"

Shade's eyes flicker up and left. "*Cub*, I think." Shade smiles, the lines around his beautiful, full mouth—his white teeth flashing against tan skin—making me choke with longing. He's the first male, human or fae, I ever slept with, and he will always be the one who makes me feel safest. He pats my arm like I'm a child with a scraped knee. I suppress a growl. "Because you look small and nippy. I will not do it again if it bothers you."

"It's fine." I wait, waiting for him to say something more. To remember. To at least narrow his gaze in thought.

Shade does narrow his gaze. "You seem to be having trouble focusing, Leralynn. Did you strike your head?"

I swallow a curse. "No. Just recovering from an intense day." I clear my throat, waiting while Shade palpates my head despite my assurance of its intactness. "Why is your hair wet, Shade?"

Shade blinks, reaching back to brush his hand over the glistening strands. His befuddled gaze skitters to the window before returning to me. "Same reason yours is, I imagine. It's raining."

"Your clothes are dry."

"I changed," Shade steps away, snatching up a bandage that's gotten away from a basket of others. For a moment, the only movement in the room is that of Shade's deft hands rolling the cloth. "I'm going to check in with Coal. River should be here shortly as well, then it is off to bed with you."

"Not quite yet." I pull the blanket tighter around myself. "I'm leaving the Academy."

"So I've heard." The utter lack of surprise or regret in Shade's kind tone cinches my decision. He squeezes my shoulder. "But you should wait until morning to head out, for the sake of your horse if you won't believe me about your own body."

With that, Shade steps out through the side door separating his workspace from what seems to be a study. I glance over, catching sight of Coal leaning against the wall before the door closes.

"Is she all right?" Coal's voice trickles through the walls. If I wasn't so exhausted, I might feel guilty about eavesdropping on a conversation that the human they think I am would not have been able to hear—but as it happens, I feel nothing of the sort.

"Surprisingly yes, though she'll hate you tomorrow. Did

you lose your mind?" Shade asks, his voice more curious than angry. The shifter may have been more discreet with me, but plainly, he's got other plans for a fellow instructor.

"Apparently," says Coal.

A sigh. Shade's voice hardens. "If you imagine you can use your cock to get yourself kicked out of an undesired assignment—"

"I wasn't using her, you bastard." The violence behind Coal's quiet words is enough to make any sane being run for the hills. "And if you are about to ask whether I used my position to—"

"Stand down, Coal," Shade says harshly. "I was not going to ask that, no. But if I did, you would bloody well sit here and take it. After what you just let your cock do, that is the least of what I expect. Are we clear?"

Silence.

I brace for the walls to crumble.

"Understood," Coal says finally, his voice deflated.

"Then I've said my bit as your commanding officer, though I little envy you River's wrath. If Headmaster Sage learns of it… It would be better if that didn't happen."

"I'll be careful. On all counts."

"Good." Shade snorts. "Though as your friend, I'd say you need to lose your mind more often—not with a cadet, but with *someone*. You look better than I've seen you since we pulled you out of the islanders' dungeon."

"And you look worse." Coal's voice drops lower, until even I can barely make out the words. "You look like bloody hell itself. For a moment there, I wasn't sure whether it was you or Lera who I'd worked to exhaustion today."

Silence. Steps. A soft growl matching a second, equally demanding one.

"It happened again, didn't it, Shade?" Coal says. "You lost time."

"No."

"How long was it?" Coal demands.

"Lady Leralynn?" The door to the treatment room swings open after a brief knock, and Rabbit—one of the Academy's young pages—slinks inside. The boy takes one look at my half-naked body and drops the parcels he's carrying.

Heart still pounding from both the males' conversation and Rabbit's unfortunate interruption, I take a deep breath before schooling my face and voice to something that passes for civility. "Yes?"

"I-I was asked to bring this to you," Rabbit sputters, thrusting the first of his dropped packages into my hands, his eyes darting about in search of someone else. Someone who he clearly little wishes to find. Ever. "Master Coal—"

"Is unlikely to smite you on sight," I say, ignoring the boy's "you know nothing" look. Glancing inside my bag, I find a set of my own clothes, as River promised. No gray uniform in sight, thank the stars. "If the other delivery is for him, I'll make sure he gets it."

Rabbit skitters off before the words finish leaving my mouth. In the study, the males' conversation has gotten too quiet for even my ears. Damn. Letting the blanket fall to the floor, I pull out the delivered dry clothes and don the soft black pants, their warm, thick fabric soothing against my skin. I pull out the vibrant tunic next, jumping slightly when something heavy slips between the cloth and falls to the marble floor with a high-pitched clink.

Following the item down, I feel my whole body go rigid as I behold a round rune-inscribed disk spinning like a top on the marble. Even here, in the mortal realm, the disk's magic sings to me, naming itself precious. Beside it, a scrap of paper nearly flutters from the tiny breeze.

Picking the paper up with shaking fingers, I unwrap the scrap.

I THINK THIS IS YOURS.

NO NAME. No signature. Just a note and the key to Mystwood.

LERA

Questions and excitement thunder through me, my hands fumbling in the hurry to tuck the precious disk away before anyone might see it. With the trousers unfortunately missing pockets, I slide the key into the waistband, covering it quickly with the provided tunic. The clothes are mine, so whoever put the precious amulet there had access to my room. Or else intercepted Rabbit on his way to deliver the clothes.

Still, who? Gavriel is the only one who knows the truth of my situation, and he'd have little cause to hide the artifact in some clothes. The note itself sheds no information, but I throw it into the fire nonetheless, lest someone recognize the handwriting that means nothing to me. With what Gavriel and Coal have both confirmed about the situation, just being associated with the fae-crafted disk could land someone in a dungeon.

Reality thuds through me. *I have a way back.* It's real now—I'm leaving. Leaving the males and going for help. It's the right thing to do.

Isn't it?

"Master Shade!" The smooth, musical voice comes from the corridor just as the flame finishes lapping up the note. A fist knocks against the doorframe. "Master Shade, we need your help!"

The side and front doors to the workroom open together, one to admit Shade and Coal, the other to reveal a horde of five young women all circled around Tye. In his training grays, Tye holds his shoulder, which looks utterly in the wrong place, his face tight with pain. Seeing me, the male's emerald eyes focus through the glaze.

"Are you all right, lass?" Tye asks.

Princess Katita's flashing teal glare is hot enough to burn me, though her porcelain features smooth to concern as she turns to put a hand on Tye's back. "Can you see to Tyelor, Master Shade?" she asks again. "He's injured himself in training."

Tye shifts his weight away from Katita, his nostrils flaring in a way that makes heat rise to my face. My damn males are all too familiar with my scent. And each other's. Despite a taut face, Tye manages to raise his eyebrows at me, wiggling them with a hint of an amused grin that makes me want to both slap him and wrap my arms around his neck.

At the back of the room, Coal grabs the bag Rabbit left for him and disappears to change, the marks my nails left on his strong back catching in the firelight.

"What happened?" Shade wades through Tye's sea of female admirers to clear a path to the worktable. "Ladies, I believe I can take care of Tyelor from here. Thank you for bringing him."

"Yes, everyone *out*," Katita says, her voice one used to giving orders and having them obeyed. "Tyelor doesn't need you hovering about him, and Master Shade needs room to work." Hand crossed over her chest, the tall blond princess watches with satisfaction as the other girls step back at once, yielding to her command as quickly and gracefully as they will probably one day do in the throne room. With her gorgeous curves and long legs, Katita owns the long blue-green silk dress I'd be tripping over, making me feel positively stumpy. When Katita's gaze falls on me, her brows tighten. "Are you deaf, wen—"

"I would not finish that sentence if I were you, Cadet," Shade says, his quiet voice reverberating through the workroom. A pair of the girls on their way out pause for a moment, their wide eyes sprinting between the most powerful young woman in the human realm and the ethereally beautiful healer, whose kind eyes flash with a predator's gaze.

The air tenses, only the crackle of the fire and Tye's tight breathing to be heard. Shoulders spread wide, Shade steps between me and Katita, each step a careful placement of an animal's padded foot. Coal once warned me that Shade truly is a wolf—and to be careful about confusing his good table manners with what he tears into for supper. Now seeing the transformation from the side, I truly understand what he meant. A muscle tightens along Shade's jaw. "Lady Leralynn is my patient. But even if it were otherwise, I expect you to address her—and everyone in the Academy, from Headmaster Sage to young Rabbit—with respect."

Katita steps back before seeming to realize she is moving. "I'd not realized the lady was ill," she says with a tight bow to Shade. "I do hope it is nothing serious, Leralynn." Clearing the way for Tye to walk to the treatment table near where I'm standing, Katita follows in his wake, her brilliant eyes flashing a silent warning to me when Shade can't see. "Of course, not being a healer myself, I find such things difficult to judge, but perhaps Tyelor's condition is the more urgent at the moment?" Katita says with unwavering politeness. "Would you agree, Lady Leralynn?"

"Coal, give me your boot knife," Shade calls toward the side room, stepping aside as the door opens and a glinting dagger flies through, jamming into the wall. The hilt vibrates. Rolling his eyes, Shade pulls the blade free. "Sit down, Tye."

"Actually, I can wait for Leralynn to be treated," says Tye, eyeing the knife in Shade's hand. Katita's anger tinges the air with a bitter scent.

"Good stars." Shade twists the knife for a better working grip. "I'm cutting your shirt, not you."

"I worked that out." Tye swallows the last word, covertly leaning on the table's edge, the beautiful lines of his face tight with pain.

"I don't practice medicine by democracy." Shade's patience snaps like a bow string, driving Tye's mouth closed as he hops onto the table. Even Princess Katita finds nothing to add.

"What happened?" I ask, the world tipping just a bit when my gaze brushes the deformed line of Tye's shoulder.

Tye's eyes find a spot on the wall, his jaw tight as he keeps his face under control. "Bad flip," he says, the words strained.

"Tyelor was training as per his usual schedule," Katita injects, addressing Shade in a voice of authority on Tye's regimen. "Though moving quite stiffly through the routine. The shoulder shifted while he was trying to catch himself after a double flip above the bar. Do you think he needs to warm up better from now on?"

"There isn't a problem. I just didn't account for how wet the bar was," Tye says quickly. His voice drops, his face turning to Shade, whose knife is already slicing through his shirt's fabric. "Shade. Please. Not now."

My brows narrow. Trying to delay inevitable pain is my

signature move, not Tye's. In fact, the male usually takes the opposite tack. What the bloody hell is he up to, then?

Shade's gaze sweeps from his work to survey the room. When his attention brushes my face, his voice softens. "Tyelor has a dislocated shoulder, Lera. He will feel better once I put it back into place, but it may look worse before it is better—and you already look pale as milk. Please take a deep breath and find a place to sit before you fall and I've another injury to deal with."

"What is going on here?" River asks, letting himself in to take stock of the situation. His deep gray eyes flick to me, then away again just as quickly, unreadable. Shade cuts away the rest of the fabric, the remains of Tye's shirt pooling on the floor just as River addresses him. "Tyelor, are you all right?"

"No." I don't realize I've spoken until the word has escaped my mouth. My hand tightens on the edge of Shade's neat countertop, my eyes on Tye's bared back. Emerald-green eyes meet mine and look away quickly. The real reason for Tye's resistance to undressing now shows in sets of long livid bruises covering his corded shoulders. Bile rises up my throat. These aren't marks from the same mishap that caused his shoulder injury, or from a sparring match. These are from a beating.

I turn toward River, eyes blazing.

The male lifts one brow in silent answer. *Yes. I did that. Surprised, are you?*

A chill that starts in the pit of my stomach spreads through my core, Tye's morning visit replaying in my memory. Because of our going over the wall against orders, I was to see Coal this afternoon and Tye was reporting to River. For *this*. Because of me. Because I went over the wall and he came with me.

Throat tight, I step up beside Tye, laying a hand on his good arm. "I'm sorry, Tye."

"It looks worse than it feels, lass." Tye gives me a tight smile. I have to stop myself from cupping his cheek, running my thumb over his blanched lips.

"Liar," I whisper.

Tye gasps, his face losing all color as Shade grips his shoulder and stretches the joint as if it were no more than a set of pulleys to be manhandled. With a sharp twist, the dislocated bones come into alignment and snap back into their sockets. Tye draws a stuttering breath. "*That*, on the other hand, felt worse than it looked." He rolls the shoulder tentatively. "Much better. Thank you."

"Shade?" River prompts.

"He's all right. For now." Shade glares at the shoulder as if personally offended by its actions. "I'd ban the Prowess Trials if I bloody could, though. Why do we have people risking maiming themselves over applause?"

"That would be my exit cue." Tye hops off the table, both Katita and I converging on him.

"Let's find you some willow-bark tea, Tyelor." Katita shoves her body between Tye and me, trampling on my feet to stake out territory. Tye's scent of pine and pain mixes with the princess's rose perfume and the sharp tang of Shade's workspace. In the firelit room, the deep purple of Tye's welts look the color of sickening plums, and I twist to let River see the depth of my fury.

Katita's foot shifts, catching the back of my ankle hard just as Tye starts walking toward the door. The surprise registers too late, my slow, exhausted feet bracing against the floor only to find Tye's discarded shirt in the path. I feel myself going backward like an absurd doll, my hands grabbing anything within reach—which turns out to be Katita's own tunic. The girl's gasp does nothing to keep us upright, until Tye's solid arms wrap both our waists, all three of us spinning about to get steady. For a moment, I'm certain the whole mess will end up on the ground, but my legs find solid footing just as River and Shade move in to lend their own support.

As we pull apart from the mess, the mix of irritation and embarrassment washing over churns into blood-chilling fear— for on the floor, in the center of the short-lived scramble, the dropped key to Mystwood now glints in the firelight.

LERA

Blood leaves my face. The spot against my back where the disk was tucked into the waistband suddenly feels empty. Cold. On the floor, the tiny clank vibrates against the marble as the uneven disk finishes its spin. The room stops, all eyes—even those of Coal, who has slipped in through the side door—focusing on the bit of metal. On the unspoken implication that it should not have been here.

The tiny streak of magic trickling from the disk settles around me. The males' tense muscles say they feel the pull as well, even as they understand nothing about its vital purpose. The key to Mystwood. The way between Lunos and the mortal realm.

River snatches the disk from the floor, his gray eyes hard. Closing his callused hand around the amulet, River surveys Tye, Katita, and me with a searching glare that spurs my still heart into a drumroll. The very artifact River questioned Tye about a day past, now fallen amidst a tussle of students—one of them a known rogue.

Katita recovers first, her hands and chin rising as she looks at the silent force of menace River has become without moving a muscle. The planes of his face carved marble, his shoulders even broader, his body towering over everyone in this room without trying.

"Whatever you just picked up, sir," Katita breathes hurriedly, "I assure you I've never laid eyes on it before now. I also submit that I've the funds to *purchase* any jewelry I might require, without resorting to theft."

"I am inclined to agree, Your Highness." The gaze River turns on Tye is ominous enough that Tye's bruised back tightens in a reflexive flinch even as his beautifully angled face remains the same—just a hair short of bored. His silver earring glints insolently in the firelight, doing nothing to help his cause. "Tyelor?"

Tye rocks back on his heels. "Is that the trinket you've been searching for? As it happens, I was just bringing it back to you."

"With me, Tyelor," River says quietly. "Now."

"It was me, not him!" I cut off River's path before he can take two steps to the door, my neck craning to meet the male's gray eyes. Cold, hard eyes, the emotion behind them reined in so tightly that the air pulsates with tension. As the entirety of River's attention settles on me, his woodsy scent and heady masculinity clouding my senses, his broad chest rising in slow, controlled breaths, I feel like the cub Shade called me, standing before an immortal king. My breath quickens, my fists tightening beneath spurts of anger.

"Lass." The warning in Tye's voice is so sharp, I'd need to be deaf to miss it. "You are a terrible liar. Don't dig a deeper hole for yourself over misplaced good intentions."

"Tye did not take your damn pendant any more than he forced me to go over the wall last night," I tell River, ignoring Tye's valiant defense. Stepping forward until the heat of our bodies mingles into one blazing furnace, I bear the full force of River's steel-gray gaze and rigid jaw.

A voice in the back of my mind informs me that there is a more diplomatic way of conveying my point, that yelling at River is as safe as carrying an open flame through a hayloft. Yet, despite the the danger sizzling along my skin, I can't make myself stop. River—*my* River—is somewhere in that thick-skulled head, and he needs to be put in his place. "You are better than your groundless accusations, *Commander*. So stop using Tye as a convenient whipping boy and ask some basic questions before you strut about showing off your bloody authority."

The air in the room chills, everyone's gaze suddenly on River and me. Katita makes a tiny noise, but even that is swallowed by the silence. My mouth is dry, my hands crossing over my chest. "I had your bloody trinket. So keep your damn hands—and your switch—off Tye and deal with me."

The seconds ticking by in the ensuing silence grow heavier by the breath. Finally, River clears his throat. "Give us the room, if you please," he says quietly, the words more menacing for their calmness. His voice carries the pure undiluted command that makes my body sing like a taut bowstring despite my own pulsing fury.

Princess Katita gives me a pleased smirk as she walks out at Tye's side, the male looking back at me with worry-filled eyes. Coal's and Shade's gazes are unreadable as they follow as well, Coal only pausing to acknowledge an unspoken *you and I still have business* glance River throws him. Even once the door closes, River doesn't speak, and I realize he is listening for the sound of departing footsteps. Making sure that we are truly alone.

"Would you like to try that again, Cadet?" River's voice is ice.

"I'm not a cadet."

"Good." River holds his hand out toward the door, his very broad chest tight beneath a high-laced red shirt. The tightly leashed ire rolling silently from his strong jaw, his rigid straight spine, his woodsy masculine scent, make River's quiet voice seem to echo from every wall in the room. The voice echoes inside my core well, igniting each fiber until my body feels too small to contain the pressure building inside me. River's fingers flex. "Then this conversation need not happen. Allow me to escort you to the stable right now, Lady Osprey. I will have your things sent into town tomorrow morning for you to pick up."

I don't move. I can't. I don't want to.

River grabs my forearm, his grip iron hard. Painful. His breath comes fast as he invades every inch of my space, looming over me until there is nowhere to look but into his unyielding eyes.

My racing heart mirrors River's own pulse, pounding hard enough that I can see the *tic tic tic* of his pulse in his neck, my immortal ears close enough to his chest to hear the booming strikes. Heat rushes through me, filling the cold void.

I go to pull my arm free of his grasp, but there is no give, no matter how hard I jerk.

"Start walking to the stable," River orders. "Now."

Leaving off fighting River's unyielding hold, I raise my chin, showing River the canines he can't see. My own need and power twine together, giving my voice a power it never had before the males walked into my life. Before they shaped me into a warrior. "*You* lost the disk. *You* accused Tye. *You* took a damn lash to a warrior who fought beside you last night. And now, you can't wait to be rid of the one person who calls you to task."

A flicker of a reaction too fast for me to read races across

River's face, the hard lines returning to stone in a fraction of a heartbeat. "Are you done?"

My fists clench at my side, the helplessness of it all boring through my core. Here in the world of Great Falls Academy, River can do as he wishes. No matter what I say, the moment I'm gone, he can take his tension out on my males. On *the* males—not mine anymore, not here. "And are you going to hurt Coal while you're at it too? Maybe give him another scar or two, since he doesn't have enough?" I swallow, choosing my last words to the male before I walk out of the Academy. "What the bloody hell happened to you?"

In the ensuing silence, I listen to the ringing of my own words, each hitting River's chest as hard as it hits mine.

You happened, Lera. You did this.

Under the heavy weight of River's beautiful, achingly familiar gaze, the truth unfurls so painfully in my gut that I can't breathe.

When you broke that rune. When the quint split up.

Stars, I've been so focused on how the males' aloofness stings my heart and hinders the mission that I've given little thought to what the separation might be doing to *them.* Shade losing time. Coal sinking back into nightmares he can never escape, because he knows nothing of the truth. Tye, the highest caliber of immortal athlete, slipping on a simple bar. And River, the weight of the world still on his shoulders, trying desperately to hold things together—never realizing that it's the quint he truly commands, not an Academy of human nobles that has existed without him for centuries.

If anyone has a chance of helping the males now, it's a weaver. Me. And yet here I am, plotting my escape just when things are getting hard. Autumn might hold more answers than River right now, but leaving the males—already under the assault of the veil amulets—is too high a price to pay.

They might not *feel* the quint's magic, but it still takes a toll on their bodies and souls. A strain that will grow tenfold if we are apart. *Stars take me.* Quints don't do well apart. I draw a shaking breath. In one frozen moment, I regret it all—my brash anger, lashing out at River in front of his subordinates and students. Even if I wanted to stay, it might now be too late. "River—"

"No." The iron control River has held on to since our conversation started cracks to flaming ire. "You've stepped too far." He snarls, releasing my arm, the loss of the connection hurting more than the grip did. River's chest heaves, his nostrils flaring with short harsh puffs of air. "I suggest you make a very fast decision, Lady Leralynn of Osprey. You will either shut your mouth, go to the stables and ride the hell out of my Academy, or you will go to my study and experience firsthand the very discipline you find so objectionable."

I halt, suddenly finding myself on the edge of a precipice I'd not realized I was climbing. River is serious. River, *River* is threatening to strike me. Naming the one cost that scares me to my core. Zake's whip isn't so far in my past that I don't still feel it in vivid, excruciating color. If River does this, it will be his face I see in my nightmares. I swallow the bile already rising up my throat, together with the pleas I know Zake wanted from me and never got.

River snorts, reading my face. "That's what I thought." There is nothing kind, nothing understanding in his voice. "Get out."

"No. I mean—" My hand closes around the fabric of my tunic, my voice hitching despite my best effort to still it. No, I won't beg that River do something else, *anything* else. I'll do what I've always done. I'll survive. "I'll accept the punishment for the disk, and whatever you intended for Coal too. But leave Coal be and don't charge Tye with theft—he truly did nothing. Does that sound fair?"

"What?" River blinks. "No."

"But—"

"I don't *want* you here." The male's shoulders spread like wings, his square jaw clenching with impatience.

A shudder runs through me, and for the first time, I have trouble meeting River's eyes. "I thought it was Academy policy that cadets must self-select to leave," I whisper. "Was I misinformed?"

"No. You were not." River's words are clipped, something between speech and a snarl.

"Then I am not withdrawing. So you must keep me on your books, by your own rules." I speak on a single breath, fearing I'll lose my nerve if I stop. "You can't punish both Tye and me for stealing the same disk now, can you? And as for Coal, he thought I'd already quit the Academy before bedding me, so you can lay the entire blame at my feet." I swallow. "If you want someone to break, break *me*. Take *me*. Not them. Please."

This time, the silence settling around us is so loud, I feel as though the deep boom of a phantom gong vibrates through the room.

"I accept your terms," River says, his voice slicing into me like a knife. "Come with me, Cadet."

1 8

RIVER

ood stars. River turned to the door faster than dignity dictated, but he needed to get outside. Away from Leralynn's intoxicating lilac scent, which, together with River's own fear and fury, made thinking impossible. The girl didn't understand how River's heart stopped when she claimed ownership of that damn disk. With Princess Katita in the room no less. A disk with symbols that could only be of the fae, that would have had a noose around Leralynn's neck so quickly, she'd not have a chance to yell at the executioner.

A fierce, great-hearted, idiotically brave life snuffed out in a single snap. Like Diana's.

Diana. Yes, her similarity to Diana had to be the reason Leralynn was getting under River's skin, rousing every protective instinct he had. River really needed to quit mixing up a new beautiful auburn-haired *cadet* with the soul mate he'd lost.

River's fist tightened, a growl rumbling through his chest. Speaking of cadets, what the bloody hell was the girl thinking, not just going nose to nose with him, but doing it in front of an audience? How did she imagine the conversation could end? It was bad enough that Lera challenged River's authority; she'd said things he couldn't now ignore. As for how Lera had gotten hold of the disk in the first place, River dared not ask and hoped to hell she would not offer. These were dangerous times. Perhaps the damn thing had found her the same way it had found him, appearing one day in a locked drawer, calling to him with its preciousness.

Inhaling the crisp evening breeze, River savored its post-rain sweetness as he listened to the quiet squish and splat his boots made on the puddled cobblestones—though Lera's light steps barely made a sound behind him, as if she knew precisely where to place her feet. In the lateness of the evening, most of the students and staff were indoors, the windows alight with lanterns and candles. Turning right, River chose the longest available path to the keep, giving Lera time to think.

The fear pulsating from Lera was so strong that River could scent it from several paces away, its tang making him queasy. With each step, River waited for the girl treading miserably behind him to change her mind, to stalk for the stable, to stammer explanations, to accidentally fall and twist her ankle so she could run and hide behind Shade's infirmary wall. Except she didn't. Leralynn was terrified and was keeping pace with River as surely as any warrior in a battle.

Yes, behind that small, exhausted body, heart-wrenchingly beautiful face, and chocolate eyes, Leralynn hid a will that would best a general. Unfortunately, her understanding of the dangers surrounding her fell far short of her courage.

Inside the keep, River led the way up the winding stairs to his study in the southern tower, notched archer's windows at every turn letting in cold blasts of night air. He opened the door to let Lera precede him inside. As she did, the girl wrapped her arms around her breasts, the slight rise of shirtsleeves showing a shadow of bruises on her right wrist. A dusting of fingerprints, no more. Except that they were prints River had left. On a woman who looked and acted—and, stars take him, smelled—so like Diana that River still could not draw a full breath when in her company.

The door closed behind them with a final bang that River was not ready for, trapping them in the suddenly claustrophobic room. The fire River had finally gotten around to lighting a few hours ago still crackled softly. Now, Leralynn's delicate scent of lilac and fear filled up every inch of air, and River didn't know if he'd rather drown in it or open a window. He needed more time to think, to work his way out of this mess that threatened to take his soul and everyone else's with it.

The disaster in the infirmary was Leralynn's fault. The events leading up to it, however, those lay at River's feet. It was River's disk that fell, River's guards who let the cadets cross the wall unmolested last night, River's weak stomach that pushed off the duty of dealing with Lera's earlier indiscretion to Coal. Most of all, it was River who so feared spending another moment in Diana's—in Leralynn's—company, that he would drive away from the Academy the one cadet who, by all appearances, had the potential to grow into a true leader. Maybe more so than any other student here, with the possible exception of Tye of Blair.

Yes, they were both at fault. And now it was time to fix it. Whatever it took.

Leralynn stopped in the middle of River's study, taking in his neat surfaces and dark wooden paneling with wide eyes, her breath so shallow and fast that she had to be getting dizzy. River surveyed her carefully. Muscles tense, skin pale, a glistening of sweat touching her temple despite her obvious chill. Eyes wide and—despite all attempts to look at nothing in particular—darting about. Searching for whatever it was she expected him to use on her. *Stars.* Leralynn wasn't merely anxious, she was utterly petrified.

River's hand tightened into a fist, his nails digging into his palm, and flame flared through him. Someone had *hurt* the girl before. Not punished, but hurt. And she was willing to face it all again to protect others.

"Where do you want me, sir?" Lera asked. Her voice was impressively steady.

Sir. She was making an effort at the rules, thank the stars for that. "Just where you are."

Walking around his desk, River pulled out his leather chair and sat down, taking out paper and ink. With a long glance at the girl, he wrote out a few lines, his neat writing filling the space with a small scrape of the quill. That done, River sprinkled sand on the ink before carefully blowing it off and finally folding the note in half.

Lera flinched when River returned to her, her eyes shutting tightly.

"I'm not going to hit you." River set a steady hand behind Lera's shoulder blade lest the girl fall, her soft warmth and lean muscles sending a wave of heat through his whole body. If River could rip the throat out of who had truly hurt her, he would. This very moment. River swallowed the sudden befuddling flash of fury. Yes, he was feeling protective, but surely he'd feel as much for any of the students. He was their deputy headmaster—he should be protective of them. Shaking off the thought, River focused on the still-trembling girl, who seemed not to have heard his promise. Or didn't believe it. "Leralynn. Lera." River lowered his voice, keeping it filled with command but softening the bite. "Open your eyes and look at me. There is nothing in my hands that will hurt you. All right?"

Her eyes opened, deep brown pools that could drown a man's soul. Narrowed. "Why?"

"Stars take me, you really want to argue this point?"

Lera swallowed and shifted her weight, but never pulled away from River's supportive touch—which sent an inexplicable satisfaction through him. "Because it won't accomplish anything," he said truthfully.

Lera's chin lifted. "Tye and Coal—"

Large-hearted, loyal cadet.

"I am keeping my word, Leralynn." River handed her the folded message. "You will give this to the stable master when you report to clean out stalls an hour before dawn tomorrow. You will return for the same chore after dusk, this time working for two hours. This will continue for a month. Longer if I note a single change in the attitude I expect." He waited until Leralynn took the note, her hand shaking slightly as her large chocolate eyes stared at him with such relief that River's stomach turned. "This is my attempt to keep you too busy to get into trouble. Into *more* trouble. For stars' sake, learn the rules."

River stepped away, already missing the feel of her smooth back beneath his hand, as if the girl belonged against his body. Fit there.

Stop it. It's bad enough one instructor lost his mind to his cock. The Academy little needs two *idiots.* Despite the reprimand, River waited for a pang of irrational jealousy. None came. Oddly enough, despite the pull Lera had on his soul, River didn't begrudge Coal bedding her—oh, he was furious at the male, but the anger came from the impropriety of Coal having taken a student, not envy. Just as Leralynn's protectiveness of Tyelor and the appreciative glances she snuck at Shade when she thought no one was looking roused no resentment from River's heart. Which wouldn't be unusual if River didn't also feel like ripping out the throat of anyone *else* who might covet Lera.

River might chalk his feelings on Coal and Shade up to friendship, but why Tye? *Stars.* It made as little sense as the urges the girl stirred in him to begin with. And mattered even less. River was the deputy headmaster, and Leralynn a first-year cadet. No number of aching cocks or similarities with Diana would change that.

"Do you have any questions?" River asked.

"No, sir," Lera said softly. "And… Thank you."

River nodded. "And you as well. For reminding me of something important." He jerked his head toward the door, and Leralynn left at once, clutching the work order.

With the door closed behind her, River took out the disk that had started this latest disaster. He couldn't be sure how much Princess Katita saw of the object before he snatched it from the infirmary floor, but if she'd glimpsed the details, there could be trouble. Katita was ruthless and, given the princess's envy over the attention Tye was paying Lera, volatile. River's position in the Academy offered him protection from cadets' wild claims—Lera's did not. For her sake, it would be better if the relic never existed, lest it provide some proof for future accusations.

River swallowed. It was time he followed Leralynn's own example and did the right thing, no matter how connected he felt with the disk, how inexplicably frightened the thought of its loss made him. Before he could reconsider, River took out the small axe he used to kindle firewood and brought its dull head down on the strange disk, shattering it into crumbling pieces before feeding them into the flames.

PART III: SCENT OF A WOLF

1

SHADE

Shade woke to the smell of grapevines twining around the gazebo and small stones digging into his ribs. Overhead, the sun was breaking through a blooming orange horizon, as if the previous day's storm had never happened. Shade drew a shuddering breath and rose to his knees, rubbing his face. The Academy's reflection garden spread away from him in both directions, with beds of dew-covered hyacinths and giant cone flowers, their tall stems and light green leaves holding up bright yellow flowering heads.

Yes, Shade was outside. But how the hell had he gotten here? From the slight ache along his ribs and memories of a dream where he'd chased a deer, he'd fallen asleep here. Fortunately, his presence would unlikely raise suspicion—the garden was large and filled with thick concealing greenery, lacy fern beds, and stone-walled nooks designed to give refuge to students seeking solitude amidst the Academy's bustling life. He wasn't the first or last of the garden's overnight visitors. But all the others knew how they'd gotten here.

Shade didn't. He'd lost time. Again.

Shade forced his mind to sort through the last memories he had. He remembered the infirmary last night, when Coal brought Leralynn of Osprey in to be seen after a punishing run that had plainly morphed into more than discipline. That was when his body first started playing tricks on him. The girl's lilac scent and deep brown eyes—not to mention her supple, creamy skin under his hands—had driven him insane, made it an effort of will to keep himself in check. To remember his duty. To remember that she was a *student*, for stars' sake. To ask the right questions, make the right decision, use the right damn salves.

Leralynn's pull on him made as little sense as waking here did. Perhaps it was the state she was in, just on this side of misery, that brought out a healer's natural instincts to protect. Or the scent of coupling that had clung to her and Coal both—a scent that would make *any* man hard. That had to be it. Plus, Leralynn reminded him of another auburn-haired, chocolate-eyed woman who'd once owned his soul.

Shade shook himself before the memory could pull him in deeper. The problem of Leralynn of Osprey was the simplest to solve—keep the hell away from her. Incidentally, that was the same advice he'd given Coal last night—and that man usually had the better restraint of the two of them. Fortunately, the girl was planning to leave the Academy.

Infirmary. Shade forced his mind back to task as he walked to the nearest garden exit—a stone archway nearly hidden in the hedgerow, covered densely in rustling green ivy. He'd been in the infirmary, tending first to Lera, then Tye, when all hell broke loose over an odd fallen disk that Shade knew instinctively was important. The cold, restrained fury in River's face had been enough to send a chill down Shade's spine, despite having known the man for years. Shade had seen kings with less internal power than what always simmered beneath River's cultured manners and speech. The man could wield more authority with a look than others did with a whip or sword. Even Shade, who considered his commander a friend, knew there was a line not to be crossed. Everyone did.

Except one Leralynn of Osprey.

Stars, the girl had no self-preservation instinct. Shade didn't know whether he was more relieved to have missed River's tearing her into shreds or more afraid of how the duel might end. He blinked. After that, he recalled emotions and smells more than events. Yes, he'd been afraid for Lera, had wanted to see whether she was all right. But he'd wasn't some idiot to stand and watch the door to the student dormitory—he'd gone back to his own quarters.

Hadn't he?

How, then, had he gotten here, to the reflection garden? Had he been drinking?

Reaching behind him, Shade pulled his hair into three parts and braided it quickly, creating the appearance of an officer up and ready early in the morning instead of one who'd passed out beneath the stars. Whatever was happening with him, Shade needed to get to the bottom of it quickly. And quietly.

"Shade?"

Spinning toward the sound of River's voice, Shade found the impeccably dressed commander striding out from the keep as if unaware of the hour. The tallest man Shade knew, River always kept his dark brown hair neatly cropped, his black boots mirror shined, and his storm-gray eyes unreadable. Eyes that seemed to have the eerie ability to focus on every place and person in the Academy at once. A pair of guards hurrying to their duties snapped to attention at the sight, their faces pale though River did nothing but nod courteously to them. At the moment, Shade knew how they felt.

Straightening his rumpled, damp gray sweater, Shade joined River at the edge of the courtyard, where he stood rock still, eyes trained on a point in the distance. "Waiting for something?" Shade asked.

"Some*one*. I issued some orders last night I would like to ensure are followed. Ah—there she is."

Following River's gaze, Shade saw the one person he was really hoping to avoid. Leralynn. Trudging out of the cadets' barracks, her smooth skin and long auburn braid glowing in the rising sun. Despite the breathtaking curves that made even a gray uniform look delicious, Lera's curled shoulders and stiff shivers against the chill spoke to undeniably sore muscles. Shade straightened his back. "I thought she was leaving us."

"She changed her mind." River's voice was tight. Disapproving—almost beyond what the situation seemed to call for, though when it came to Leralynn, Shade wasn't one to judge well.

"I see." Shade's stomach clenched. "And what do you have her doing?"

"Mucking stables for three hours a day for a month." The utter lack of emotion in River's words cut Shade's hearing. For whatever reason, the punishment made River uncomfortable enough to put effort into burying his thoughts. For all his stoic masks, River saw entirely too much, which boded poorly for Shade's own predicament.

Shade cleared his throat, finally working through what River had said. "You are taking three hours a day from her for a month?" With the Academy's workload, that would leave a first-year cadet with no time to sleep. "Isn't that a bit severe? A simple thrashing would have done."

River's face did tighten then. "I couldn't," he said quietly. "And I need her too exhausted to get into trouble for a while."

Shade rocked back on his heels, saying nothing—he didn't trust himself to keep from uttering something that might expose his own turmoil to River's too perceptive eyes. As for River... In the whole time Shade had known the commander, River had never hesitated to punish a student or soldier, male or female. River was never cruel, but he was efficient. And fair. And consistent. Until now.

What was it about this beautiful cadet? First Tye. Then Coal. Shade himself. Now River. Leralynn of Osprey was touching souls. Which made her as tantalizing as it did dangerous. A fact that should have made Shade turn away, and made him hard instead.

2

———

LERA

"*T*ouch your ear," I tell Coal, my heart quickening. I can't help it. I need to show Coal his true nature. Need to try.

Coal glances at me, his metallic scent mixing with the lingering tangs of sex and sweat. Shirtless, the male is pulling his blond hair back into a bun, the muscles coiling beneath taut skin. "My own ear?" *he asks.*

"Yes. Your own ear. Touch it."

I feel as if I'm moving through molasses, focusing on Coal's still, calm face. This is a nightmare, *some part of my mind shouts.* Just a nightmare. *But a nightmare on repeat, four times, five times in one night, each iteration forcing me closer and closer, making me relive each moment.*

Coal reaches for the bottom of his ear. I capture his hand, redirecting it toward the pointed tip.

No! Don't! *I scream at myself, almost watching from above. But I don't listen. The Lera lifting Coal's hand doesn't know what's coming.* Wake up, wake up, wake up, *I beg, knowing it's no use.*

Coal's strong hand is trusting beneath my touch as he makes contact with the proof of his fae heritage—and screams in agony. The pain in his voice tightens my chest, making bile rise up my throat.

241

I pull away.

Coal rocks on his knees, his head between his hands, his body shaking as I've never seen. His glazed blue eyes see nothing.

"Coal!" I take the male's bare shoulders, now blazing hot as if with fever. "Coal!"

SITTING UP IN BED, I inhale lungfuls of cold air. *Coal is all right,* I tell myself, as I have all night—but I'm an awful liar, even to myself. Coal doesn't scream in pain from anything short of torture in the dark realms. And yesterday, from me. *Stars.* The male might recall nothing of the episode, but I remember enough for us both.

Marking the rising sun, I slip to the floor and pull on my gray uniform. Stable duty. Right. Trudging across the Academy courtyard toward the stable, I listen to my footsteps echoing off the stone walls in the cool dawn air. My veil amulet swings dully against my chest, feeling extra heavy this morning. I haven't been able to take it off while sleeping lest Arisha wake up and catch sight of me in the night, and my mind is longing for a rest from the magic-spun half-truths.

In fact, everything feels heavy this morning. The irony isn't lost on me. Once, mucking stables in Zake's estate was my life —right up until Coal, River, Shade, and Tye rode into my world and turned it on its head. And now I am right back at it. At River's orders no less. The irony would be morbidly funny if memories of Zake didn't still make me break out in a sweat. If the thought of getting on the wrong side of River again didn't frighten me so much.

As if summoned by thought, I note the male watching me from the edge of the courtyard. Even from this distance, River's broad shoulders, commanding height, and square jaw take my breath. With hands clasped behind his ramrod-straight back and his hooded gray eyes trained unblinkingly on me, River wears strength and responsibility with the same casualness that others wear coats. Beside River, Shade's predatory perfection coils beneath a sharp-boned face framed by black hair and piercing golden eyes—though my sharp fae vision notes deep shadows under those beautiful eyes. Shadows that I could smooth away in another life, but not here. The sight of them together sends heat pooling between my thighs even as I quicken my pace.

This is what normal people must feel in the males' company. When the magic bonded us, everything happened so quickly that I never truly felt the full weight of their power before seeing past it—before becoming friends and lover. Mates. To me, River has always been *River*. But he isn't. He is the king of one of only three Lunos courts, a commander of legendary warriors whose centuries of battle-honed nerves and minds are matched only by their physical allure.

Now that I see them from beyond the walls of intimacy, the distance between us feels insurmountable.

My foot catches a loose cobblestone, and I wince as I hope to keep my balance. After spending half a day with Coal running me into the ground and the rest shivering like a sapling—with one notable exception that most certainly did not give any of my muscles a rest—I hurt. My arms hurt. My legs hurt. My shoulders hurt. I think my eyelashes hurt too, but keeping my eyes open is so great a chore that I am not quite certain.

Slipping into one of the paths through the thick shrubbery wall separating the Academy's east and west sides, I hear a familiar voice calling my name and frown. Gavriel. What could the librarian want with me at this hour?

Cutting over toward the sound, I find Gavriel in one of the small round alcoves. Seeing me, the man rises from the crescent stone bench, his leg unusually stiff in the morning chill. Despite the obvious soreness, Gavriel's brown eyes lively are too lively for this hour of the morning, his tattered robe fluttering behind him in the cutting breeze.

"I heard I might find you here, and here you are," he says, holding out his hands in greeting. "Though I must say, this stable-mucking business is highly counterproductive to our needs. River certainly didn't force such a time waster on his star athlete. Perhaps I can speak to him about an alternative—"

"I'm fine with stable duty, Gavriel," I say quickly. *So long as I'm not late for it.* "And good morning to you as well. Is there something you needed?"

"To discuss tonight's mission with you, of course." Gavriel beams at me, mouth opened in a wide grin to reveal slightly crooked front teeth—as if offering rare wine instead of a way to get me killed.

I stare at him. "Because the last one ended so well for me?"

"Don't be so hard on yourself." Gavriel pats my shoulder. "You'll get the hang of it soon enough, I'm sure. Now then, tonight—"

I put out a halting hand, stopping Gavriel midsentence. Heat seeps into my blood and I draw a breath full of earth and sap and pine. Yes, Gavriel and I have plainly been talking past each other these past days, but pushing away the one person who knows the truth about me would be unwise. Still, after what happened yesterday I need to steer us to a different course—preferably without making me late for stable duty. Closing my eyes for a moment, I gather the clearest words I can find. "We need River, not me, leading the charge to close the magic's leak. If you wish to help, then work out how to get the males' memories back. I tried to force it yesterday, to make Coal feel the top of his own ear and… it didn't end well."

Instead of the expected curiosity, Gavriel's eyes widen for a moment. "No, I wouldn't imagine it would." The man's brows pull together as if chastising a belligerent child. "Good stars, Leralynn. What made you think it wise to meddle in magic you don't understand?"

"Because I needed to show Coal what he is." My chin rises. "I thought evidence of his origins would push Coal to override the amulet's illusion."

"And instead the veil attacked him," Gavriel snaps.

Bile rises up my throat as I shove down the phantom echo of Coal's agony-filled bellow. Attacked. Yes. That is what happened. When challenged, the amulet flooded Coal with pain until all traces of the attempt were ripped from his mind. I rub my face. How does one go about apologizing to someone who remembers nothing of the incident?

Gavriel sighs, his voice softening. "It sounds as though the veil's magic is fighting for its own survival. You are fortunate that—this time—your experiment ended with only a bit of pain." Gavriel straightens his sweater which does little for his overall appearance. "I must point out that I've been telling you to forget the males all along. I do hope you've learned your lesson, Leralynn, and are ready to listen to the parameters of today's mission."

My eyes narrow, my heart thudding against my ribs. "That's it? Your solution to the veil's attack on Coal is to ignore it?"

"Coal isn't the Protector," Gavriel says with exaggerated patience. "You are. Now, I expect clear skies tonight, which you will certainly wish to take advantage of to…"

I stop listening, the simmering heat filling my veins giving way to a roar. This is war, the amulet's attack the first shot fired. And I... I can't fight it on my own—clearly—not without making things worse by several magnitudes. Gavriel won't help either. Which leaves one single course of action: wait for reinforcement from Lunos, hold the line until help comes. Eventually, with no contact or results, someone in the Elders Council will decide to send a scout to check on us. And if not the Council, Autumn surely will.

I wish I had a way of getting in touch with Lunos, but I don't, so I will make do. Being immortal, we've the time to wait—so long as I ensure we are all still here, alive and sane when help comes. So long as I don't do more harm to the males than I've done already.

"Are you listening?" Gavriel demands, his voice rising. "You are the Protector, Lera. The least you can do is pay attention."

My head snaps to him, the thoughts spinning in my mind finally stopping. Gavriel cares nothing for me or the males, for the fact that the five of us are shattering, each in our own way. And I'm done with him. With all of it. "No." I meet the man's eyes, my chin lifting. "I'm not your personal prophetic puppet."

Gavriel rocks back on his heels, as if struck. "But the Protector—"

"I don't care." I step in front of Gavriel, cutting off the man's path. My chest feels heavy, my nerves raw. If River were here, he'd probably be going over the wall come hell or high water. But he isn't. I am. And the world is better—safer—without my meddling. That is a proven fact. "I don't care about your prophesies, about the magic seeping into the mortal realm. I care about *none* of this. So leave. Me. Alone."

For the first time since I've met Gavriel, the man's self-assurance falters, the depth of his disappointment in me clear in his eyes. When I start walking, the librarian doesn't call after me.

3

LERA

$\mathcal{P}$ulling open the stable door, which slides smoothly on well-oiled rails, I inhale the familiar, wonderful scent of horse and hay. The Academy's grand stables are the largest I've seen, with long rows of large stalls, an overhanging loft with hay, and a grain room for storing oats and feed. True to what I'd expect of a military academy, everything is kept in simple, gleaming order, the rafters and stalls built from a pale pine wood that's been polished to a high sheen, not a speck of dirt or hay out of place. The hostler, who is standing to meet me, is much less welcoming, his heavy-lidded gray eyes saying exactly how he feels about having to climb from his bed just to hold a pitchfork out to me.

"This is your bloody punishment, not mine," he mutters under his breath, thrusting the handle into my hand with more force than necessary. "Stalls are here. Horse shit is inside. Wheelbarrow is somewhere. If you've questions, figure them out yourself or ask the damn horses."

Right. I'm near certain the man is sleep-talking and cringe as he nearly walks into the wall on his way out into the cold and toward his bed. You'd think the stable hands would be grateful for the assistance of a student made to muck stalls for several hours daily, but at this hour of the morning, all bets are off.

Closing the door behind him, I survey my battlefield, the pitchfork in my arms too heavy for my aching muscles. Curious heads of gorgeous horses hang out of their stalls, looking at me with a mix of curiosity and hope of an early breakfast. At the end of the aisle, I see a gorgeous gray stallion standing on the crossties, a tall and equally gorgeous young woman rubbing down the horse's coat. From the looks of it, the pair were out exercising. I blink. Rub my eyes. "Katita?"

The princess turns to scowl at me. "What are you doing here?"

I raise my pitchfork in answer. "What are you doing here?"

"I don't like riffraff touching my things." Unclipping the stallion, she walks him into a large corner stall and adds water to his bucket before closing the door. "Keep your hands off my horse," she says, striding past me to the exit. "Don't exercise him, don't brush him, don't bloody look at him." Stopping with her finger on the handle, she turns, blond hair swinging in a perfect arc, blue-green eyes flashing. "Actually, that goes for everything that is mine. Stay away."

Right. I wait for the door to close behind Katita before shaking my head. I remember Katita's cold eyes on me in Shade's office yesterday as she ushered in Tye, and I think I know what "everything" she's talking about. In the stall beside me, Coal's stallion, Czar, glares at me, clearly relaying that trampling me into the ground would be his preferred way of spending the morning.

"Get in line," I mutter, reaching into my pocket. Empty. I've not been to the dining hall and thus have apples neither for the horses nor myself. Walking to the other side of the aisle, I burrow my face in my mare Sprite's neck.

Sprite snorts softly, her breath tickling my skin. At least someone here remembers me.

"Let's get your stall cleaned, girl." I reach for the lead rope hanging at the perfect height for someone a head taller than me—and yelp like a cat with a stepped-on tail. If I thought reaching *down* to pull my boots on this morning was difficult, reaching *up* toward a hook is damn near impossible.

"Good stars, lass, what are you doing?" Tye's voice, coupled with the soft whisper of the opening door, jerks me around.

Tye stands in front of the door, slid closed once again, studying me with a feline mischief in his emerald eyes that sends a wave of heat through my body. Even in the barn's dim morning light, the male's tall, muscular body, sharply angled features, and thick floppy red hair have an ethereal beauty that makes my head spin. Mine and everyone else's at the Academy—I'm certain Katita has the male listed on her property inventory.

"Have ye swallowed a stick?" Tye asks in his low, lilting drawl. Dressed in a tighter version of the Academy's training grays, Tye moves with a stiffness few but I and the males would ever notice behind the well-rehearsed swagger. The memory of his bruised back—a whipping from River for sneaking out of the Academy with me—makes my jaw clench.

The one *damn thing you need to do in order to not make things worse, Lera. That includes not pitting the males against one another.*

"What are you doing here?" I ask Tye.

Tye winks at me. "Looking for something I desperately need."

My skin heats, but I step back. I swear I can see through

the thin fabric of Tye's shirt to the injured flesh beneath. *Do no harm.* "You've an odd notion of what you think you need."

"No, I don't think—I'm certain." Tye points overhead to one of the sturdy horizontal beams crossing the aisle. "It's one of the best bars in the place, outside the proper training grounds. Mother Shade won't let me train on the outdoor setup because of the shoulder mishap, and I can't afford to miss the morning. So, here we are."

Hopping up to the bar, Tye hangs loosely for a moment before pulling himself up in a slow, controlled arc. Touching his chest to the bar, the male then lowers himself down again, his body just as taut and controlled as before. Up again. Down. Up, his bare arms intricate fields of flexing, twitching muscles, though he hardly seems to be straining.

Shaking off the hypnotizing perfection of Tye's movement, I point my pitchfork toward his shoulder. "If Shade is so worried about your shoulder, why is he letting you train at all? It doesn't seem like indoors should be any different from outdoors."

"Och, he isn't." Tye grins, swinging back and forth with increasing speed. When the male lets go, I barely have time to pull the pitchfork away before he lands a foot from me, his powerful thighs flexing slightly to absorb the landing. "But if he happens to stop by, I'll just claim I came for this." Leaning forward, Tye impertinently presses his warm mouth over mine.

4

LERA

I gasp, and Tye deftly brushes his tongue between my parted lips, inviting himself in. His warmth, his taste, are achingly familiar. My mouth tingles, the sensation racing through my nerves and spine. The male's exercise-kindled heat spreads over my skin, his clean masculine scent filled with pine and citrus. Before I can consider the wisdom of what we're doing, my treacherous body responds to Tye's provocation, mouth opening to let him take me deeper. Pulling him against me until our bodies are flush, his breath hitching at the invitation.

But he takes it no further than that, simply sweeping through my mouth with slow, savoring strokes. A sweet kiss. Kind. Delicious. Polite. But not predatory. The Tye my soul calls to claim my mouth and body—this one aims to please. Nothing more.

I pull away, clearing my throat. "What was that about?"

"A thank-you. For standing up to River last night."

I feel a flash of reflexive indignation—that Tye should give a kiss as a thank-you gift, assuming it's wanted—but it sputters out just as quickly at the memory of Tye's bruises. "It was too little too late." I shake my head. Nothing I can say will make up for the stripes Tye wears because of me. In fact, probably the less of me he has in his life just now, the better. "I am sorry about your back. It looked painful."

"Lass." Raising his hand to my face, Tye brushes a lock of hair aside, his thumb coarse as it scrapes my cheekbone. "It wasn't my first thrashing. Or third. Or last. I little mind it once it's over. And given the choice, I'll take a thrashing over mucking stables."

I pull back. "I mind."

"I noticed." The mix of concern and incredulity in Tye's eyes—as if despite his own protective nature, the male can't imagine another caring for what happens to him—tightens my chest. Shaking himself, Tye puts a knuckle under my chin and lifts my face, his mouth twitching mischievously as his tone lightens. "I also noticed you can't move to save your life just now." The thumb that traced my cheekbone moments earlier now presses against a neck muscle so sore that I rise onto my toes, a sudden exquisite pain rippling from Tye's touch.

"Stars take me." I glare at the male. "That was a low blow."

Tye whistles. "Forget sore. You're halfway crippled, lass." Easing the pressure, Tye's fingers spread to my shoulders, finding a whole field of agony-filled balls beneath my skin. Ignoring my yelping, Tye works the knots for a few minutes before shaking his head with a sigh. "There is no chance in hell you will be moving like anything resembling a human by morning training. That said, I think we might get you to be a slightly better imitation of a stick figure before Coal has a run at you. Come, I'll stretch you out a mite."

"Oh no, you won't." I step back. The last time Tye stretched me—at the Council's orders to lead serious training

—the pain was enough to bring tears. As sweet as the male can be, he also takes anything athletic to absurdity. In an odd way, Coal is more gentle.

A frown skitters over Tye's perfect face, and for a second, I wonder if he's remembering the same exercise. Then he shakes his mane of red hair, and the memory, if it was ever there, disappears from his gaze. "You'll thank me later, I promise," he says, his long arms collecting me easily. Turning me around until my back is toward him, Tye slides his hands down over my arms with tantalizing slowness.

"Deep breath," Tye says, pulling my arms open like wings, his hard body pressing into my back. His lips brush my ear, the hypnotic whisper tickling the sensitive skin within. "Twenty. Nineteen. Eighteen." The pressure grows with each heartbeat, shifting between pain and molten pleasure. "Seventeen. Sixteen."

A soft moan escapes me. Then a hiss as the pressure keeps growing. Pain. We are definitely heading into pain. My shoulders. My arms. My chest. Everything. "That hurts." I struggle against Tye's hold, discovering it as unyielding as iron. "Let me go."

The bastard chuckles. "I've seen more flexible stones, you know."

"Then go torment them." My words come between clenched teeth, only the solid feel of Tye's body against my back grounding me to safety.

"Breathe, lass," Tye murmurs, a firm note of command beneath the sympathetic tone. "Halfway there." Tye's hips press into my lower back, arching me like a bow. "Nine. Eight. Sev—"

"—tree was watching you?" a male voice calls from the outside, the noise getting closer to the stables. "Did it chase and bite you as well?"

I jump away from Tye with a muffled yelp, suddenly painfully aware of how little I appear to be working right now —for all I know, River too actually measures the change in manure levels.

"That's not what I said," a younger man answers, his adolescent voice breaking and strained. "I just felt watched. And then this happened."

Releasing me, Tye massages my arms as he returns them to my sides. By the time the barn doors open, the male and I are both busy distributing flakes of hay to the horses, my chest and shoulders tingling through recovery. They do feel better— though I won't be telling Tye that.

"Tell me one thing, Rusty, why is it that things *just happen* only to greenies?" A tall black-mustached guard in his forties steps aside to let Rusty through, their horses following. The young guard's blue eyes glisten, his whole body hunching around one of his arms while he struggles to keep a stoic face. His reddish-blond hair is drenched in sweat, and his face is a sickly gray. The older guard whaps the back of the boy's head. "You'll find that no one here takes kindly to wild stories, so you might as well speak the truth. What are the pair of you doing here?" The last is barked at Tye and me.

"The lass is here on punishment detail from Headmaster River," Tye says, dropping the last of the hay in his arms into Sprite's stall. "And I'm around to try and get under her skirts." Tye grins so broadly that for a moment, both the guards and I only stand blinking like owls. By the time we return to our senses, Tye has already taken Rusty's horse and subtly maneuvered his body between him and the older guard, creating an illusion of privacy. "What happened to ye, lad?"

"N-nothing." About sixteen, the boy shifts his weight from foot to foot, plainly mapping an escape route that I know Tye doesn't intend to give him.

"Stupidity," the other guard calls, huffing as he goes about putting away his mount. "Mix a lack of wit with an abundance of imagination, and you can brew up anything."

Tye raises a brow, his gaze intent on Rusty's tight face.

Coming up on Rusty's other side, I feel a sharp tang of corruption tickling my nose, similar to what I smelled on the sclices two days ago—when their own stench of rotting garbage wasn't overpowering it—but different too. Something all its own. A quick glance at Tye shows his own nostrils flaring delicately, his emerald gaze concerned behind a mask of cavalier ease. The *nothing* that happened to Rusty doesn't belong in the mortal realm. Another symptom of the cracking wards and ripping fabric. My heart pounds.

Summoning the brightest smile the early morning allows, I reach for the boy's arm. "Can I take a look?"

"It's nothing. Like Mic said." Rusty tenses, readying to bolt. His blue eyes have grown even more glazed in the short time we've spent with him, darting about wildly.

"Rusty," Tye drawls, jerking his chin toward me. "Which would ye say rates higher on the cadet—the breasts or backside?"

"What?" Rusty and I say in unison.

Tye's gaze sharpens on mine for a heartbeat, somehow holding both a warning and an apology, and flicks to Rusty's arm. By the time the silent order registers, the male is already back to blinking conspiratorially at Rusty. "I'd rank the breasts higher myself, but with those curves, it's a tough call."

The boy's face reddens.

Tuning out discussion I will castrate Tye for later, I peel away Rusty's sleeve. Patches of bubbled yellow skin cover the boy's forearm, looking almost like wrong-colored burns. Several of the sores grow before my eyes, the leaking pus carrying a corrupted stench that makes my stomach churn.

"Master Shade warned me to watch for poison oak around these parts," Tye says, loudly enough to ensure the boy's partner overhears. "I wouldn't risk Shade's wrath myself by keeping this from him, but that's me."

"That is no poison oak," I mutter once the pair of guards departs. "That's—" I don't finish my sentence. *That* is exactly the mess I need to be steering clear from until someone who can differentiate his ass from his elbow—magically speaking—can draw me a bloody map. With my track record, I'd trek the *that* all over the Academy.

"I'll pass word to Shade about Rusty," Tye says, his voice low. "If the lad doesn't find the infirmary, it will find him. But that's as far as I go. Challengers have been barred from the Prowess Trials for lesser reasons than meddling in fae craft."

"The Prowess Trials are—" I catch myself cold, Coal's agony-filled scream echoing again through my memory. I'd been about to blurt something unamendable, telling Tye that his Prowess Trial track is nothing but a spun illusion.

"Are what?" Tye says.

"Are coming up sometime after Ostera celebrations, right?" Reclaiming my pitchfork, I busy myself with cleaning a stall, breathing deep against sudden panic. This is further proof that I have to be careful—very careful. Perhaps keep clear of the males altogether until I can get my tongue under control. The veil's magic is no jest. Just as my veil kept memories of Zake alive in Leralynn's new backstory, Tye's veil didn't invent Prowess Trials for him—it built on wounds already there.

Once, before the quint call bonded him to River and the others, Tye was destined for the top athletic title in Lunos. He and his family had given up everything for Tye's training, including his connection to the tiger that his soul yearned to shift into. Tye was a commoner born into nothing, whose talent and training and sacrifice let him challenge the crown prince himself. Or would have let him, if the night before the final challenge, the prince—in a message left in Tye's mother's blood and broken bones—hadn't forced Tye to forfeit the game forever.

Yes, the Tye standing before me remembers nothing of that, but the wounds went nowhere. The Prowess Trials are the magic's stand-in, and ripping Tye from them just might tear his soul into bloody strips.

Realizing Tye is waiting me to say something, I clear my throat. "The Prowess Trials are something. I little blame you for doing what you must."

Tye steps back toward the wall, though he keeps from actually leaning back against it. For a while, neither of us says a word as I return to my work. Scoop manure. Toss it into the wheelbarrows. Hold back the wince of pain the movement evokes. Repeat.

Finally, Tye clears his throat. "I am not bedding Princess Katita, in case you're wondering."

My heart skips a beat. "I wasn't."

He grins, but I can feel the tension behind the jest. "Of course you were."

I give Tye a vulgar gesture, which only makes him grin wider and jump right back onto the overhead bar, this time raising and holding his legs at a right angle to the floor. "I'm not going to bed you either," he adds, his attention on his bar.

My hands tighten on the pitchfork. Instead of mucking Sprite's stall, I set my sights on one farther away and walk toward it with purpose. There is simply no response to that bit of presumptuousness, especially when it happens to be true. We aren't going to sleep together—and not just for whatever reasons he's come up with.

"Lass." When I look over my shoulder, I find Tye still

hanging above the ground, trying and nearly succeeding in holding on to his cocky expression. Almost. I know the male too well to buy the lightness and smiles, not when my own immortal senses let me see the heaviness behind his gaze no matter how far down the stable aisle I am. "It isn't anything against you," he says, the reason behind this morning visit suddenly becoming clear. A thank-you. An acknowledgment. And a line drawn in the sand. He clears his throat, his vibrant green eyes suddenly shadowed. "My training and entanglements don't work. Trust me, I've tried. Some things are best said up-front. What we did the other night... That can't happen again."

I grit my teeth and force my shoulders into a shrug, ignoring the trickle of acid in my throat. Of course it can't happen again—I've already come to the same conclusion myself. The kissing and more against that tree hadn't been real, and I let myself enjoy them anyway. I've no regrets. But it burns to hear him say it, as if it's his decision alone. As if I hadn't been the one who'd warned him not to read anything into the kiss.

And all of a sudden, with a surge of anger that simmers my blood, I realize that I've made yet another—more grievous—miscalculation. While wondering whether the males would still care for me without the magic's bond, I'd overlooked the fact that I might not care for them. And this Tye, who thinks his kiss is a thank-you gift I should savor, I don't like one bit.

Reaching the other end of the stable, I look at Tye over the thick metal prongs of my pitchfork. "Message received. Now, I'd appreciate you choosing some other place to tempt Shade's wrath. Unlike Princess Katita and her ladies, I find little amusement in watching you strut about like a cock at sunrise and even less in explaining to River why my work isn't done."

5

LERA

I think I might actually be moving better by the time I head across the neatly trimmed grass and raked sand of the training yard toward Coal's morning sparring lesson, groups of gray-clad students and shouting instructors blurring in my side vision. I wonder whether Tye attends morning practice as well, and what the poor human in charge of him makes of the male. Lack of qualification—that is one problem *my* sparring instructor certainly doesn't have.

I, on the other hand, do. What I—usually—have in physical prowess, I make up for with a desperate lack of academic preparation. The veil might have convinced the Academy that I've had an educated, noble upbringing, but it didn't condescend to make me read better or do sums without the help of my fingers. I've already heard mutters on that score, my too-sharp hearing eagerly picking up hurtful tidbits. I turn my face up, letting the warm sun and clear sky lighten my mood. After the soggy disaster of yesterday, at least the weather seems to be on my side today.

The weather, however, quickly reveals itself as my *only* ally.

261

As class starts, the difference between "moving better" and "keeping up with Coal" is as clear as the clouds. My mind functions little better, unable to shake Tye and River from my thoughts no matter what I do—the former's cocky assumption that I'd want to bed him in the first place, that *he* was letting *me* down. The latter's cold gaze across the morning courtyard, gray eyes so neutral that I almost couldn't recognize my own commander in them. Where does the veil's magic end and the truth of the males' nature begin? Where was that line when the magic bonded us in Lunos? How are—

"Osprey!" Coal snaps just as my practice sword bounces pitifully off Katita's own raised blade. "Are you attacking or giving her a bloody massage?" He glares at me with piercing blue eyes, as professorial and distant as if yesterday never happened. Clad in his usual black leather in defiance of any uniform and wrapped in his masculine metallic scent, he crosses his sculpted arms over his broad chest—the same chest I felt against my skin yesterday, when the powerful beast Coal keeps leashed tangled with my own.

Unbidden heat floods my core, my sex clenching around the emptiness that so recently throbbed around Coal. *Instructor. Cadet. Not happening unless you want to be squirming before River again. Or worse. You aren't in Lunos and won't be until help comes.*

The princess grins, white teeth flashing in a perfect face. "It must be the latter, sir," Katita says, sweeping her sword into a wide arc before threading it like a needle between my body and sword arm. Arms thus wrapped, Katita yanks me close enough to murmur into my ear, "Though I do prefer my ladies-in-waiting to bathe in water, not horse piss. Just to let you know for the future."

I stumble as Katita shoves away from me, her coldly beautiful face shifting to deferential respect quicker than any warrior's strike as she glances at Coal. "Might you work with me instead today, sir? I have been having difficulty with a lunge-attack sequence for some time, and nothing I do seems to fix it."

Coal's brilliant blue gaze weighs me, my throat tightening at the mess I know he sees. A rumpled, too-large uniform stained with sweat and manure from the stable, shaking arms that keep dropping the blade, shoulder curled in to protect my aching body. Worse still, with me standing beside the princess whose every line oozes power and self-confidence, the resemblance between me and a drowned rat is hard to miss.

Even knowing all that, it still hurts when Coal nods to Katita and plucks my practice blade right out of my hand. "Osprey, join Arisha for basic strength work," the warrior says, pointing to where my segregated roommate friend is attempting to conquer push-ups. Without waiting for my response, Coal squares off with Katita, his gaze intent on the princess's movement as she walks him through the troublesome combination.

Keeping my face a stone, I find a place beside Arisha and drop gracelessly to the ground. She turns her head to look up at me, her scrunched brow damp with sweat, her brown hair sticking out wildly from her head in two collapsing braids. I smile in commiseration, but she only looks away quickly, focusing on her shaking arms. I swallow a stab of hurt. Ever since I returned to our dorm room last night, she's been acting differently—quieter, not looking at me full-on. Almost like... almost like she's scared of me.

"Arisha—"

"Silence on the pitch," Coal calls out without pausing his movements.

As I straighten into a basic push-up position, I'm hard-pressed to say what hurts more, my protesting muscles or the sight of Coal and Katita dancing with blades. Their matching blond hair gleaming in the sunlight—Katita's flowing behind her in a ponytail, Coal's in a tight knot—their paired beauty is almost painful to look at. I can sense the males of our group trying not to watch Katita as determinedly as I try not to watch Coal. Her smooth midriff shows each time she parries high, her hips flaring in perfect proportion from her slim waist.

Watching Katita's sharp, crisp strokes, I suddenly wish that King Zenith's daughter and heir to the Ckridel throne was less well trained, less diligent, less bloody perfect as she faces down one of Lunos's greatest fighters without a shred of fear. When Coal lands smarting blows on the princess's shoulders and ribs and thighs, Katita takes the rebukes with gracious nods of acknowledgment even as they make her wince. Damn her. That's *our* dance, Coal's and mine.

Or maybe it isn't. Maybe crossing blades with Coal was special to me, but to him—to the male who's lived with a sword for centuries—I've always been just another novice to be trained.

I try to straighten my arms too quickly, my palms slipping to send me face-first into the sand. Grains of grit fill my mouth and eyes, which—from the sound of nearby chuckles— must look much as it feels. The one and only class in the day where Cadet Leralynn of Osprey has something of worth to offer, and I'm failing even that. Right in front of Coal.

I struggle up again, my back sagging in a form so poor that a child would mark it. Face tingling, I watch Coal switch drills and continue down the line of cadets to make correction to form. Every time the warrior's muscled hands align a student's shoulders or settle on a cadet's hips to twist them into proper position, his blue eyes a wall of professionalism, a claw rakes over my chest. It little helps that the women of the group can't hide their pleasure at Coal's attention. One, a slight, black-haired first-year, even seems to press into Coal's hands like a purring tabby cat.

Back in Lunos, Autumn once jested that she could name a dozen females who'd likely find release just from seeing the bastard naked—plainly, Coal's allure is no less strong in the mortal lands. Masculinity streams off him in his scent, his chiseled features, his bare, corded arms. Arms that didn't hesitate in flipping me over and taking me from behind only yesterday—

"He is an instructor," Arisha says, her voice so low that even I can barely hear. Crunching up to touch her elbows to her knees, she waits for me to mirror the position, her cheeks flushed under their constellation of freckles.

My heart jumps, my abdominal muscles protesting so vividly that I see stars in the brilliant blue sky. "What?"

"Master Coal. He is an instructor. Instructors teach." Arisha follows my gaze to where Coal stands behind one of the female cadets, his broad palms bracing her arms as he guides her upper body to follow through a blow. "I'm saying it doesn't mean anything other than that."

My body tightens, my skin blazing. Arisha couldn't possibly have smelled what happened between Coal and me yesterday, which means my current pining is pathetic enough for her to have taken notice. "So long as I'm not in his sights, I little care what he does." I bite off my words, then instantly wish I could take them back. Arisha may be unable to run across the road without getting winded, but the girl is no idiot. She deserves better. I sigh. "I'm not blind to beautiful bodies. So long as I keep fantasy and reality well separated, there is little harm in looking."

"Hmm." The girl makes a noncommittal sound, and I excuse myself to get some water before Arisha can share any more of her too on-point thoughts.

6

COAL

*C*oal turned his back to Lera lest she caught the hint of amusement that made the corner of his mouth twitch. After the smooth athletic sword dance of the previous afternoon, today the girl couldn't so much as lift her arms. Her smooth curves and lean muscles were a stiff, strained mess. Anyone who'd trained hard knew the feeling, which made it entertaining to watch another suffer through the same fate.

On the sand in front of him again, Princess Katita brought her practice blade to ready guard, her keen teal eyes watching for an opening that Coal supposed he should give her. Let the princess try to mount an attack. Maybe see how well Katita could split her attention between offense and defense when the pace picked up. The princess was certainly trying, working with her whole heart. She deserved more than Coal's bored indulgence, no matter how well he knew he hid it.

Coal's jaw tightened with irritation at himself. He had two

dozen students in the corral and yet couldn't keep his thoughts from swirling around Lera—who wasn't even training today.

Before him, Katita took the offered weakness and attacked, her body moving with all the technique a training master could demand. Plainly, the princess not only had had good trainers but had also put in the work to go along with instruction—and yet as far as a *conversation* of blades, Coal had little to say to Katita's perfectly textbook movements.

Especially after he'd crossed blades with Leralynn the previous afternoon.

And then done more than that. Unbidden, the memory of Lera moving beneath him in the cave's moist air gripped Coal's cock. Even now, he couldn't help seeing how Lera's full breasts had bounced with his movements, her chest heaving with desperate breaths, her taut legs wrapped around his waist like a vise. It almost felt like it'd happened to a different person—like a different man's cock had been buried to the hilt in all that lilac-scented warmth—especially since it could never happen again.

Unable to help himself, Coal glanced over to where Lera was doing basic strength training with Arisha. Her rich auburn braid swung over her shoulder as she lowered into push-ups, the choppiness of her usually ethereal movement so absurdly unlike her that it was all Coal could do to keep from cracking a smile—especially as Lera fell halfway through a push-up, landing with her face in the sand. Watching her sit up and rub the dirt away, Coal waited for the string of colorful curses that was sure to come.

Instead, the girl's skin darkened as she struggled back into plank form, her jaw tightening with humiliation.

The amusement faded from Coal's chest so quickly that he nearly left a welt on Katita's unprotected shoulder for no reason beyond his own distraction. Surely Lera understood that soreness after yesterday's ordeal was normal. Not a sign of weakness. Not a sign of anything beyond the effort she'd put in to withstand the misery he put her through.

The color of Leralynn's skin said otherwise. She gritted her teeth as she started moving jerkily again, injured pride and frustration rolling off her in waves. Stars take him. What did the girl expect? Yet even knowing that Lera's demands of herself were unrealistic, Coal could no longer take any gentle humor in her predicament. Or forgive himself for not having watched closer, for anticipating a reaction from a girl who was anything but predictable.

Especially after River told Coal what she'd done last night.

Lera had tried to protect him. Offered to face something terrifying, just to spare Coal—the man who'd just punished her. What woman did that? It had shaken River enough that he'd shared the conversation with Coal—along with his suspicion that someone had hurt Lera before. Having seen the scars Lera's old master left on her, Coal knew River's guess was right. When the time was right, when trust was rebuilt, Coal would need to work with her through that. A fighter couldn't freeze up in terror at the thought of being struck—an echoing circumstance could too easily come up in battle.

"Rotate!" Coal called over the training grounds, turning his face up to the wind while the cadets scurried to new positions. He'd acted like an idiot. *Again.* He should have anticipated Lera's unrealistic expectations of her body, done something to subtly defuse her pain. Instead, Coal had let the whole class watch her flail.

The bloody reality was that Coal deserved the very thing Lera had spared him from. He was an instructor. He'd been responsible for every breath she took yesterday. And instead of protecting the girl, Coal had let his cock do the thinking.

Leralynn had been weak and hurt and exhausted. She hadn't been thinking straight—but he should have been.

A rush of heat slashed through Coal's core, making his cock twitch in memory of Lera's blazing, clenching sex. He certainly *hadn't* been thinking yesterday; he'd been…reacting. The scent of Lera's arousal had woken something primal inside him, the strength radiating from her matching the power coiled in his own soul. The bedding hadn't been gentle. It had been raw and exhilarating and made him feel more alive than he had since escaping the islanders.

It was how Coal had imagined bedding the woman who'd helped him survive captivity would be.

"Nothing of consequence happened here today," Leralynn had told Coal in the cave. That might have been true for her, but not him. Coal had wanted her so deeply that his soul howled with the need. Still did. Not that it mattered.

The sound of cracking wood and gasping students jerked Coal's attention back to the corral. With a start, Coal realized that he'd not only taken a swing at a practice post, but hit the wood hard enough to shatter the practice blade. Stars take him. "Can I help you all?" he demanded, the students scattering back to position at once.

Grabbing a fresh sword, Coal snuck a final glance at where Lera was doing push-ups again. Coal had hurt her. Many times over. And now he could offer no comfort. Because it wasn't his place to. And because he didn't know how.

Putting distance between them was the only path to take. "Rik, Puckler," Coal called, waiting for Katita's bulky cousins to take a place before him. The twins had inherited much of the princess's status and arrogance without the wits or work ethic to go with them. Bringing up the tip of his blade, Coal decided to see how many times he might make the pair blunder into each other before the bell rang.

7

———

LERA

*I*t takes three full days before I can move normally again, and I'm surprised to discover how easily I've slipped into the invisibility that saved me most of my life before I met the males. Aside from the uncomfortable conversation about Coal, Arisha still seems to be keeping a distance from me, finding reasons to be out of the room whenever I'm there and reading through meals. I try not to let it hurt too much—but I miss her. Even in the short time I've known her, her easy, clumsy friendliness was a welcome balm against the coldness of the Academy. Perhaps she's discovered that I attract too much trouble. I can hardly blame her there, especially since Tye, Coal, and River have plainly come to the same conclusion and stay clear of me as well. With no injury to complain of, I see nothing of Shade at all.

At least I'm not making things worse for everyone, which should count for something.

With dinner approaching, the keep has raised a rich gold standard in place of the morning red, marking the Academy's daily shift from a military protocol to the evening palace court atmosphere. Around me, the manicured courtyard walkways are filled with cadets in attire suited for their high birth—long satin and taffeta gowns in every color of the rainbow, carefully made-up faces and gleaming hair. Clusters of young women move together toward the dining hall, laughing and whispering as they eye matching clusters of men in crisp evening suits. Lifting my face into the breeze that seems to forever course through the open spaces on this exposed hilltop, I inhale the scent of young grass and fresh-cut shrubbery, the satin magenta dress I've chosen sliding coolly over my hips.

I scowl at my choice of attire. The open back and thigh-high slit give the long sleeves no chance to offer protection against the elements, which take perverse delight in perking my nipples—a fact I notice the same time as a boy walking toward me does, his gaze sliding across my chest and hips. I hug my books to my chest, ending the show, my body too new and foreign for me to feel comfortable in.

If Autumn were here, she'd enjoy taking in the different fashions of the Continental Alliance kingdoms, from the billowing skirts with bamboo ribbing favored by the ladies in the north to the sensual, revealing silks of the southern kingdoms. If Autumn were here, she'd likely have me decked out like a new doll each day. Except, she isn't.

"Perhaps Osprey is weak of mind?" a girl's voice says. For a moment, I think someone is beside me, but quickly realize my immortal ears are a little too adept at picking up conversations—this one being carried from a group of ladies ten paces away.

"I believe she is bright enough," the girl's companion answers thoughtfully. "It's something else."

Ah, that would be the growing commentary about my class performance.

A third girl clicks her tongue. "She's simply spoilt. Allowed to indulge in swords and horses with no mind paid to tutors—I've a brother of that same ilk. Too bad for her Master River will not put up with such nonsense for long."

I quicken my step to get out of earshot, the mere mention of River's name sending an uncomfortable shiver though me. I've barely seen him in three days, and when I have, he's as remote as ever. I shudder to imagine his response when my lack of prior education does finally reach his attention. My attempt to sit in on one of Arisha's tutoring sessions with Tye diffused any desire to try that route again—and not just because my body and mind couldn't agree whether I wanted to kill the male or kiss him. The reality is that with math skills extending little beyond sums and only enough reading ability to make out instructions, the whole mess was as humiliating as it was useless. My failure to turn in an assignment for Master Erik's *Understanding Islanders' Goals and Strategies* has already earned me extra work, which I've no way of completing. By week's end, I'll be in the same predicament with Master Briar's mathematics.

How the bloody hell am I supposed to stay in the Academy long enough for Lunos to send help when I can't do even the basic coursework? I want to tear off the amulet around my neck and grind it into the dirt. Why did it give me a student persona if I had no ability to be a student? Why not make me something more suitable? A scullery maid, perhaps, or a stable hand.

The dormitories are deserted by the time I make it there, with everyone already at dinner. Holding up my books as a ready explanation should any stranger wonder why I'm walking in the wrong direction, I climb the external stone stairs to my floor, then walk quickly down the torch-lined hallway to my bedchamber. Perhaps I might skip dinner altogether today, keeping the empty room company and sparing Arisha awkward conversation.

Sliding my key into the lock, I feel my body stiffen at the lack of resistance. The door is open. My heart quickens, my senses wakening. Arisha would have been in last, and she *never* forgets to lock a door. Or fold a shirt. Or anything except how to braid hair and swing a sword.

Reaching to draw the boot knife Coal gifted me back in Lunos, I find the sheath empty and swear softly. I used the blade in the stables to cut the twine, and after getting distracted with Czar throwing a fit over Sprite being in heat, I never tucked the weapon back. Damn it. Forcing myself to breathe, I slowly open the door and inhale the stench of undiluted terror.

Arisha. Rushing inside, I find the girl pressed tightly against one of the dorm room's high white walls, her small freckled face drained of blood.

"Arisha—?"

"Shh." She seems unwilling—or unable—to move a muscle, even to turn her head in my direction. Dressed in nothing but smallclothes—a white chest wrap and undershorts—with her uniform grays folded neatly on the bed, the girl seems to have been in the middle of changing for dinner when…

When what?

Dropping the books to the floor, I survey the room…and see nothing. With the smell of Arisha's fear so thick, I can sense little else on that front as well.

"Behind you," Arisha whispers, still not moving a muscle. Her blue eyes are wide, her chest rising with shallow rapid breaths. "Under the bed. Move very, very slowly or it will—" She gasps as a low growl fills the room. "It doesn't like movement."

My back tightens, my body shifting protectively between Arisha and the bed as I glance around for a weapon. "What is *it*?" I ask in a voice too calm to be mine.

"I don't know." She swallows. "But it has teeth. And yellow eyes. And…a tail. Gray."

Eyes, teeth, tail. A feather of disbelief runs down my spine. Turning around, I narrow my eyes into the under-bed darkness.

"Grrrrr." The darkness replies in a lupine whine I know too well.

8

LERA

My eyes widen, my heart stuttering for a beat before leaving my chest. The instinctive unbearable longing to throw my arms around Shade's warm neck flashes through my soul, stopping short against a cold kind of terror. Arisha already thinks something is wrong with me. How do I explain a bloody wolf in our room? If she makes an accusation… If Arisha makes an accusation, it won't be just my head in the noose. River will have the whole guard searching for Shade's wolf. And if he keeps being this reckless, eventually they'll find him.

Think, I order myself, drawing a covert breath. *Think, think, think.*

Facts race through my mind, shifting like rules in a mathematics formula. Shade is under my bed. No, Shade's *wolf* is under my bed. Arisha has seen the animal, and I can't make her unsee him.

"That's my dog," I blurt to fill the pounding silence. "Ruffle. I didn't think he'd follow me all the way from Osprey. I'm so sorry he scared you, Arisha."

The girl points a trembling finger at my bed. "That thing isn't a dog."

"I mean, he's tame. *Like* a dog." I need to do better. How does one make a humongous wolf seem harmless? Grabbing a pitcher of water from the small hanging shelf in the room, I head for Shade's hiding spot. "Look. I'll show you."

Before I can reconsider the wisdom of what I'm about to do, I swing the pitcher, emptying the cold liquid into the growling darkness.

Arisha's high-pitched screech hurts my ears, the noise mercifully stopping a heartbeat later when a large yellow-eyed wolf belly-crawls from beneath my bed and shakes himself off, hundreds of tiny droplets flying at both me and my bedding.

Shade's wolf tilts his head as if finding the concept of a talking girl to be fascinatingly curious, his black muzzle opening into a gentle, easy-to-please pant. Then, with great lumbering laziness, the beast arches his back down, indulging in an extended stretch.

Arisha whimpers.

"See? He's friendly." The words tumble from my mouth and I beg the stars to make them true. The amulet around my neck remains cool, spinning no veil to explain Shade's appearance. A wolf belongs in the mortal world, after all. Even if he'll be hunted. My voice turns desperate. "Please. Just let me introduce you. He won't hurt you. Won't hurt anyone. But I don't know what Masters River and Sage might do if they find him."

"Wait." Arisha closes her eyes and draws several deep breaths, her strained breathing filling the silence. When she opens them again, her shoulders are set in a fair imitation of bravery, though her hands wring each other until they're bone white. "Is it... Stars. I can't." She shakes her head. "I shouldn't say—"

On the other side of the room, Shade is now circling in place, his wet nose chasing a slowly moving tail. When Arisha takes a step, however, the wolf snaps his teeth, and she cowers back against the wall. I swallow a curse. Shade's wolf scents my fear and, with no one else in the room, has concluded Arisha to be its source.

"Stop that," I snap at Shade. Turning back to Arisha, I hold out my hands placatingly. "What were you going to say?"

"Is that your f-familiar?" Arisha says quickly.

"A familiar?" I blink in bewilderment. "Like…in children's tales about witches?"

She nods, her face reddening.

"I'm not a witch." I clear my throat, not sure how to react. "Witches aren't actually real. I mean, so far as I know." In Arisha's defense, witches figure in human tales and legends as much as fae, the difference being that the latter aren't fiction.

"No. Of course not. I know that," Arisha says quickly, then cringes at her own words. "I mean, I'm not gullible—I just didn't want to assume things."

"For the record, I understand what you just said about as well as I understand my mathematics homework."

Arisha rubs her face. "Well, we've proof of fae and not witches, but how can one prove that something doesn't exist? It's like proving a negative. You can't prove a negative. And that isn't a dog. There has to—"

"You are babbling," I tell Arisha.

"And you are fae," she shoots back. "So that makes us even."

Silence settles through the room. Arisha hugs herself. I cross my arms over my chest, my head cold and blank. Shade growls. The silence grows thicker, heavier. Outside our tall open window, the slowly lowering sun casts a warm peachy light over the spring evening—a bizarre contrast to the tension in this room.

Something. I have to do something. Say something. But what?

Arisha covers her face with her hands, rubbing her forehead. When she speaks, her voice shakes slightly, as if she's fighting her own better judgment. "Gavriel is my uncle. So I know…everything." She lowers her hands. "It's not just gossip. I'm training for the Guild, so he had good reason tell me. And yes, I *know* it's forbidden to interfere, but whoever wrote that rule wasn't stuck in a room with—" She waves her hand at Shade's wolf, now snapping at a fly daring to buzz around his head, "Ruffle."

I drop onto my bed, sitting right atop a still very damp Shade, who somehow managed to sprawl across the covers when I wasn't paying attention. The wolf huffs his displeasure before shifting over. A hollow ringing fills my ears, as if someone just struck me over the head with a club. "How long?" I ask.

Arisha looks at her bare feet. "Two day after you came. When you were out with Coal."

"Is that why you—" I pause as the rest of the words Arisha said finally catch up with me. "What did you say about not interfering?"

"The Guild is not supposed to do anything to influence any fae that might cross—it's one of the Guild's tenets," says Arisha, plainly regaining her footing with a chance to offer up information, reminding me so much of Autumn for a brief moment that my chest squeezes. "The ancients were very clear on wanting no fraternization between the worlds, hence the wards and Mystwood and all. And more practically, it keeps the peace. Without the noninterference vow, you'd have the whole Guild maneuvering to try to influence the Protector instead of cooperating and sharing knowledge."

"Wait." I hold up my hand. "What you are describing is not Gavriel."

"You're telling me," she says with a snort. "That's why the Guild threw him out... He didn't tell you that part, did he?"

"No."

Arisha blushes. "It looks like I'm little better. Stars. All the rules make so much sense on parchment, but reality is never quite so clean."

"Is this why you've been avoiding me?" I ask, biting my lip. I hadn't realized just how much I'd been missing Arisha's friendship until this moment.

The wave of relief rushing through me at Arisha's nod makes me sink into Shade's fur.

Shade.

I straighten up, suddenly remembering how we got into this conversation. "So, about the wolf. Could you possibly not mention him to, well, *anyone*?"

Arisha eyes Shade warily. With his head resting on furry paws, the wolf seems to be following the conversation, one long ear flickering now and again. With new attention suddenly on him, Shade lifts his black snout and sneezes, sending a new cloud of gray fur and lupine drool into the air.

"Is he really a pet from Lunos?" Arisha asks, her face filled with momentary curiosity before her eyes widen again. With a shriek, she rushes to grab the bedspread off her cot, hastily covering her still mostly naked body. "It's one of them, isn't it? One of the four males. Stars. Coal? Is that Coal in our room? Did you empty a pitcher of water on bloody *Coal?* I was already doing badly enough in his lessons—"

"It's not Coal," I say quickly. "I promise."

Arisha's gaze narrows. "But it is one of them?"

I wince. So much for keeping my head down until rescue arrives. "Shade."

"I'll never step into the infirmary again without turning so red I set the walls on fire," Arisha whispers hoarsely.

"If it makes you feel better, Shade won't be aware of this. I mean, the version of Shade you think you know doesn't know he's fae, much less that he shifts into a wolf now and again." I drop flat onto my mattress, ignoring the wolf's indignant rumble. If he wants to take up the entire mattress, then he can hardly complain when I use him for a footrest. "It's a mess all around."

Arisha tilts her head in consideration. "All right. So will you tell Shade the truth? I imagine waking with a belly full of meat—or whatever that beast you are using as a pillow does with its teeth—is rather disconcerting."

"If I accused you of being fae while also claiming that everything you think you know about your life is an utter lie and that you secretly turn into a wild beast, what would you do?"

"At best, I'd think you daft. At worst… I'd think you were conjuring an accusation as a threat—that you are thinking of making the claim to the inquisitors." Arisha winces. "And by the time those inquisitor bastards are done seeking proof— wait. Proof. What if you had proof?"

"I tried that," I say, recounting what happened when I forced Coal to touch his own ear, my stomach turning at his phantom screams. "The veil magic is fighting for its survival, and I think it attacks when cornered. That means I stay the hell clear of anything that might provoke it until someone who knows what they are doing comes."

"Right." Arisha nods slowly. "For all we know, each time the veil reacts, it might grow stronger, like a muscle. All right, so no placing the males in the crossfire between the real truth and the veil magic's truth."

I bite my lip. "What if I didn't tell Shade that *he* is fae, but just took off the amulet to show him who I am?"

"He'd likely turn you in, Lera," says Arisha. "Or else be in danger just for knowing the truth. It seems that when the males absorbed their veil amulets, they truly inherited the fictional personas. If the amulet is fighting to keep the veil's illusion alive, it may very well compel Shade to turn you in, just to protect itself."

I curse softly. Arisha has a point.

"We'll work this out," she says softly.

I tense, turning my head to find her gaze. "We?"

"We." Arisha stands, squaring her shoulders before remembering she is still half-naked and yelping as she snatches up her sheet. "If I'm going to break *some* of the Guild rules, I might as well break all of them. Unless you'd rather I not—"

Bouncing off my bed, I throw my arms around Arisha, holding her slim body so tightly that I'm not sure the girl can breathe. "I want *we*," I say into Arisha's shoulder, not realizing my eyes are stinging until I blink back the moisture. "I want there to be a 'we' very, very much."

The *dong* of the dinner bell breaks us apart in a distant reminder that the Academy's life is flowing on, whether we are ready or not. Despite my assuredness that Shade will have no memory of what his wolf sees, Arisha insists I keep his attention while she changes into evening attire.

"Go on ahead," I tell Arisha, helping her tie the back laces of her midnight-blue gown. "I want a few more moments with this beast."

A quarter hour later, I'm within scenting distance of the dining hall—the smells of roasted lamb and baked apples making my stomach growl—when a horse's distant whinny reminds me of the knife I forgot in the stable. At once, my weaponless boot feels too light. Promising my stomach that lamb is not far off, I turn down a narrow courtyard path toward the tall row of flowering mountain laurels separating the Academy's east and west sides, the plants' thick fragrance enveloping me as I pass.

My delicate high-laced boots and low-backed magenta dress look as out of place on the dirt-packed trails as the cadets' training grays seem in the luxurious breakfast hall. My stomach growls. Picking up the pace, I hurry toward the stables, the vast training corrals—perfectly mowed and raked for the coming morning—ghostly around me. Everyone is eating—cadets, guards, hostlers. Everyone except me.

I freeze, quickly amending my assessment.

Everyone except me and whoever is shrieking inside the barn.

9

LERA

*P*ulling the stable door open, I brace myself for the sight of a rampaging stallion knocking some unfortunate soul into the wall. Instead, amidst the sweet-smelling hay and the warmth of the horses' scent, I find Princess Katita's three cousins—the dark, heavyset twins, Puckler and Rik, and the slightly older Lord Nolan—surrounding the scrawny page everyone calls Rabbit. With Nolan gripping the front of his shirt, the nine-year-old lad stands on his toes, shaking in fair imitation of his namesake. A livid bruise peeking out from beneath the threadbare fabric of his tunic matches the set of leather reins in Puckler's meaty fist.

Hot fury rushes though me, my face and muscles blazing while my magic thrashes against its shackles.

Puckler raises the leather again, Nolan maneuvering the boy to make him into a better target.

Rabbit cringes, bracing himself while hiccupping little sobs escape his throat.

"Belay that!" My bellow echoes through the stable, turning

heads, human and equine alike. My fists curling at the sides of my flowing dress, I advance on the group. The rage inside me is so loud, I hear it whistling in my ears. Inside me, River's shackled earth magic pounds fiercely enough to bring down the barn if given the chance.

Still holding on to the front of Rabbit's shirt, Lord Nolan turns to flash a set of crooked teeth at me. "If you bothered to look first and speak later, you'd know we are doing the lad a favor." The tallest of the bunch, Nolan has a thin blond mustache, a nose too pointy for his face, and an expensive jacket cut to make the most of his lean features. The cadet's gaze slithers across my body before finding my face. I can almost feel the oily trail left by his hard green eyes. Pulling a thick gold sigil from his pocket, Nolan flashes the piece at me. "The little shit picked this from my pocket. Now he is paying for it. Unless, of course, you think I should report him to Commander River instead?" Nolan's small eyes gleam at the boy. "How would you like a beating from the deputy headmaster, boy? Right before he throws you out of the Academy with the rest of the garbage."

Rabbit sobs, shaking his head. "No. Please."

"Seems Rabbit has learned the lesson you have so generously taught him," I tell the three. Thunder still ringing in my ears, I close my hand casually around a pitchfork leaning by the stable wall. My mind screams that this is the opposite of keeping to myself. I ignore it. "Since everyone is in the mood for favors today, I'll offer one as well. Let the boy go *now*, and I won't break your noses for you."

Standing closest to me, Nolan releases Rabbit and shifts his weight, loading up his right fist. The obvious movement says fighting isn't the lord's strong suit, and I imagine the sudden bravery comes from being a head taller than me. The dubious glance that the twins shoot toward Nolan is absurdly satisfying. And very fleeting.

Nolan swings his fist at my head.

I swing the pitchfork's handle against the back of the lord's knees.

Rabbit takes advantage of the commotion to skitter away.

My strike on Nolan lands first, his legs flying out from under him as he topples backwards. He lands on the stable floor with a soft thud, a pile of fresh manure cushioning his head. I step back quickly, crouching in readiness.

"Filthy wench," Nolan shouts to grunts of agreement from the others, who now converge on me from both sides, eyes flashing. "You'll regret that."

Built like barrels, the twins have shining eyes the precise color of Katita's and tightly pulled-back black hair. The brutality in their mirrored gazes sends a shiver down my spine. They were *enjoying* hurting Rabbit and, with that taken away, little want to be left empty-handed. I may be fae and they human, but I'm still adjusting to my new fae body—a body that is far smaller than theirs—and three to one are not good odds.

On my right, Puckler swings the leather reins he used on Rabbit, the thick material making a whooshing sound as it cuts through the air. On my left, Rik has located another pitchfork—though unlike me, he holds it with the sharp end forward. Across the aisle, Sprite is kicking her stall, and even Coal's Czar is whinnying his displeasure.

Rik swings the pitchfork first, the metal teeth flashing toward my head.

I duck and slide sideways, letting Rik's momentum carry him to stumble into the wall. Just as I do, a line of fire explodes along my left ribs. Puckler. I gasp at the pain, twisting to see him swing the leather reins back for another blow. The whooshing sound makes my stomach clench, my memory flashing in remembrance of Zake's beatings, and I know that only my having been moving when he struck saved me from the full force of the blow. I won't be so lucky next time.

Out. I need to get out of here.

My eyes slash over the three cadets. The stable. The horses. Stalls line both sides of the long, wide aisle where we are fighting, the two doors on either end as far as from me as the moon. Worse still, I'm in the middle of the boys, with the twins cutting off the south exit route and Nolan cutting off the north. The pungent stench of Nolan's fury is stronger than latrine refuse.

But Nolan is the weaker of the group. If I can get through him, it would put the lord between myself and the twins.

Throwing my pitchfork at Rik, I buy myself time to set up my attack. Breathing steadily, I lower my level. Aim my shoulder for Nolan's hip. Push off my legs. Explode.

My shoulder hits Nolan's bony frame with a satisfactory thud, the lord's body yielding to my force. Falling backward for the second time in as many minutes, Nolan moans.

I don't even pause.

Jumping over Nolan's writhing form, I spring for the door, my dress swinging awkwardly around my legs. My soft boots pound the wooden floor, my lungs taking gulps of hay-sweet air. Behind me, the boys scramble off each other, their cursing egging me on. Faster. I need to go faster. The ten steps left between me and the door feel like miles. Eight steps. Five.

I'm going to make it. I can tell by the distance of the sound closing up from behind me. Just one more—

My foot lands on my dress's hem, my knee suddenly hitting fabric. With a curse, I fall onto my knees, the sting of impact nothing compared to the devastation of a hand closing around my ankle. A hard yank from one of the boys flattens me, the rough wood scraping my face.

"Going somewhere, wench?" Puckler's gravelly voice hits the back of my neck a moment before his considerable weight settles atop me. The stench of too-strong perfume fills my nose. "You think you have leave to assault members of King Zenith's court?"

I move on instinct honed from too many minutes spent flattened beneath Coal's unyielding body. Rising to my knees and elbows, I turtle up to protect my stomach and head. Wait for my opening. Compared to the immortal warrior, Puckler is an awkward sack of rocks—but he is large and one of three. I can't stay here in my turtle position for long.

There. The slight shift of Puckler's weight is all I need to twist out from under him.

The moment I do, Rik is there, forcing me right back onto my hands and knees while his brother restraddles my back. The two failed escapes press on me as roughly as Puckler's considerable weight.

"Well, this is convenient, isn't it?" Nolan's thin, nasal voice holds a note of vicious amusement. "I do love breaking a filly. Let's get a bit in its mouth."

The clanking sound of a bridle being readied shoots through my nerves. I buck to get Puckler off, having to wait patiently for a shift of weight. For an opening. Puckler doesn't budge.

The next moment, something cracks along my backside, the slap of leather an acidic mix of pain and humiliation. A second lash.

Atop me, Puckler grabs my hair while Nolan's manure-covered palm shoves a bit into my face.

The rush of fury that overtakes me is enough to rival a storm.

1 0

TYE

With the others busy at dinner, Tye swung on the horizontal bar in the center of a quiet training pitch as the sun slowly sank below the Academy wall, gaining more momentum with each flex of his body. With an easy exhale, he gave himself a final push and flew into the air.

Cool air nipped his face, his body's tumbling in defiance of gravity sending a rush of exhilaration through him. In that instant of soaring above the bar, with nothing but the control of his body and trust in momentum keeping him in the air, Tye felt that elusive completeness.

He felt *alive*, his heart pumping hard in celebration of nothing but the now.

The moment ended as Tye caught the bar on his way down, his too recently dislocated shoulder screaming its protests. With a swallowed wince, Tye let himself down, landing neatly on the forgiving sands. After the high of soaring through the air, the return to the ground was deadening.

Clap. Clap. Clap.

Tye turned toward the applause, a trained smile on his face as he saluted whoever it was. Katita. Again. Tye's jaw tightened. Pretty, intelligent, and ruthless, Katita was King Zenith's heir and Ckridel Kingdom's—Tye's kingdom—next queen. For all the uniforms and Academy rules that technically made the upperclassman Tye a superior to first-year Katita—there was no denying the reality of power. Ckridel was hers, and by extension, so was Tye.

"Impressive," Katita said, ending her applause. "I'm not sure what Master Shade would say about stressing the shoulder, though." Dressed in a pair of billowing black pants and a short silver jacket that let a sliver of taut belly show, her blond hair tied up in an elaborate nest of coils and braids, Katita was accustomed to drawing the eye of every male at the Academy. Yet her toned body failed to captivate Tye in the least. Not that it would be polite—or wise—to inform her so aloud.

Tye summoned a grin wide enough that he knew it made his green eyes seem to dance—which usually confused people long enough to give him time to escape. He didn't like to abuse his effect on others, but sometimes it was worth it. "What Master Shade doesn't know can't hurt him. You wouldn't be in the mood for reporting on a friend, would you, Kit?"

"My name is Katita." A mix of annoyance and pleasure.

"Is it?" Tye hopped back on the bar, which had the dual benefit of ending the conversation and making his shoulder burn. At least pain was a feeling. A something.

These days, feeling was a privilege. No matter how many people surrounded Tye, how he laughed or jested, a great slice of Tye's soul seemed to remain trapped away in some dungeon. And no matter how hard Tye pounded on the door, he couldn't get to it. Couldn't feel the range of emotions, not outside those glorious moments of flying.

With one notable exception.

Leralynn's lilac scent woke Tye's soul as only soaring above the earth did, his heart and breath quickening with the merest shift of wind if it carried the smell. Made him drunk on it. Unfortunately, it also made him stupid. Especially in the time following that first awkward run-in in the courtyard, when he'd followed Lera into the woods and let his cock do too much of his thinking. The part in question twitched even now just at the bloody memory.

At least Tye had manned up a few days ago, laying the reality bare before Lera. Tye could not get involved. With anyone. And whenever he was tempted to, he needed only to recall what happened with his fiancée Tiga, and the misplaced lust dissolved to reality.

Unlike the Academy's other students, Tye was common born—with only his talent for athletics bringing him in contact with his betters. Athletics were his life—it and the fiery, passionate Tiga whom he'd been promised to since childhood. With both of them growing up, Tiga had been certain Tye's competitions would stay behind. There was, after all, no place for a common-born peasant to go.

Until Great Falls Academy invited Tye to enroll and represent them at the Prowess Trials. Until Tye had accepted, standing firm through Tiga's tears and pleas.

The morning after the argument, Tye awoke to a note on the pillow freeing Tye of all obligations. No destination, no address, no promise of return. *You made your decision,* Tiga's loopy handwriting leaked with hurt. *And now I've made mine. I hope you find it worth it.*

A week later, Tye returned from a grueling run to learn that a villager had found Tiga's body at the bottom of a ravine. A note tucked into her bodice said goodbye to no one in particular.

No. Tye was never doing that to anyone again. Not getting involved with anyone he didn't wish to hurt. Training and relationships did not mix at all. *He* and relationships didn't mix.

Which all still left the void Tye struggled to fill with what he could. Tempting gravity, tempting fate, even tempting River. He'd go over the Academy's wall again in a moment, no matter how many beatings it earned him. Feeling pain was better than feeling nothing at all, and the thrill of Lera's nervous excitement—the first he'd felt with any woman since Tiga—was worth any amount of discomfort. Tye could still feel the heat of Lera's body, her pulse beating hard enough to be heard, her eyes widening as he slid his hands along her hips.

Lera, that small, glorious lilac girl, was so alive that even Tye's locked-away soul sang in her presence. Her similarity to Tiga in appearance little hurt either.

Keep your cock to yourself, you bastard, Tye told himself as he completed a twenty pull-up set and hopped back to the soft sand. *Flowers are to be savored, not trampled on.*

The last dinner bell sounded from the keep tower, and Tye's stomach gave a dissatisfied rumble at being out here when food was elsewhere. Well, it could join his cock in complaining, Tye still had things to do. A run, to start with. Then more strength and flexibility work. He could always talk a cook into some bannocks later, but with the others busy eating, there was no one to tell him what he should and shouldn't be doing with his shoulder. Katita might tsk and fawn, but she wouldn't interfere. And she certainly wasn't going to run with him.

Tightening his laces, Tye looked toward the moat of woods planted to create the illusion of a forest instead of a wall, his attention catching on a small body sprinting fast as a frightened squirrel past Katita and into the training corral.

No, not a squirrel—a Rabbit.

TYE

*C*atching the lad, Tye crouched beside him. The small, curly haired boy was panting, tear tracks plain on his dirty face.

"What's keeping you from dinner?" Tye asked, narrowing his gaze on Rabbit's trembling shoulders. Tye had been small as a boy as well, and knew firsthand that only events of grand magnitude could make the lad skip a meal. "Have the guards been giving you a hard time?"

With no family, Rabbit had somehow talked his way into a position as a page at the Academy, mostly running messages around the grounds. With no other children employed, the adults had differing ideas on what the boy's exact role should be—especially since, despite months of regular meals, Rabbit couldn't help picking the pockets of anyone careless enough to leave valuables there.

Tye understood that as well, and, being of a belief that anything worth doing was worth doing well, was unlikely a good influence.

"Le—Leralynn. Nolan and his… Surrounded." Rabbit's

skinny chest heaved with panting breaths that left him unsteady on his feet. "Puckler. Rik too."

A chill spread down Tye's spine, the world around him suddenly silent. Irrelevant. "Where?"

"The stable, I presume." The cool answer came from Katita, now standing beside them, her turquoise eyes cold, her blond hair gleaming in the setting sun. She snatched Rabbit's ear to pull the boy away. "At least that is where my cousins took this rubbish to discuss his recent activities. He must have escaped."

A flash of heat lit Tye's blood. "Let him go."

To Tye's relief, Katita released Rabbit's ear, her gaze turning slightly amused as she folded her arms over her chest. "Better?"

"Yes." Shoving past the princess, Tye started toward the stables.

"Stop." The amusement in Katita's voice was gone now. Stepping in front of Tye, she pressed her hand into the middle of his chest. "Leralynn must have interfered. Let the royals handle it as they see fit."

"Are you insane?" Tye fought the urge to grab and snap that slim wrist. His mind raced, his gaze darting between the princess and the stable. "Come with me and put a stop to whatever is happening, Katita."

"No." She closed the distance, her movement for once void of sensuality. "Leralynn interfered with *royals*, Tyelor. After today, I imagine she won't repeat the mistake." Her voice lowered, the soft threat raking like nails on slate. "Don't make the same mistake she just did."

Tye burst into the stables in time to hear a high-pitched male wail. This came from a doubled-over Lord Nolan, who, judging by his popping eyes and straining vocal cords, wouldn't be siring any children in the near future. Or ever.

Just beyond the downed Nolan, Lera had control of Puckler's back, her arm wrapped around the cadet's thick neck. Unable to reach the ground, Lera hung on to the choke while Puckler flung her about like an angry bear. Puckler's twin, Rik, circled the pair in search of an opening that his own twin wasn't giving him. Granted, given Puckler's increasingly darkening face due to lack of air, the mindless thrashing was understandable.

Stars. Lera was half the size of any one of them, and holding her own better than any Academy guardsman could have.

For a heartbeat, Tye's swell of pride for the fierce little tsunami made him hesitate to interfere. Then Puckler twisted around.

Welts and bruises flashed through the rips of Lera's tattered magenta dress, bits of manure covering her vibrant hair and flushed skin. Another bruise ran along her mouth, her lips swollen and bloody. She'd not been winning; she'd been surviving. And she was hurt.

Tye was already moving from across the stable when Rik finally managed to grab Lera's hair and haul her off Puckler. In the same motion, Rik slammed her chest-first into the wall so hard that the boards rattled. Without missing a beat, Puckler grabbed Lera's free arm with one hand, the other rubbing his reddened neck. With Puckler and Rik now pinning Lera to the wall, Lord Nolan snatched a thick leather girth from a hook.

Leralynn froze, the scent of her sudden terror filling the air—and kindling an explosion of primal violence inside Tye.

Tye's vision darkened. He was still a pace away when

Nolan swung—just as Puckler realized they were no longer alone and shouted a warning.

Tye discerned neither Puckler's words nor his twin's answer. Tye heard nothing but the pounding of his own heart as he grabbed Nolan's thick blond hair and shoved the bastard headfirst into the horses' drinking trough. And then Tye held him there, beneath the water, while the tall lord thrashed uselessly. In outrage. In fear. In desperation for air that Tye was never going to let him have.

The twins' eyes widened, the righteous excitement in their faces fading to disbelief.

Puckler shouted something. Lifted his hands. Stepped away from Lera.

Tye didn't know what Puckler said. Didn't hear. Didn't care. Not with Lera's frightened scent still spinning his head, the sight of the marvelous, ethereal creature who'd faced down three of the Academy's largest royals being made vulnerable.

Beneath Tye's grip, Nolan kicked wildly. Seeing his cousin's jerking spasms, Puckler swung a hammer-sized fist toward Tye's jaw.

Jerking Lord Nolan's head from the trough, Tye used the lord's face to intercept Pucker's blow. The crush of bone and spray of blood chilled the stable's air to ice. For a moment, no one moved, Nolan holding together his broken nose while Puckler stared at his own bloody fist.

Tye, his hand now free to curl into a fist, twisted about the battle scene, ready to finish the males. To rip their throats out with his teeth.

"Walk away." Lera's quiet voice skittered across the stable. Not aimed at Tye, he realized through his haze of protective instincts, but at the royals. "Move slowly. No running. No sudden moves."

The royal cousins glanced at each other once before obeying, and it was all Tye could do to keep himself from pouncing on the pathetic figures and clawing them to shreds. His chest heaved. Yes. He longed to hunt them down. To kill them. To protect Leralynn from anyone who dared harm her.

LERA

Choking down the pain and fear still filling my lungs, I wait until the doors close behind the escaping cadets before stepping toward Tye. The male's chest heaves, fiery hair damp with sweat, his green eyes still flashing with a primal fury. The fury is as much Tye's as that of the tiger he doesn't know he shifts into—the tiger he only started connecting with earlier this year.

"Tye?" I say softly.

The male finds my gaze, his own still unfocused. Still primal and savage and as dark as the blood that gushed from Nolan's broken nose. Unlike Tye, whose veil-covered mind remembers nothing of me, the tiger must still feel the mating bond pulling at his soul. Just as Shade's wolf does.

My breath hitches. Unlike Shade's wolf, Tye's tiger form recalls nothing of his fae partner even in Lunos. With the mortal lands further choking the magic, if Tye ever shifts, the resulting predator would think nothing of ripping half the Academy to bits and eating them raw. I can't let that happen.

"Tye? I-I'm all right." I swallow, forcing a smile into my

lie. Leaning against the wall for support, I try to ignore the throbbing as welts and cuts check in from all over my flesh. "I'm all right. It's over."

Tye shakes his head, his mane of red hair swooshing about him. When he steps toward me, his glazed eyes slowly regain their reason. Distantly, I notice that, unlike me, he's not dressed for dinner—he looks to have come straight from training, in a cut-off gray uniform tunic and black pants.

I hold very still. Doing nothing that might further wake the predator.

Tye blinks again, his gaze lucid, and it's all I can do to keep from burying my head in his shoulder. As if all the strength and courage I've borrowed have now fled. That's what I would do with my Tye—but this is not my Tye.

"Leralynn." Tye crouches beside me, his hands brushing my wrist. His perfect features are sharp with focus now, his silver earring glinting in the barn's low light. Concern and anxiety roll off him in waves of warm scent, the gaze that held murder moments earlier now focused entirely on gently probing my flesh. "How are ye, lass?"

"Sore." Very bloody sore. The bastards' crude attempt to turn me into a pony flashes in my memory, making my jaw clench. "It's mostly my pride that's injured."

"Why don't I believe you?" Tye asks, his thumb stroking a bead of blood from my lower lip. Penetrating green eyes brush my body, seeing every rip and welt and cut. The clean pine-and-citrus scent of him mixes with sweat—and determination.

Before I can move away, Tye snakes his arms around me and lifts me into the air. I gasp, struggling as I find myself held tightly against the male's broad chest.

"I-I can walk." I should walk.

Tye's arms tighten, his heart pounding so hard that I hear it through his chest. "You are currently wearing magenta strips of silk," he says, his light voice utterly at odds with his heartbeat. "While the Academy would no doubt enjoy the spectacle, I'd like to keep this little secret all to myself just now."

I open my mouth to protest, to ask where Tye thinks he's taking me, but shut it without speaking. I hurt. And for now, just being cared for is enough.

With most everyone in the dining hall, the grounds are near deserted. Wherever Nolan and twins ran off to, I see no trace of the royals as Tye navigates the convenient rows of trees and hedges he plainly has experience using as concealment. Five turns later, even I am lost as to our destination until the low stone bathhouse looms before us. The *men's* bathhouse.

"Wait!" My protest comes altogether too late as Tye shoulders the door open, crosses a locker-lined antechamber, and brings us into a large, softly lit room filled with sprawling bathing pools. From a heavily steaming pool in one corner to a tiny round one steeped with mugwort—which gives it approximately the smell and color of black tea—to a deep, clear pool that looks unheated and long enough to do laps. The thick wet steam caresses my skin, and I inhale a lungful of blissfully warm air. Unlike the female baths, where vases of spring flowers provide splotches of color amidst a white interior, the men's bath has patterns of smooth round river stones laid into the green tiled walls and around shelves holding soap and towels. The sloped floor takes advantage of a cleverly routed branch of the Great Falls river to easily circulate the water, while always-burning braziers keep hot water readily accessible.

Setting me down on the farthest pool's lip, Tye closes the drain and tips a flow of scalding-hot water to mix in with the burbling, cool liquid already there. His muscles flex and shift under his skin in the low lantern light. The bathing pool thus drawn, Tye pulls off first his boots, then my own, his deft hands moving with the skill of centuries spent undressing women.

"How did you know there was trouble?" I ask. Next to Tye's perfectly lithe movements and sweat-mussed hair made only more perfect by its wildness, I look like a tattered rat rolled in muck.

"I was training nearby and Rabbit fetched me. It didn't make Katita pleased at all." Tye adds the latter under his breath, as if the words are intended more for himself than me. "Pitting yourself alone against three royals—I don't know whether that makes you the bravest or most reckless Great Falls cadet. And I'll have you know, I currently hold the most reckless title, and I'd rather not give it up."

Tye was with Katita. A jolt of pain I've no right to feel twists my stomach. Free of the magic bonds, this Tye is kind and smart and brave—but he isn't mine. He's made that clear enough. Which is *good.* The farther we stay from each other, the less chance of me provoking the amulet.

Stripping down to his undershorts, Tye slips into the water, planting himself between my open thighs. I do everything I can not to stare at his bare torso—the broad flare of his pectorals and shoulders, the hard ridges of his abdomen, bulging even at rest, sun-kissed by many shirtless training sessions—but it's a losing battle. His calloused hand cups my cheek gently. "Let's see the damage, lass. From the little I caught at the end there, you've something to show for the encounter."

I open my mouth, but no words come out.

Taking my silence as consent, Tye pulls down the tatters still holding the top of my dress to my shoulders, letting my breasts tumble free—which, instead of making me rightfully furious, sends a shiver of excitement along my skin. Warm water swirls around my legs, reaching up my calf. When my arms come up to cover my breasts, Tye flashes me a quick grin. "You know that just makes me want to look closer?"

Face heating, I focus on the steam rising above the water in little curls. Curls that look so like the coarse hair I know is to be found around my companion's cock that I quickly realize I need to be looking elsewhere. But where?

Tye's fingers probe my ribs, his intense green gaze so focused on my body that my breath hitches. One white canine, dulled by the veil amulet's magic, scrapes his lower lip in concentration. When his hands slide around toward the front, slipping beneath my tender breasts, I bite my lip and try to pull away.

Tye shakes his head, dismissing my efforts. "I don't think anything is broken," he says, pearly drops of water running along the grooves of sculpted muscles. The focus of his gaze makes the rest of his broad, trained body even more beautiful, the tension singing beneath his skin sending vibrations right to my apex. His touch gentles. "But you've some bruises to match the night sky."

"Stop it." Pushing Tye back, I gather my dignity and slide off the pool's edge into the water—which has the opposite effect of what I'd intended. Instead of providing greater cover, the water that only reaches Tye's waist now slaps gently against my breasts, the soft bounce drawing a clear swallow from Tye. Adding to the mess, the remaining bottom of my dress yields to the water's pressure and billows up to my waist. The welts along my backside sting, but I dare not rub them just now. Dare not do anything that may bring us closer to the line we've decided not to cross.

Friends. We are friends. Not even that now. Acquaintances. Partners in crime. Tye came to my aid just as I came to Rabbit's. There is nothing more in this than that.

With a soft curse, Tye turns his gaze to the ceiling, drawing several deep breaths. When his attention returns to me, the male captures my waist. Sitting himself on an underwater bench, he draws me to stand between his legs. With him sitting and me between those corded thighs, our faces are level. "You are beautiful, lass," he growls softly. "So much that a man can't help wondering if you taste as good as you look."

Line. Not helping.

The thought of Tye's mouth on my sex is enough to make it clench. Ignoring the wetness slowly coating the inside of my channel, I splay my hand on Tye's broad chest, feeling the warm, velvety skin damp with steam, the muscles contracting beneath my fingers. "You are obnoxious, Tye. Or have you forgotten that we've no interest in bedding each other?"

A shadow passes over Tye's face, gone so quickly that I'm not sure I saw it. "Aye, but if I stop being a prat, you might notice that I've been busy removing the rest of your clothes."

I blink, realizing the male has, in fact, been busy handling my dress, and now lifts the remaining fabric over my head. I jerk backwards, which proves a mistake when Tye's large hands close on both sides of my bruised bottom.

I yelp.

The amusement in the male's face fades, his whole body tensing as he beholds the full results of the royals' handiwork. "I am going to rip them apart limb from limb."

I reach for the soap, determined to be wearing at least something, even if it's only bubbles. "I don't imagine princess Katita would thank you for it."

"That might be the best part," Tye says, his earring glinting dangerously, a match to the silver flecks in his eyes. This close, I can see his constellation of freckles and suddenly long to trace them with my lips like I used to do in Lunos. His fingers trace the tender bruise around the curves of my cheeks, my resulting shudder having nothing to do with pain. "Do you want to know what I'm thinking now?" he whispers roughly.

"No." My voice comes out in a croak. My sex clenches around the emptiness inside it, my whole body longing for Tye —the real Tye, my mate. Longing to finish what we started against the tree. The heat pooling between my thighs is enough to warm the bath with no help from the brazier. My pulse quickens, the aching along the insides of my thighs radiating through my core and burning away all common sense.

Tye's teeth flash, leaning forward until his lips touch my ear. "I am thinking that I can't stand the scent of those royals on your skin. And that if I don't dive into a frigid bath right now, I'm going to lose the battle to replace their scent with mine. Very, very fully."

13

TYE

What in the names of all the bloody stars did Tye think he was saying?

The truth.

The wrong truth. The impermissible truth. Beneath the water, Tye's cock strained so hard that it actually pulsated with his rising heartbeat. The bruises covering the girl's skin looked even more livid than before, and the thought of someone—some male—having laid his hands on her waking a primal beast inside Tye's chest. The same beast that smelled Lera's arousal as he towered over her small form, tracing her curves with his hungry gaze. Another moment and Tye would lose all control altogether.

And that wouldn't be fair. Not after what he'd done to Tiga.

Releasing Lera quickly, Tye curled his hands around the edge of the pool. Lifting his chin toward the ceiling, he forced air into his lungs. Focused on the sounds of gently gurgling water and dripping condensation echoing off the tiled walls. Anything to relieve the hold on his shaft.

It didn't work. No. Everything inside Tye suddenly demanded his scent—yes, *scent*—all over the lass before him. Needed it. And the part of his mind that had any rational thought left, the one telling him that men did not do such things, was quickly becoming irrelevant.

He had to go. Run. That was the only way this would end without him inside Lera, taking her so hard that her screams echoed from the bathhouse walls.

Lera stepped forward, her knee bumping against Tye's throbbing shaft. The sudden jolt of sensation made him leap to his feet.

A glaze settled over Lera's deep-chocolate eyes. Her nostrils flared delicately with her quickened breaths, her engorged nipples tantalizing atop the gently bouncing breasts. Even the light touch of freckles along her perfect cheekbones was bloody arousing. She'd been so blazing hot when he'd fingered her against the tree, the thought of what that channel would feel like around his shaft stole Tye's air.

"Tye?" Lera breathed, her fingers touching the crest of his hip. The sensation went right to his engorged cock.

"I wasn't kidding about the scent," Tye said breathlessly.

"I know." The way Leralynn said it made Tye think she really did know. Understood it in a way that he couldn't himself.

That did it. What little self-control Tye had remaining fell apart as a deep possessive instinct had him gripping Lera's head.

Tye pressed his mouth over Lera's, her lips parting hungrily to let Tye's tongue slip inside. He'd intended as much. Planned to savor her sweet lilac taste. To linger there and then muster control and pull away. Right up until Tye tasted the drop of blood on Lera's split lip and felt his world blur around the edges.

Tye cupped Lera's face, holding her steady as he plunged into her sweet mouth, claiming every tantalizing taste of her. His. His. His. Tye took Lera deeper, swallowing the moan that escaped her mouth, the sound vibrating through his aroused nerves.

Her fingers dug into his back, pulling him closer. The molten heat from Lera's mouth reached so deep inside him that Tye's heart raced, tripping over its own beat. Deeper. Deep enough to kindle a flame that had lain cold since Tiga's death.

Cupping Lera's lush thighs, Tye hoisted her up onto his waist. The girl's legs wrapped instinctively around his hips, her toned muscles linking their bodies like pieces on a perfect puzzle. *Stars.* Such a small, strong, vibrant creature.

Lera's foot kicked at the top of Tye's undershorts, struggling to pry off the wet cloth. Tongue still savoring her mouth, Tye released one hand to loosen his front flap, his cock springing free so hard that he and Lera both inhaled at the sudden smack.

With his hand still low, Tye brushed it along Lera's opening, discovering a wet, warm slickness that made him groan with need. Tightening the arm holding Lera against him, Tye plunged a finger into her channel.

The needful moan that evoked was the most beautiful sound Tye had ever heard.

His second finger went in, teasing and stretching her blazing tightness. A third.

Lera's channel clenching around him, the girl broke the kiss with a frustrated growl. "I. Want. *You.*"

Tye attempted to chuckle—he prided himself on making women soar, drawing out their pleasure and frustration for a climax that would shatter their world—but the attempt came out raspy and strained. He couldn't play. Tye needed to take her. Now. Fast and hard and permanent. It wasn't just his cock, with its engorged shaft pulsating in anguish, but something much deeper that demanded he connect. That he *mate*, as if he were a wild predator instead of a man.

Panting, he gazed up into Lera's face. Her muscles strained, her heart pounding so fiercely, he could see the pulse at the side of her neck. A droplet of sweat beaded her temple, close to her glazed brown eyes. The thought of being inside all that heat and power drove Tye as mad as Lera's lilac scent, which spurred his heart every time he inhaled.

Flashing her teeth, Lera bent her head and bit Tye's ear. Hard.

He roared, his voice echoing around the tiled room, and buried himself deep in Lera with a single stroke.

14

LERA

I gasp, suddenly unable to fill my lungs. Despite longing for the very cock that's suddenly inside me, the sheer size of Tye's intrusion makes my whole body tighten. Too big. Too long. I want to scream even as my hips rock against the male hungrily. My sex clenches around the thick, thick shaft, finally full after days of mindless craving.

Tye's hands grip my bottom roughly, the sudden sting as he lifts me up and down along him turning to molten pleasure that curls my toes. I push my hips forward, greedy for more friction. A familiar undeniable need to hold the connection between Tye and me consumes my body and echoes in Tye's dilating eyes.

Not want. Not desire. But a *need* for a mate's connection, the kind that broke many otherwise productive evenings back in Lunos. Broke many beds too. The impossibility of feeling the mating bond through the veil flitters inside my head like a small annoying fly. My body little cares for what's possible, only for what exists.

I breathe in the pine-and-citrus scent of the powerful male

inside me, the *slap slap slap* of wet skin hitting skin echoing through the bathing chamber. Each thrust hits a spot so deep that the vibrations spider through my core, raising me to a greater height from which to fall. My heart quickens in rhythm to the pulsing cock slamming into my channel.

Thrust. Thrust. Thrust. Hard. Fast. Deep.

And yet not enough. Still not enough.

"Tye." I don't know whether I mean his name in plea or command. Just that after so long apart, the primal part of my soul is so very ravenous.

The male's glazed eyes flicker, and he claims my mouth in response, a clash of tongue and lips. He slaps my bottom, the shocking sting magnified by the water and abused flesh, and swallows my guttural moan, never slowing his deep thrusts. My taut nerve endings ride the wave of sensation, a tsunami that turns pain to pleasure to desperate need.

I try to retreat from the onslaught. Tye holds me firm and thrusts deeper than ever.

My muscles spasm, clamping around his cock. My mind blanks, the coming release inevitable. With the next heartbeat, the wave I'm riding finally shatters. Pulsing waves of dizzying pleasure radiate from my throbbing sex, making my breath race. Tye's thick warmth fills my channel.

"Stars." I mean to scream, but the words come out as a panting gasp. Tye's arms come up to support me, his lips brushing mine in a kiss so sweet that I let myself relax into it, savoring its—*ow.*

"You bit me." I pull back, looking indignantly at the male.

"Did I?" Amusement dances in Tye's eyes, their glaze sharpening to a roguish emerald focus. A warning bell tolls in the back of my mind, growing louder when I try to get down and find myself trapped against the muscular male, his arms as implacable as steel. Tye licks his lips, his gaze brushing down my naked body. "I just recalled that I meant to taste you, lass. I think I'll take that treat now."

My fuzzy mind tries and fails to follow Tye's meaning. Now? What does he mean now? After the climax of moments ago, my whole body feels like a lump of dough. My exhausted sex stirs and—my eyes widen. Not only is Tye's shaft still inside my channel, but it is hardening again.

I gasp as Tye hoists me out of the water and lays me flat on my back at the bathing pool's smooth edge, my backside hanging free over the lip. Tye's strong hands stroke the skin along the inside of my thighs, cupping my bottom gently before pulling my knees apart and stroking the folds of my exposed sex. He licks his fingers slowly.

"Mmmm," says Tye.

That quickly, I want his hardness right back inside me.

Green eyes dancing with a roguish flame, Tye hoists my legs atop his muscled shoulders and blows a long hot breath over my apex. Jolts of sensation zing along my thighs and calves and toes, making me squirm.

Tye's hands clamp along my thighs, restraining me in place. A moment later, his tongue replaces the breath, trailing luxuriously along my folds. Flicking his tongue over the hood covering my bud, Tye swirls it around as if savoring a sweet.

A tiny vibration starts deep inside Tye's chest, and I suddenly realize the male is purring. Him or else the tiger coiled so tightly beneath the magic's shackles that he cannot escape—yet still wishes to share in his partner's pleasure. In all our pleasures.

I let out a contented sigh. The moment I do, the bastard between my thighs scrapes his teeth along my engorged apex.

The world blinks. My nerves rouse with sharp need that takes my breath. Makes me so wet that the dampness tickles warmly as it slithers down my thigh. My sex clenches, the fire exploding between my folds unbearable after the release I had earlier. I flex my hips. Shift my bottom. Buck.

Tye's iron hold keeps me in place, an added punishing nip to the inside of my thigh warning against further squirming about. Ordering me to endure each glorious, maddening *flick flick flick* of his skilled tongue. *Stars.* The throbbing inside me is already echoing along my spine. How can my body take more?

Not that Tye seems to care, his tongue moving ruthlessly over me. Left side of my bud. Right. Each touch sends zings of intense sensation. Left again again again before stopping a single rough stroke away from toppling me over the edge of the abyss I cling to.

My hands dig uselessly into the floor, finding no purchase. With Tye's powerful arms holding my legs against his shoulders, I can't move. Can't do anything but feel each and every touch. And lick. And *suckle.*

A mangle of scream and groan escapes my lungs, need raking each inch of my skin. The pressure inside me is so intense that my muscles tremble uncontrollably, my breath coming in quick little gasps I can't slow. One more lap of Tye's tongue and I know I will tumble in the abyss again. I brace myself.

The lap never comes. Instead, Tye's fingers claim my channel.

With a frustrated moan, I clench greedily around the intrusion. The skilled callused fingers tease my channel, forcing my desperation higher still while always stopping a hair short of release no matter how much I try to rock against them.

"Please," I finally whimper. "I can't. Tye, please."

Tye returns his tongue to my bud with a growl, his fingers still sliding back and forth inside me. *Flick-thrust, flick-thrust,* the duet of tongue and fingers plays me like a tuned violin, plucking a new sensation with each precise touch. My thighs press in, blocked by Tye's wide shoulders. *Flick-thrust. Flick-thrust.*

The approaching abyss widens its maw. My whole body shakes.

"Now," Tye says against my bud. With a self-satisfied growl, the male takes my whole engorged apex between his lips and sucks.

Need explodes in shards of howling bliss, a blaze that tightens every muscle in my body. Again. Again. The spasms come in waves, one crashing atop the next until I can barely draw breath into tightened lungs. The molten heat between my legs spreads through my backside and spine, rolling down the backs of my legs with pleasure so intense, it hurts. My head swims, my core sated down to every tiny crevice, even as my body shudders in the aftershocks.

As the last one subsides, I realize Tye has pulled me off the ledge and now cradles me gently against his chest. The feel of his warm cheek resting atop my head is so perfect that I know I could stay like this forever and be absolutely content.

And yet we both know I can't.

LERA

"In Tye's defense, he said he wouldn't *bed* you," says Arisha the following morning, eyes trained pointedly on the sprawl of papers on her desk, a faint pink blush rising up her cheeks. She's told me that cadets couple up at the Academy all the time, in spite of it being technically against the rules—which doesn't make it any less scandalous to my by-the-book roommate. "And it sounds like there was no bed in sight. Does this mean you two are——"

"No. We are friends. Possibly friends. Maybe ones who enjoy a tumble in the sheets now and then." I cringe, thinking of the searing look Katita gave Tye and me from across the cobblestone courtyard when we snuck out of the men's bathhouse—our sex-glazed eyes damning us as surely as my borrowed-from-the-baths clothing. Was it simply bad fortune that the princess happened upon us as the Academy was bedding down for the night—or something more? The notion that Katita may have been waiting, watching for us, fills me with a new type of dread. I've been in the mortal lands for less than a week and have already crossed one of the most powerful people here. For an interloper who is supposed to be keeping her head down, I'm doing a damn poor job of it. I clear my suddenly dry throat. "Anyway, this Tye doesn't know me well enough to even consider anything else. Now, how do I look?"

Turning about in the center of our narrow dorm room, I display the dress uniform the quartermaster's courier delivered for the Academy's monthly parade inspection. The short-cropped red vest sits snugly across my chest, the gold trimming shining between the double rows of buttons. Lower, the pants flare in a bow to feminine sensuality, the material flowing along with each movement. A glorious mix of military discipline and courtly elegance. Neither of which I displayed last night.

"Perfect. It shows off your swollen lip in the best possible light." Arisha's head never comes up from the notes and sketches littering her desk. "I don't for the life of me understand why normally sane and reasonable people lose their wits for a day each month to have the whole Academy turn up in dress uniforms on the courtyard lawn. It literally accomplishes nothing with the exception of seeing whether the pants still bloody fit."

"There is something to be said for gathering everyone together," I say, recalling River's crowning ceremony in Slait a few months back. For all River's stoic tolerance of Autumn's elaborate planning, when he finally strode out to the dais to take his vows, the energy of the court hummed so loudly that it made my very blood sing. And not just my blood. I turn quickly, lest Arisha looks up to read too many delicious memories in my face—not the least of them being the sight of River striding back into the antechamber, his epaulettes gleaming with the same molten heat as his eyes.

"There is something to be said for seeing Tyelor in his

dress red." Arisha shuffles her journals. "Let's return to what happened with you two last night again. For scientific study."

My eyes narrow. "Are you just seeking gory details, or is this actually helpful in working out the veil problem?"

"Both." This time, Arisha does flash me a sly grin. "Plus, as I little expect to be bedding anyone—much less the upcoming Prowess champion—any time soon…or ever, I'm entitled to live vicariously through you." She frowns. "Wait, no. Being you would mean dealing with all four of them, wouldn't it?—Because I don't want to spend an extra moment in a room with Coal or River, forget a bed. As for Shade… Well, he was a swoon, but now I can't look at the healer without remembering the hair his wolf shed onto the clean linen." She shifts in her chair. "Now that I think on it, I've the better end of the bargain."

"They aren't as they seem," I say, weaving a thick braid down the left side of my head. Despite all that happened the previous day, I feel better than I have in some time. Energized. Alive. "For a time there yesterday, Tye and I connected the way we're meant to. It was the same with Coal. Coupling has always woken a deeper magic between us, even when I was human. It was how I was first able to harness my power."

"Well, shall I write 'bed the headmaster early and often' at the top of our to-do list, or can you recall that one on your own?" Arisha blinks at me innocently, and I throw a shirt at her from my dresser top. It falls short, snagging on her bedpost. Her mischievous grin fades as she seems to realize something, clicking her tongue. "I wonder if we've not been going about this the wrong way."

"I've been going about things the wrong way so much that the laws of probability say I should have stumbled into something correct by now," I mutter. "What are you referring to?"

"What you just said, about the males not being as they seem. Everything I've read about the veil amulet and what you've told me of yourself contradicts that statement. The veil doesn't change someone's essence, only their explanation for it. Both Lera of Lunos and Lera of Osprey had the same childhood emotional experience—just dressed up in different clothes."

"So?"

"So, instead of waiting until the males regain their memories, maybe you need to accept their personas as they are. Stop calling them 'not real' and forge bonds with these males who are here now, frightening as it may be. You five may need each other's strength long before a magical key drops from the skies to reverse the veil."

"I'll think about it," I say, trying and failing to sound nonchalant. Tye is right. I can't lie to save my life. Everything about Arisha's theory is bloody reasonable, except the one gap that is so wide, not even Tye's athletic prowess can leap over it: the males' new personas have no room for me in their busy lives. The energy I gained last night starts to fizzle.

"You should talk to River," Arisha says.

I swallow, my gaze searching for somewhere else it needs to be just now. Outside on the swaying branches or maybe the book on my desk in case a strong desire to study should suddenly strike me. My back stiffens in spite of myself, and the smile I force onto my face feels like it's cracking through dry lips. Stupid. I clear my throat. "Talk to him about what?"

"About the fact that you all know—from that first time you went over the wall—that there are magical threats to the Academy. That you want to be a part of the solution. He can't tell others about the magic for fear of unwanted attention on the Academy—or worse, prosecution from fae hunters—so it limits his options. Let him invite you—" She stops, her eyes narrowing on my face, on the flush that's probably rising there. "River intimidates you."

"I'm not afraid of my own mate." My jaw tightens, the only defense I have against my pounding heart. "I refuse to be." I pause. "It's just that, although River has always been our quint commander, before now, it's simply meant that he had the final word on our missions, not on what time I need to be in my room."

Rising from her chair, Arisha wraps her arms around me, her frizzy hair tickling my cheek as her comforting scent of parchment and ink calms my nerves. "Now, you listen to me, Leralynn of…of wherever you're from," she says, pulling me away enough to look at me over her round glasses. "River is the best deputy headmaster this Academy has ever had. You don't know what it was like with only that weasel Sage here. What I'm saying is that River is a good man just as he is a good male. That's one."

Something I didn't know was raw inside my soul quiets as I nod. "What's two?"

Arisha squeezes my shoulder, her small pointy features soft with kindness. "Two is that you really are a cadet now. Not River's equal. And we are *all* a little terrified of the deputy headmaster. You feeling the same as the rest of us just means the veil is working as intended—not that something is wrong with you, or him, or the bonds you had in Lunos. Which brings me to thing three."

"You really like lists, don't you?"

"Thing three," Arisha continues as if I hadn't spoken, "is that if you intend to be digging into Coal's nightmares, and Shade's losing time and all the other dark little festering wounds that make the males uncomfortable, they will likely dig into yours as well. So consider yourself warned."

"Yes, ma'am." The smile I give Arisha must be genuine, because the girl nods and walks back to her books.

"Now, on the less romantic side of things, I think there is a Yocklol tree near the Academy."

"Is there a reason I should care about a tree?" I stride over to look at Arisha's drawing.

Arisha does not meet my eyes. "It isn't truly a tree. It just looks like one," she says, laying out a spread of several pencil drawings depicting burns similar to what I saw on Rusty's forearm, as well as a rough sketch of a yellow-looking trunk with an eye in the middle of it. Scrawled notes, lists, and calculations line the margins of the pictures. "But it moves about."

A sudden chill runs along my spine as I look at the blight. It is precisely the type of magical corruption I'd told Gavriel I won't be fighting. Can't fight. Not without the others.

"If I'm right, Yocklol is what burned a guard recently," Arisha continues. "Shade had to amputate the man's arm last night."

My hand closes over my mouth, my chest tightening. Rusty. The young guardsman from the stables who'd smelled of wrongness. When I told Gavriel I had no intention of prancing around to put out whatever magical fires he found, I'd not thought about the costs. There is no winning, it seems. If I turn into a one-woman stealth operation, I'll be pitting myself against the males instead of working toward reuniting us. If I do nothing, innocents get hurt.

Reaching over Arisha's shoulder, I gather the papers into a heap with more roughness than I'd intended. "You shouldn't have these out of the library. First, it's disgusting. And second, it is about as far from safe as it gets. If the wrong person catches sight of your drawings—" I don't even have to finish the sentence for understanding to dawn on Arisha's face.

Sometimes she's so like Autumn that it hurts—the girl can think her way out of a locked box, but then trip over that same box on her way out of the room. "In fact, we'll drop this horror trove off with Gavriel before the parade."

Taking the papers from my hands, Arisha expertly knocks them against the table, arranging everything into a neat pile that would have taken me a quarter hour to replicate. How can a girl who has a place for every pen and sheet of parchment be equally incapable of taming her hair into anything resembling braids? I reluctantly pick up my amulet from my desk—with Arisha in the know, it's been a relief to take breaks from it in our bedchamber—and I fasten it around my neck. The weight of magic settles over me instantly, making my skin too tight, my body too heavy and awkward.

Winding around the densely ivied walls of the reflection garden, Arisha and I step onto the grand cobblestoned courtyard to find it already filling with a sea of red dress uniforms waiting for the ceremony to start. Voices echo gaily off the high stone walls surrounding us, the parade having not yet forced everyone into silent order. Bright morning sunlight glints off the keep's many glass windows, and the ten Continental Alliance kingdoms' flags fly from its cornices. Sparrows flitting about from rooftop to ground give it all the lighthearted atmosphere of a festival.

My immortal sight lets me make out the details of River standing on the grand keep steps, towering over everyone about him—especially Headmaster Sage, who stands with his shoulders hunched and coughs into a handkerchief, his bald head almost glowing in the light. Each time someone walks close to the steps, the moment they note River's presence becomes obvious in the slight faltering of steps and hasty bows.

Arisha and I skirt the edge of the courtyard, aiming for

the library before the horn signals the ceremony's commencement—a ceremony I've no notion of how to follow. "There is so little thought to it that even Rik and Puckler can manage," Arisha promises. "Stand prettily in a line while the instructors strut about like—well, much like *him.*" She rolls her eyes toward the approaching male.

"Braids, do you recall my solution to supply calculations last week?" Striding up to us in the male version of dress reds, Tye is breathtaking in a tailed coat that shows off his taut stomach and broad chest. When his gaze touches my face, he swallows, his silence a tension-filled string of memories of last night. Sleeping on it doesn't seem to have made Tye any more comfortable with the intensity of our coupling than he was in the dark of evening outside the dorm rooms last night. Clearing his throat, Tye bows to me, his attention returning to Arisha. "Because your hair looks about as well put together."

My blood heats. If Tye regrets our evening together, he has no right to take it out on my friend. I step into his path.

Tye steps around me, his movement feline quick. "Turn around," he tells Arisha, the fingers I know too well yanking her hair ribbon loose. "Let's see if I can't do a bit better."

Arisha's face turns the color of her coat, her mix of surprise and pleasure tickling my nose so strongly that I sneeze, blinking in my own bewilderment. What's Tye about now?

Giving no indication of anything beyond his signature cockiness, Tye runs his dexterous fingers between Arisha's frizzy brown strands, separating the hair into three neat bunches. "Maybe we can try one braid today," he says. "It will be a good look for you. And maybe easier to…err…count. Just remember, anything not inside the braid is out of place."

Arisha shrugs as if she couldn't care less, but her eyes fight to stay open under the relaxing pressure of Tye's hands.

Knowing those fingers—and exactly what they can do—I can almost feel them on my own scalp.

...And the hint of a smile on Tye's lips says the bastard knows that.

I open my mouth to call Tye a bastard, but close it quickly at the sight of the approaching figure.

"Well, isn't this pretty?" Katita says, the red silk of her pants swaying from long legs and perfect hips. With her inky-black lashes and glistening blonde hair, the princess looks as feminine as she does powerful. "Your bloody lip goes well with that uniform, Osprey. Perhaps you should wear marks more often."

"Is there something you needed?" I stride forward, cutting off Katita's path.

"I need to know which part of keeping your hands off my things your empty mind found confusing." Katita smiles, stepping so close that her rose-scented perfume stings my nose. Her voice drops. "You made a grave mistake yesterday." Katita's gaze flickers from my lip to the space over my right shoulder, where I can hear Arisha arguing with Tye over ribbons. "And there will be a penalty for it."

"Noted," I say, pushing past Katita as if she'd just warned me about a new divot in the road. "Excuse me."

"I'm not done." Katita grabs my upper arm, her grip firm and trained. For a human. For someone who's not had Coal as an instructor for the past year, no matter what his veil amulet tells her.

"Yes, you are." Clamping my hand over Katita's wrist, I put my thumb between her first two knuckles and twist. My heart pounds hard and steady, the simmering fury condensing to ice.

The girl drops to her knees beneath the pressure. A scream escapes her as she tries to free herself from my hold.

One flailing attempt at a strike bounces off my thigh. The next—

"Arisha!" My warning lands at the same time as Katita's wild leg sweep. It misses me entirely but catches Arisha midstride as she rushes to my aid.

With a gasp, Arisha windmills her arms for balance, the books and papers in her hands flying into the air before scattering across the cobblestones. Papers with drawings of sclices and Yocklol trees and fae. Papers so dangerous that I made Arisha bring them with us to drop off at the library for her own safety—all fluttering open in the chill breeze before the princess of Ckridel. My heart stops.

LERA

*A*risha's face pales. She scurries to collect the fallen documents, tripping on her own billowing pants in the process. When Tye trots over to help her, the pictures laid plain before him turn his scent from concern to utter, unfettered fury. *Challengers have been barred from the Prowess Trials for lesser reasons than meddling in fae craft,* Tye had told me in the stable. He'd not wanted to so much as discuss Rusty's injury, much less be caught consorting with fae sympathizers.

Beneath my hold, I make out Katita's gaze likewise tracking the documents through a glaze of pain. The entitled cruelty in the princess's eyes freezes, morphing slowly to a very different type of hatred.

"Fae craft." Katita hisses at Arisha as Tye jams the remaining books into my friend's chest and backs away. "I knew you were poison."

"Katita—" My voice is breathless, my pounding heart making it hard to think. To come up with an explanation. A plea. Anything. *Stars.* This isn't how my staying clear of magic was supposed to go, with others pulled into the line of fire.

"I will see a noose around her neck. AHH!" Katita howls over a soft snap that I feel as much as hear beneath my hands. My preternatural fae strength rearing its head right when I least needed it.

Gasping and releasing the wrist I've just accidentally broken, I step away from the princess, who is now curled around her hand. The blood rushing through my ears is as loud as a waterfall. From the corner of my eye, I see the guards running toward us, hear someone shouting for help. I can feel the stunned, quiet courtyard around us as our commotion ripples through the crowd, the somber faces pressing in from all sides.

"Fall into parade formation, all of you," one of the instructors shouts to the mass of perfect uniforms, the other picking up the call to form the cadets into lines. Keeping them busy despite the glances they try to steal our way. When Tye takes a step to join the lines, Katita bares her teeth at him.

"You stay," the princess says, nodding to a guard who cuts off Tye's path. "You are a part of this too."

For a second, my instincts roar for me to bolt, but then a pair of iron-hard hands grips my wrists from behind, Coal's metallic scent informing me that I am not going anywhere.

"Get Commander River," Coal snaps at one of the approaching guards. "And Shade."

"And Headmaster Sage," Katita says, raising her face. "I've a matter for him. Please tell him I invoke a tribunal."

WITHIN MINUTES, we're crossing the courtyard in front of two hundred sets of heavy, curious eyes and climbing the wide, flaring steps to the keep. A procession of instructors and guards and us. Coal walks beside me as if ready to tackle me to the ground at the slightest misstep, an ironic echo of our march through the woods four days ago.

My mind tells me I'm in trouble—very real trouble—even as my heart whispers that it isn't so. Can't be so. My males are here, they know me in their cores, they'll recognize me when it matters most.

One step ahead, Arisha sobs, the breaths heavy from the mix of fear and the never-ending climb up the steep twisting stairs to the top of the tower. I wish I could comfort her somehow, touch her hand, anything, but we're separated by a cluster of tall armored bodies. Katita, having refused to be taken to the infirmary at once, is pale but holds her back straight while two guards gently keep her steady. Tye is silent.

The passing minutes are punctuated by nothing but racing thoughts and heaving breaths as a dozen sets of feet climb to their destination. At the head of the group, Sage coughs into his handkerchief, stopping on several of the landings to clear his lungs before proceeding. Upon reaching the final floor, a pair of guards steps forward to swing open the double door into what must be the Academy's equivalent of the throne room.

In contrast to River's neat, practical study, with its wooden paneling and small crackling fire, Headmaster Sage's office showcases tapestry-covered walls, intricately carved gold-gilded chairs and a heavy desk so polished that it reflects the torchlight sconces bathing the room in shifting light. Sitting behind his desk, Sage points to a worn spot on the carpet, where Arisha, Katita, Tye, and I are supposed to stand.

When Tye doesn't move, Coal shoves him to the carpet. Giving me a cold gaze, Tye steps as far away from me as the space allows. As if it's my fault that he is caught up in all this. And maybe it is. If I'd not turned my back on Gavriel, I'd have known what Arisha was researching. Kept it out of our room. Taken care of the damn Yocklol tree.

River jerks his head at the guards, clearing the room of our escorts. Coal leans against the door, arms crossed over a broad chest. His chiseled face is hard. Cold. River steps back to stand beside Sage's chair, his stormy gray eyes and beautiful sculpted face as implacable as ever. To them, I'm just another unruly student—perhaps the most unruly they've ever had the displeasure of contending with.

Before anyone can speak, a confident knock sounds twice against the doorframe. Shade lets himself in at Sage's bark of acknowledgment. The healer has a satchel slung over his shoulder, the gold of his dress uniform bringing out the sun-kissed bronze of his skin and length of his dark lashes that are too beautiful to be on a male. Shade's glistening hair is plaited back, his yellow eyes somehow adding warmth to the room without even trying.

"With your permission, Headmaster Sage," Shade steps around me to lay a gentle hand on Katita's shoulder, "I would like the girl sitting down while whatever this is about rolls out."

"Of course, do take care of the princess," says Sage in his pinched, wheezing voice. "However, as she is the one to have invoked a tribunal, I will require she speaks." He shifts in his seat to better address Katita, who is now trying to refuse Shade's insistence that she sit on an ottoman. "Princess Katita. It is most...unusual...to have a cadet request such a meeting. I, of course, have nothing but the greatest respect for King Zenith and his throne. How might I be of service to his daughter?"

River shifts his weight, the movement nearly unnoticeable except for the waves of displeasure rolling off him. "If I may," he says, his voice even, "it appears that two cadets had an altercation just now, which led to the injury we see. An unfortunately not unique incident amongst youth. For the consistency of Academy discipline—and to avoid the appearance of special treatment that students from other kingdoms might read into this meeting—may I propose that I oversee the matter?"

"My request has nothing to do with the squabble, sirs," Katita says quickly, shrugging at her broken wrist as if it were hardly material to the matter at hand. "I've discovered that Leralynn of Osprey meddles with fae craft and appears to have co-opted Arisha of Tallie and Tyelor of Blair onto the same path. I ask they be turned over to the authorities in Grayson for further investigation."

My breath stops. Beside me, Arisha gives a strained sort of gasp. Sage sputters into his handkerchief for so long, I'm certain he is buying himself time to think. Only River's face remains utterly devoid of expression as he clasps his hands behind his back and stares down at Katita. "Your proof?" he says levelly.

"My initial suspicions were roused four days ago, when Leralynn of Osprey claimed possession of a medallion with what appeared to me as fae-crafted runes," Katita says smoothly. "I dismissed the notion at the time, as you, Commander River, seemed to have recognized the disk."

Beside me, air catches in Arisha's throat.

Shooting Arisha a quick glance, Katita returns her attention to River. "The unnatural effect Leralynn appeared to have on Tyelor of Blair further bothered me, sir. In retrospect, I believe Leralynn may have used fae craft to coerce him into associating himself with the disk as well as making other choices that are of benefit to Leralynn to Tyelor's detriment. However, that was only the seed of my suspicion. The proof came just moments ago, when I caught

Leralynn's roommate carrying fae craft documents. If left unchecked, I fear she will summon the beasts depicted."

Katita gestures to Arisha's papers, which River retrieves from my friend's hands. For a few moments, no one says a word, the sketches laid out on Sage's desk speaking for themselves. Finally, River taps his finger on one of the sclice drawings, dark brows drawn in thought. "This is a likeness of the hog beasts Leralynn of Osprey assisted us in putting down a few days back, sir," says River. "I agree the creatures are not of this world and question Leralynn's judgment in describing them to her artistic roommate, but she certainly isn't trying to summon the things."

Thank you, River. The wave of relief hitting me is so strong that I nearly sway.

Katita's chin rises. "You mean these hog things have already appeared near here?"

"Yes," says River.

"No," says Sage, before pursing his lips at the obvious conflict of words. "What I mean is that there is no longer a problem, Your Highness. The situation was handled swiftly, leaving no danger to the students. King Zenith can be assured of that."

"With due respect, sirs, then this is the *second* confirmed incident of fae craft that is tied directly to Leralynn of Osprey," says Katita. "After two centuries of no problems, we have two within a week of her arrival."

"The second?" Sage asks, taking the bait.

"I make a habit of visiting injured guards, sir," says Katita, the stark similarity to what River and Autumn do back in Slait slicing deep into my gut, though I imagine Katita's motives may be somewhat more calculating. "This morning, I spoke to the young man named Rusty who lost his arm. It appears that several days ago, Rusty scratched his arm on patrol. Upon returning to the stable, Rusty ran into Leralynn, who was mucking stalls as per her punishment detail. Rusty admitted to acting in a manner not befitting a gentleman, making crude comments regarding Leralynn's body. In retaliation, Leralynn insisted on meddling with the small injury he sustained—which started growing worse before the guard's very eyes. Unnaturally worse. The spread of magic-rooted corruption continued until the boy lost his arm late yesterday evening. Tyelor was in the stable at the time. I imagine he can vouch for the account—unless he played a larger part than witness in the events."

"No." My blood simmers, my hands curling into fists. "Rusty was hurt, and his partner was pressuring the boy to downplay the injury." My voice rises with each word, and it's an effort of will to rein in my tone. "I looked at the wound. I didn't cause it. And Tye helped ensure the boy went to the infirmary."

Sage coughed into his handkerchief, shifting through the paper laid out before him. "And yet your roommate carries images of the wound, along with predictions of its spread and notes on the magic that causes the blight." He holds up his hand. "Commander River, did you not issue a decree that not so much as the word *fae* was to be uttered in my Academy?"

"I did, sir," says River.

Sage sighs, rubbing his face. "Then it is safe to presume that this isn't an accidental bit of research."

Bile rises up my throat.

Katita nods, a shawl of triumph settling over her shoulders as she sweeps the room with regal gaze before focusing her attention right back on the small man sitting behind the large desk. "With all that, Headmaster Sage, I request Leralynn of Osprey be taken before a magistrate for further investigation and trial immediately. I believe Arisha and Tyelor are likely victims of her wiles and not true accomplices, but that is for the court to determine." Katita raises her delicate chin, standing tall despite her pallor. Her voice drops. "To be clear, my lords. I speak now not as an Academy cadet, but the heir to the Ckridel throne, which you all have pledged your lives to."

"None of this is true," I hear myself saying. What the bloody hell am I supposed to say? My breath halts, the tension in the room vibrating like the string of a violin. The males —*my* males—are silent. Willing to protect me no more than I was willing to protect the mortal realm.

No. Something. I have to be able to do something to save Arisha and Tye at least. I will do something.

Beside me, Arisha grips my hands, hers damp with sweat. "You can't do anything, Lera," she whispers, her voice shaking. "Katita is the heir to the throne. She can do as she wishes."

"Lieutenant Coal," Sage says, his nasally voice filling the chamber. "Take them into custody. We are an academic body, not a court. The magistrate can work this out."

Coal steps forward, his ice-filled blue eyes meeting mine. I wonder what he makes of having bedded me in the cave. Whether he regrets the entanglement now. Whether he feels anything at all. Coal's hand reaches for my wrist.

The roar that sounds from the back of the chamber has nothing human about it. My heart stops, the room in a momentary silence. Then Arisha, Katita, and Sage all scream in unison as a large gray wolf pounces on Coal's chest, knocking the male away.

1 7

LERA

Coal stumbles back, drawing his sword in a single motion as a new terror rushes through me. Voices rise in explanation. Katita screaming, Sage gasping, River barking orders for everyone to stay still. The amulet against my chest grows hot trying to force an explanation into my foggy mind.

Shade left for medical supplies. The wolf rushed in just now through an open door.

Shade's wolf snaps his teeth, his yellow eyes flashing at Coal. Circling him. Nipping at his sword arm and ankles.

Coal swings his steel with one precise motion, not a dull practice blade, but a razor-sharp edge aimed for Shade's jugular.

"No!" With a scream, I launch myself in the middle of the pair, burying my fingers in Shade's warm fur. Beneath my hold, the animal's sides vibrate with flesh-shuddering growls. "Don't fight."

Coal's gaze snaps toward me, penetrating my eyes as if seeking answers.

My mouth is dry, my heart racing my breath. Shade's wolf holds its position against my thigh, hackles raised.

You know this wolf, I shout at Coal in my mind. *Remember him. Bloody remember.*

"Fae craft." Katita's voice shatters the silence. "Osprey summoned a wolf to her aid."

"He walked through the door." Beside Katita, Arisha's thin voice sounds barely above a whisper. When gazes turn to her, the girl blanches but stands her ground. "The wolf wasn't conjured. He walked through the open door. We all saw it."

My amulet heats, agreeing with Arisha's words. Slowly, the others nod along despite themselves. They can't help it. The veil tells them what to believe, and Arisha plays to the veil.

Arisha swallows. "And he didn't just appear. That's Lera's pet. Ruffle. I've seen him before."

The amulet stays cool. That fiction I made up all on my own.

"It doesn't matter. Only a fae would have a wolf as a pet," Katita says, recovering her wits first. "Put him down, Master Sage."

"You can't do that," I gasp, gripping Shade's thick gray fur desperately. Stomach bile claws at my throat, and my eyes dart around the room, looking for a single sane face. She can't. I can't let her.

"I don't think you understand how this kingdom works, Lera," says Katita.

"Katita is the heir to the throne," Arisha's voice reminds me. *"She can do as she wishes."*

My gaze flows to River, his intelligent gray eyes watching me. Watching everyone. As he always does. Watching, thinking, evaluating, carrying the weight of responsibility that would crush a lesser being. Katita may be a princess of a small kingdom, but River is the king of an immortal court.

And River can't do as he wishes. Never could.

I gasp, the sudden realization slowing the world around me. I can see the room I'm in—River is tightening his brow, Sage is fingering his handkerchief, the logs are crackling in the flame—but my mind is too busy to pay attention to that. What is more powerful than the king of Slait court, so powerful that it makes the king himself bend a knee?—It is the welfare of Slait itself.

"No," I whisper, turning to face Katita, knowing the move I need to make. My *one* move. "No, I do understand how your kingdom works, Your Highness. Which is why you can't turn me over to the magistrate. Or Arisha. Or Tye. Not without announcing to the whole Continental Alliance that Ckridel has been compromised by magic. That the very Academy they've sent their children to has been under siege from those hog beasts for weeks, and your officers kept it quiet."

Letting go of Shade, I step toward Katita, my voice becoming more powerful with each word.

"Men and women around the continent have been tortured and executed for charges so frivolous that it makes the evidence you laid out today a case for the newsleafs. But that's the problem, Katita. There is no magic breach in all those other places. No magical blight. No hog beasts. Just accusations of 'fae craft' levied against people who've never seen magic. But here, in *your* kingdom, in *your* famed Academy that's stood for two hundred years, there is true danger. Enough of it that if the alliance learns your secret, Ckridel may find itself all alone. So, here is what you are going to do, Katita of Ckridel, heir to King Zenith's throne: you will get on your knees and beg everyone in this room to keep that secret."

Katita's face has gone white. I know through my bones that she has never been given such an order in her life. The danger of what I'm doing thuds in my temples, but I hold my ground.

Katita's nostrils flare, her good hand opening and closing at her side. Wide teal eyes study me, the pure hatred in them tempered only by dawning comprehension.

I take another step closer. "And after that, Your Highness," I say, my voice ringing through the room, "you will beg that we continue pooling our swords and our minds and our research to work out how to pull your kingdom out of this blight. Because those drawings and theories are all we have standing between the mortal lands and disaster."

The last is not true. The mortal realm has more than drawing and theories. The mortal realm has *me*.

18

COAL

"And did she?" Shade asked Coal, his soft voice riding under the din of dining hall conversation. "Did Katita get on her knees?"

The clink of silverware on china echoed delicately around the great tapestry-lined dining hall, the crystal chandeliers overhead scattering candlelight on all the finely dressed diners below.

"Yes." Coal dug his fork into a slice of roasted pig. He tasted none of it—though that didn't stop him from eating every bite—which he was focused on now with more industry than the task required. No matter how he angled his chair, he could not help seeing Lera at the other end of the hall, her red dress as bright as the fire glowing inside her. It was strapless, tightly hugging her breasts and torso, then flowing down from her waist in textured waves of silky crimson. She was eating. Talking. Smiling at Arisha as if she had no concept of what that dress was doing to every male in the dining hall—and, knowing her, she probably didn't. The dress, the creamy shoulders and clavicle, her fiery hair, the shadowed V of her breasts, inviting the eye lower and lower. It was enough to make a man mad.

But Lera didn't notice. She was moving on with life, doing all the normal things Coal found near impossible after the morning's near horror.

Coal still didn't know what he would have done had a bloody wolf not walked into Sage's chamber just when the headmaster ordered Coal to seize Lera. How far he'd have let things get before breaking the girl out, no matter what it took. Coal wanted to think it was because no one deserved to fall victim to the fae hunts plaguing the continent, but he knew it was more than that. Coal hadn't been *worried* or *concerned* as Princess Katita laid out her deadly accusations—he'd been terrified down to his core.

"Leralynn. Stars," Shade said softly, shaking his head. "I've little notion what just might come into that girl's mind next. And speaking of Katita—her wrist really is broken. Don't let her push it."

Coal nodded, paused, then schooled his voice to a quiet nonchalance. "When you left to get supplies for a splint, where did you go?"

Shade shifted, his golden eyes carefully impassive. "The infirmary."

"No, you didn't." Coal snatched Shade's wrist before the man could move away. "I went looking for you afterward, and no one had seen you there. You might have gone to the infirmary, but that's not where you ended up." Coal paused at a slight tic in Shade's jaw. For a moment, they locked gazes, their silence filled with the sounds of an oblivious dining hall. Then Coal slowly released Shade's wrist, leaning away from the higher-ranking officer. "You've a bloody big problem, Shade. Let me help you."

Leaning forward into the space Coal just vacated, Shade

bared his teeth. "I will tell you what losing time is like, right after you lay out the details of being held captive. Unless you want to put that on the table, stay out of my business."

Coal kept the man's gaze, letting silence trickle between them.

"Is everything all right?" River asked, his approach bringing Coal and Shade to their feet. Setting down his plate, the commander frowned. "Am I interrupting something?"

"Not at all, sir," said Shade. "Coal was filling me in on what happened at the tribunal. It appears I left just before things turned interesting," said Shade.

"I think you should move Leralynn off my training team," Coal said, turning to River. "After what happened a few days ago, it would be better to put some distance between us."

"Agreed." River's brisk reply stung despite being right. Sighing, River lowered his fork without having taken a bite and brushed a hand through his short brown hair—his only tell of turmoil within. "Except I can't. That girl brought a princess to her knees this morning, defied me in the middle of the infirmary four days ago, and—if the rumors I'm hearing are correct—started a fight with three royals twice her size yesterday in an effort to protect Rabbit. I've no one else who can handle her, Coal. The girl has a point about making use of her magical knowledge, but she is a *cadet*. A fact that she— and we—need to remember very plainly."

Coal's stomach clenched. Everything River had said about Lera was true—painfully true—except for one thing. Coal was not the right person to handle her. Not when just the scent of her threw his mind and body into chaos, brought up memories that he barely recognized as his. But how could he say one word of this to River without digging himself into an even deeper hole?

River watched him, waiting for a response. Then

something shifted in the commander's eyes as he studied Coal's face, probably seeing far more than Coal intended. "I *am* sorry, Coal," River said.

Coal shrugged.

"What about the wolf?" Shade asked. "We can't have a wild animal roaming the Academy."

"You'd need to catch him first." Coal turned to his food. He was the only one eating. "I saw the beast before. He'd been with Leralynn when she got away from me on our run. Came and left. Like today. Arisha is right, the animal isn't—quite—wild."

"And how many cadets do you propose we let him maul before we give him that distinction?" Shade asked.

"Do you truly want an answer?" asked Coal.

"This day just keeps getting better." Pushing his plate away, River tipped his head toward the sound of the Academy bell and rose. "I need to go talk Sage down from having an apoplexy after this morning," he said, rebuttoning his crisp dinner jacket. Placing both hands on the table, River lowered his voice to hard command. "In case I wasn't clear before—I want Lera under close watch, lest she graduates herself from protector of wolves, children, and instructors to a one-woman force guarding us from the immortal world."

CONTINUE the adventure with GREAT FALLS ROGUE, (POWER OF FIVE BOOK 6). Free preview on next page.

TRACING SHADOWS (Audiobook available)

UNRAVELING DARKNESS (Audiobook available)

TILDOR

THE CADET OF TILDOR

SIGN UP FOR NEW RELEASE NOTIFICATIONS at https://
links.alexlidell.com/News

ABOUT THE AUTHOR

Alex Lidell is an Amazon KU All Star Top 50 Author Awards winner (July, 2018). Her debut novel, THE CADET OF TILDOR (Penguin, 2013) was an Amazon Breakout Novel Awards finalist. Her Reverse Harem romances, POWER OF FIVE and MISTAKE OF MAGIC, both received Amazon KU Top 100 awards for individual titles.

Alex is an avid horseback rider, a (bad) hockey player, and an ice-cream addict. Born in Russia, Alex learned English in elementary school, where a thoughtful librarian placed a copy of Tamora Pierce's ALANNA in Alex's hands. In addition to becoming the first English book Alex read for fun, ALANNA started Alex's life long love for fantasy books. Alex lives in Washington, DC.

Join Alex's newsletter for news, special offers and sneak peeks: https://links.alexlidell.com/News

Find out more on Alex's website: www.alexlidell.com

SIGN UP FOR NEWS AND RELEASE NOTIFICATIONS

Connect with Alex!
www.alexlidell.com
alex@alexlidell.com